For Dad, who encouraged me to stop and smell the flowers.

CONTENTS

Acknowledgments

Writing this book has been quite a journey for me and there are a number of people I would like to thank for their assistance along the way.

My editor, Steven Manchester, for your time, knowledge, and abundant use of a red pen on my manuscript, thank you. Your editing advice was tremendously helpful and I have much gratitude.

Beki Greenwood, my friend and designer, thank you for so much: for reading my manuscript in one day, even though there are no dragons, and immediately brainstorming cover art ideas; for your formatting, design, and photography skills; and for understanding my brand of nerdy.

When my idea for this story was just forming, I sat down with an acquaintance to discuss alternative medicine and bounce ideas around. Two hours later, I had shared most of my plot and characters and knew in my gut I had a project worth pursuing. Thank you, David Freitas. You made me feel competent and inspired, and over the course of the research and writing of my book baby, you kept me well supplied with useful information and became a good friend. I have truly learned so much from you. Thank you.

Bernadette Nelson and Tammy Carvalho, thank you for reading early drafts and providing detailed feedback. Also, a big thanks to David Mazzola for reading, providing feedback, contributing several original poems and allowing me to use and adapt them to fit the needs of this book.

Thank you, Barbara Rose, for the final proofread.

Thank you Robin B. for Wednesdays at noon, listening to my stories, and helping me see my goals. Lisa Camara, I've always appreciated your tolerance for my drama, my rants, and for being my friend. Karen Anderson, thanks for the pep talk and for understanding my fears. Thank you to the WFG ladies for helping me grow. Though we've never met or even talked, thank you to Rick Simpson for providing important contributions to cancer treatment that were useful in my research and writing.

The Lakeville Public Library staff and community were encouraging and supportive, even when I talked way too much about Brian Williams, rough drafts, and when and where I was going to find figs. Thank you, Linda Connelly, Carol Cohen, and Julia Edelman for regularly asking me how it was coming along and listening as I talked about my project. Carol Magner, thank you for being my tough love guardian angel mama bird!

Finally, I have the love of my family and would like to thank my mom, JoAnn Newton, and Rainier, Jasper, Zavier and Elena Tan for years of patience and time to write. Much love.

ONE

June 2004

Dear Tessa,

All I have to give you are these words. I hope you won't hate me too much, but will understand if you do. Try not to think about hate, but don't think about love either—especially that. It will only derail you in the long run. This I know for a fact.

I cannot stay any longer. I just cannot. You're smart. You will be okay. Don't let your chance at education slip away. It's a slow crawl through life without it. Make yourself an independent woman. That's what I need to do now. I've been called many things, which I am sure you will hear now. Crazy. Selfish. Bitch. Crazy selfish bitch. I may be all of these. I may be none, but I won't find out here. I will not get well here. I need to find a place where I can heal. This life and this place are not my own.

Please don't look for me.
Mum

The letter was written on a sheet of paper torn from one of Tessa's own spiral bound notebooks that she'd left on her desk. Its back side had a few algebra equations scrawled on it. She peered into the mirror atop her bureau, brought her fingers to the gauze bandage on her face and read the letter again.

Please don't look for me.

If Tessa was being honest with herself, she knew this was coming; deep down, she expected it at some point. Her mother had been slowly leaving for years and had told Tessa more than once that her heart was dark and her head was a jumble of chaos. At fourteen, Tessa was only beginning to know what this meant. *But why now? At this moment and under these circumstances?* She could drive herself crazy with all the questions. She could analyze the hell out of it. Or she could take a pain pill, or two, and go to sleep.

For now, Tessa knew her mother had left and that the cast would be on her broken right arm for at least eight weeks. *If I focus on only that for the rest of the summer, maybe the jagged and red, stitched up gash on my face will take care of itself. Poof. Just heal and fade.* Maybe each time Tessa removed the bandage to clean it and replace the dressing, she would notice improvement—healing and fading. The doctors told her she couldn't start with the Mederma ointment until the stitches came out. *As long as it makes some progress by the time school starts in September, I'll be okay,* she'd told herself when the nurse had put a mirror in front of her and taught her how to clean and re-bandage it. She could always get some heavy duty make-up, maybe try to get in with the goth kids if all else failed. Drawing spider webs and little hearts and teardrops on her face with black eyeliner, and wearing baggy dark clothes might work to hide her sudden ugliness. Going goth for ninth grade was unlikely to bother her father. He had larger concerns now.

For this early summer night, Tessa put it all away: The

letter. The abandonment. The new ugliness. She tucked it all into her top drawer and went to bed, hopeful that the pain medication the hospital sent her home with would get her through the night.

Two

January 2015

As she wiped down the last of the tables in the dining room, Tessa looked over the counter at her father. She stuck the damp rag into the string of her apron and headed into the supply closet for the broom and mop.

In less than two hours, it would be dark and she wanted to be on her way back to her temporary home at her cousin's cottage before the sun set. Her grandmother would give her a hard time about driving all that way in the dark. *Such a long way and so cold out there tonight. Might start snowing.* She'd *tsk-tsk* at Tessa. *No sense in it. Better to stay here tonight. Safer.*

But there was no snow in the immediate forecast. Tessa and her dad had watched the weather report after the last of the afternoon customers left. Cold, yes. Snow, no. She'd have to reassure Mémère. It would be ten minutes of back and forth, with her grandmother laying guilt on Tessa; guilt and fear of driving. *I can't understand how you can drive at night. A young girl all alone. Anything could happen. You, of all people, should know that.* Her words were nearly the same every weekend, and Tessa's response was always a nod to her grandmother's concern, along with a firm statement that she needed to go. "Yes, Mem, I know. I'm very careful and if I leave now I won't be driving in the dark." Same conversation, different week. She wanted to add that at twenty-four, she wasn't exactly a young girl anymore, but that would've been futile.

"Thank you, baby," her father called over to her, as she finished up the floor and dumped the contents of the dust pan into the trash barrel. "I couldn't do it without you."

Angela, Tessa's father's regular Sunday help, had called out again, claiming a sick little boy at home. Tessa had her doubts. Angela had most likely found something else and hadn't the heart or the guts to inform her long term employer yet. She was probably milking the sick pay for as long as she could, Tessa figured.

Tessa had stepped up and worked the breakfast and lunch hours, and Saturday evening as well. It was a relief that her father decided to close the restaurant after lunch on Sundays several months ago. Breakfast and lunch were always his prime times anyway, when he caught the early risers and the after church crowd. Dinner had steadily decreased to less than twenty percent of his Sunday business for the past few years. Even still, Tessa knew it hurt his heart to flip the CLOSED sign at 3:00 PM.

"Are you just about done, Dad?" She asked her slumping, exhausted father as she switched off the dining room lights, before extending her hand to help him from the counter stool he'd been perched on for the past half hour. He flipped his ledger shut and took his daughter's outstretched hand. She couldn't convince him to go digital with his bookkeeping. "I don't roll well with change," he'd always told her. He did what worked for him and that was that.

Tremblay's Place was her father's little restaurant by the

sea, located on a narrow peninsula that was home to mostly residential properties. The strip of beach that wrapped around from one end to the other was dotted with a few small businesses and one small eatery that Benjamin Tremblay had bought, fixed up and run since Tessa was a toddler who liked to climb atop the stainless steel counter and rearrange the spice rack every chance she got. The front window provided a view of the Elizabeth Islands on a clear day or the mist-shrouded Fairhaven beach on a foggy day. He called it a diner for simplicity's sake. She thought of it as more of a café. Most of the customers came for the best hot sandwiches and pastries in town and didn't try to classify it beyond that. It had been a busy weekend now that the holidays were over, with the coffee pot brewing continuously for the steady stream of customers popping in.

Her father locked the door, as Tessa zipped her coat up to her chin and grabbed the keys off the counter. Another Sunday done. Tessa drove; her father dozed in the passenger seat as they made their way back home. She would not be at Tremblay's Place tomorrow, but at her full time job more than a hundred and fifty miles away. Weekdays were easier on him. The Monday through Friday crew had been loyal to him for years, giving him the ability to show up a bit later in the morning without too much worry, something she doubted he took advantage of, though.

They pulled into the driveway. "Kate will be pissed at me for working today," he said, as Tessa opened the car door for him.

"You seem better today than you did last week," Tessa said. "Sleep in a bit tomorrow. What time does Kate usually come?"

"Bright and early, usually before seven."

"I can call the agency and tell them not to send her so early, if that would help you," Tessa suggested.

"No. No. She won't hear of it. Wants to make sure I

take my meds at the right time of day, you know, and that I don't leave the house without them. As if I'm an invalid. An invalid with dementia."

Tessa peered at him.

"Which I am not, Tessa. I can assure you," he said. "And anyway, she's been known to check in on me at the restaurant if she stops here and doesn't see my truck in the driveway."

"Maybe if you let yourself rest more, the meds could do their work." *And the chemo could do its work.* He was in a break phase from the chemo to let his body adjust, regroup itself. Tessa tried to imagine all the good, healthy cells gathering together in a huddle to plan their attack on the cancer cells and hoped the ratio was back in his favor by now. She also wanted to tell him that the restaurant would survive if he let someone else manage it while he took a couple months off for his own good. But this was not something she could suggest. That restaurant was his life blood and he was the life of the restaurant—had been as far back as Tessa could remember. He would close it down before turning it over to someone else, even temporarily. This never needed to be said.

"No can do, Tessie baby. I need to stay busy. Keeps the old mind occupied. You know what they say about idle hands and all that."

"Yeah. Stay busy resting, Dad. I'll call you tomorrow to see how you're feeling," she said. She wanted to grab her stuff and head out, just in case Mémère had invited Frankie over for dinner again. Whenever this happened, she never got out of the house as planned.

"Don't worry too much about me, Tessa. You have your own life now," he said. He wouldn't even tell her when his next appointment was when she asked. She had to check the calendar or look for those little appointment cards on the fridge, if she wanted to know.

When he was first diagnosed, he dismissed Tessa's concerns, saying that he had a little tumor in his tubes and would take care of it. *A tumor in his tubes. What tubes? His bronchial tubes? His intestines? His coronary artery? Could people even get cancerous tumors in their coronary artery?* Months ago, she pressed him for answers, but he merely said, "When I can't get up in the morning and go flip eggs for my adoring public, then you can worry, baby. Even then, if then, *if,* baby, got that? If...then I'll deal with it, okay? Right now, I'm fit and as fabulous as ever." She hated his casualness, while he hated the thought of her worrying about him. "You've got bigger fish to fry, baby, and so do I. Now let's go. It's the weekend and people are out and about, looking for the best lunch in town. Who's going to take care of that, if you and I sit around talking?"

With a heavy sigh, she'd gone to Tremblay's' Place with him that weekend and cooked and served and cleaned up. He didn't mention it again for a while and neither did Tessa. And now it was January of the new year and Dad had not only been through surgery to remove his tumor—which had been in his large intestine—but also two rounds of chemotherapy that nearly broke him. He kept pushing though—pushing to keep his restaurant afloat and pushing Tessa out the door every Sunday after closing so she could get back to her Monday through Friday life. Any advice or suggestions she had for him were shooed away.

"Are you saving money at all?" He asked as Tessa threw items into her tote bag in preparation to leave for the week.

"A little each month," she said. *Very little.* "It's adding up, but it'll be a while still."

"What kind of place are you hoping to find...when you can?" He asked as though they hadn't talked about it many times already; as though finding her very own apartment hadn't been at the top of her goal list for months now. The cushion of her deposit, however, was a bit slow in accumulating.

He had offered a little money, enough for a first, last, and security deposit when she told him she wanted to start planning her own future, but she hadn't taken it. Saving the money on her own made it more authentic, if not also a far lengthier process.

"Oh, you know, Dad. Just something that suits me. Nothing fancy."

"Fancy's in the details, baby, and you can add those yourself."

"Yeah, I know. When I have enough saved up. A few more months and I should be able to start looking."

"You'll know it when you see it. Places are like that. The right ones speak to you and say *stay*."

THREE

When Tessa quit her job as a kindergarten teacher after two years of squashed enthusiasm and unmet idealism, she took a clerical position in the admissions office of a small college in the northwestern corner of Massachusetts, twenty miles from the Vermont state line. The pay was a few notches short of mediocre and it was more than a hundred and fifty miles from home, but it was a new start in a new location. The town was called Greenfield and somehow that was enough to intrigue her, and when she stepped onto the campus for her interview, Tessa became captivated. There was something mystical and enchanting about the place; something she couldn't quite put her finger on. Perhaps it was the air, the scent and colors of the landscaping, the old stone footbridges and white brick buildings. There was activity and serenity all at once. People moved about with purpose and grace. She felt a soothing energy that she had previously not known and took this as a good sign.

After weeks of leaving her father's house before 6:00 AM for her two and a half hour daily commute, Tessa moved into her cousin Charlotte's spare room so she could sleep an extra hour each morning. It was nice not to have to listen to her grandmother's anxiety over Tessa's driving after dark too. Charlotte's cottage was closer to Tessa's new job, in a central Massachusetts town dotted with little ponds and summer communities that owners had turned into year-round homes. It didn't bother Tessa too much that Charlotte's spare room was actually a walk-in closet under the attic stairs. It was a stepping stone to her independence.

Charlotte was a moderately successful artist who made most of her income through an online shop where she took custom orders. She had a friend named Marcus with shoulder length mahogany hair and eyes the color of autumn maple leaves, who walked barefoot around the cottage with a cup of herbal tea in his hand. Tessa learned to wait her turn for the bathroom and avert her eyes when Marcus came out wearing nothing but a towel. Charlotte kept him around because she said he wasn't a pain in the ass and there was no chance she would ever fall in love with him. "He's just for fun. We play with each other. No harm. No hearts."

Tessa pondered this and remembered her mother's words. *Don't think about love...especially that. It will only derail you.*

"No harm, no hearts," Tessa said. "What do you do with it then?"

"With what?" Charlotte asked.

"Your heart?"

"My heart's fine...usually. I channel it into my work. That way, I know it'll always be there," she responded.

Tessa let herself absorb this and carried on arranging her things in the walk-in closet, creating a space for herself in the windowless room. *One year,* she told herself. *I'll live with Charlotte for one year.* By the time the following fall came around, she'd have enough saved to get an apartment of her own. *One year.* If she did her new job well enough, she might even have a pay raise and a promotion by then.

Frankie wouldn't like it much, but that didn't matter much to Tessa. *A break from Frankie is what I've needed for longer than I can remember.* Her half-hearted attempts to cool things off with him had been unsuccessful so far. *Distance is the ticket.* It was long past time for that. She had outgrown Friday night club dates and crashing, half drunk, on Frankie's lumpy sofa bed that always smelled of bodily fluids and nicotine.

But on this first Friday evening of the new year, Tessa drove to Dad's for the weekend to find Frankie sitting at the kitchen table eating cake with her grandmother. She hadn't seen him since before Christmas. She'd purposely kept her holiday visit short, staying only for Christmas Day with Dad and Mémère. They'd gone to Mass and prepared a meal together, just the three of them.

Nobody had bothered with gifts. After nearly a year of treatment, her father was coming to the end of his second round of chemo and all she wanted for him was a return to health. He'd kept his spirit about him whenever he was in Tessa's presence, hardly sharing any details with her unless pestered. A return to normalcy for him and a step, or perhaps a leap, forward on her own path were all the gifts she needed.

"Come for a ride with me, Tessa," Frankie said, wiping crumbs from his mouth. "I have something I've been wanting to give you."

Mémère cleared his plate and set it in the sink to wash later.

"I just got home. I've been driving for more than two hours," she said, slipping her coat off and hanging it from the hook behind the door. "Where's my Dad?" she asked.

"At the restaurant, honey," her grandmother answered.

It was well into the evening.

"He's not supposed to be working so late. It wears him

out."

"He came back home and rested, a long nap actually. I bugged him to stay home too, Tessa, but you know him. That place is his life."

His life. Yes.

Frankie stood up. "So, come with me. We'll go see him. Let him know you're home."

"All right," she agreed after considering a phone call instead—knowing that wouldn't ease her mind. *One of his staff will pick up and tell me that Dad's hands are full.*

She slipped back into her coat. It was red wool and she'd had it for more than ten years, since the Christmas of her freshman year in high school. It fit her loosely now and made her feel young and safe, like a soft blanket on a cozy couch.

Mémère smiled at her and Frankie.

"It's been weeks since I've seen you, Tessie," Frankie said once they were in his truck. "I've missed you." He leaned over to her. His kiss landed hard and wet on her mouth. He tasted of her grandmother's cake and smelled of tobacco.

"Tessa," she said.

"Hmm?"

"I prefer Tessa, please. I always have. Not Tessie," she said. "Yeah, I guess it's been a little while."

It had been three weeks since she'd last seen Frankie, nearly seven weeks since she'd last slept with him. She hadn't forgotten. The memory of driving to CVS the day before Christmas Eve and the panic in her chest as she made her purchase was something that would never leave her. She had gone out of her way, meandering far from any of the four or five other pharmacies or Walmarts that were closer to Charlotte's house or to her job. Bumping into someone who might recognize her and engage her in a conversation about work or the holidays was not an option. Or worse yet, someone may notice what she was buying and wish her luck or give her unwarranted congratulations. The drive back to Charlotte's cottage was the longest twenty-five minutes of her life, and that was saying a lot for someone who easily spent nine or ten hours a week behind the wheel.

When she got back to Charlotte's and locked herself in the tiny bathroom to pee on one of the absorbent white sticks she'd bought, she tried not to let herself think during the three minutes of uncertainty. But her thoughts came anyway. She looked out the bathroom window to catch a glimpse of the pond—that slick, icy punctuation mark—at the end of Charlotte's unpaved road. In summer, there were swimmers and retirees with dogs and fishing poles who lingered near the dock. But on December twenty-third, an hour before sunset, there was only a bit of frost visible through the bare trees. Nonetheless, she let her mind wander and it became summer for those three minutes and she pictured herself walking with her toes in the lapping water and wet sand. She even let the image turn into the ocean. That's where clarity seemed to hit her. She looked out into the horizon and asked herself two questions.

Could I possibly see myself married to Frankie and living back in Fairhaven if I am carrying his child? The answer, after a bit of contemplation, was *maybe*, if absolutely necessary, and she knew he would have it no other way. How she felt would not matter. He would turn it into a practical issue and make living separately into a ridiculous, expensive scenario. *And why not get married?* He'd certainly mentioned it over their years together—had even proposed—but it had always been in a way that was impossible to tell whether or not he was serious or just trying to get a reaction from her. *But a child, a child would close the deal. It would be non-negotiable. One insurance policy. One apartment. One income. It's how Frankie thinks.* She had known him long enough to envision his entire reaction. But to Tessa, it was a closed door. Just the idea of that *maybe,* was a locked door that would take a lot of mental gymnastics to either hurdle over or break through.

The second question was: *Could I possibly see myself married to Frankie if I'm not carrying his child?* The answer came instantly, with no need for contemplation. She just knew. *No. No way. Absolutely not.* It simply was how she felt.

Tessa closed her eyes against the icy white blue sunshine that was filtering in through the window and cleared her mind of the beach, the ocean and the little neighborhood pond. She then opened her eyes and looked at the home pregnancy test on the counter.

One blue line. Just one. Negative. Not pregnant.

Not pregnant!

The relief was better than the feel of a hot shower head after a long, sweaty run. It was more welcome than her pillow and favorite quilt after a long week of working and a weekend of helping her father at Tremblay's Place. The relief at that one blue line was a gush of oxygen to her lungs that had already started closing in on themselves at the very real possibility that there could've been two blue lines.

She did the second test the following morning when there was still no sign of her late period. Again, it was negative. She breathed deeply and purposefully for several long minutes. Then she threw her coat over her shoulders and walked down to the pond at the end of the road. It was Christmas Eve and she made a decision. *I'm done—absolutely done.*

The drive to Tremblay's Place from her father's house was mere minutes. As soon as Frankie had backed out of the driveway, he announced his intention. "I have a late Christmas present for you, Tessie. We'll swing by my place, so I can give it to you."

"Can we go see my dad first? I mean, let's go see my dad first. Frankie, I need to see him." She was practicing her stern tone, stating rather than asking, attempting to make her words mean something to Frankie. She needed to make herself into more than the shadow she usually felt like in his presence. Stating rather than asking was a sign of confidence. It showed that she existed, that she wasn't just wind blowing by his ears and flying over his head. She'd read that somewhere.

"It's on the way, Tessie. It obviously makes more sense to stop before."

Tessa, not Tessie. Only her father could call her Tessie, but she let this pass.

"If it's on the way, then it's on the way back too," she reasoned, but there was no reasoning with Frankie sometimes. "I don't have anything for you, though. I didn't really go shopping this year. You know, it's been sort of crazy...with my dad and all." *Plus, my fears that I was growing a little Frankie took up any spare time I may have had to hit the stores.* Her period had only just started yesterday, an unprecedented two weeks late. "Stress," her doctor's office had told her when she'd called with her concerns. She wouldn't tell Frankie about the scare. She had quickly processed what it meant and only needed to share her decision with him, not the details.

"And besides, you're not making much at that job anyway. I know. Not to mention what you must go through in gas money with all the back and forth."

Breathe...just breathe. Inhale, exhale, she reminded herself.

Frankie pulled into the parking lot of Mullens Motorworks, the full-service garage he and his father ran together. He cut the engine and put the truck in park. "Come upstairs," he said, referring to his apartment over the garage.

"No. I'm tired. I want to see my dad and make sure he's okay. Just run up and get it quickly. We can sit and talk after."

"He looked pretty good when I saw him earlier."

"Today? You saw him today?" she asked.

"Stopped by Tremblay's for lunch, best burgers anywhere. He wasn't working too hard. He was sitting in a booth doing paperwork."

"Was he stressed? He's not supposed to be too stressed."

"Maybe a little, I don't know. He said something about being short again this weekend. He was trying to figure out the schedule," Frankie said.

"Damn it, that's why he's there now—tonight. He's trying to get someone from his weekday crew to come in early tomorrow." She knew this was what he was doing. He was promising time and a half and Monday off. Mondays were slow and easy days for the restaurant. Saturday mornings weren't. *Guess I'll be the one opening up at 6:00 AM tomorrow—again.* It was becoming a regular thing. The weekday morning staff loved their boss, but they were mostly moms who worked school hours or older ladies who woke up with the birds and liked to feel useful for a few hours. The weekend and evening crew were generally high school or college kids who were in and out in quick succession, often according to the season or semester.

"Come upstairs, Tessa. I want to show you what I got you."

"Please Frankie, as much as I appreciate that you got me a gift, I want to see my dad. I'm here for the whole weekend." She knew he would interpret this the wrong way, that he would expect her to stay the night with him, but she wanted to move him along.

"Tessie, it's cold and dark in the truck. You won't be able to see properly," he said. "And I really want you to see this."

"After I see my dad, we'll come back here and go in. I

promise. There's stuff we need to talk about anyway."

"Christ, Tessie. Are you trying to dump me again, 'cuz it's sure felt that way these past few weeks?" Frankie asked, staring over at her from the driver's seat. His right hand was on the steering wheel, his left, on the door handle. "You know how many times I've wanted to drive out to that shack you're living in with what's her name and talk some sense into you?"

"Talk sense? What sense, Frankie? And her name's Charlotte. She's my cousin and she's been very kind to let me stay with her this year."

"Only reason I don't is 'cuz it's so goddamn far. I'd be too fucking exhausted to work the next day...and you know, I don't have the option of just not showing up for work in the morning because I'm tired."

She allowed her deep breathing to be her only response.

"You seem to be coming home less and less," he said after a minute or so.

"I'm here every weekend," she said.

"Don't seem that way."

"Frankie, could you just start the truck back up and take me to see my dad now? Please."

"He's okay. You wanna talk, let's talk," he said, pulling the handle in and releasing the door. He got out of the truck and walked around to Tessa's side, opened the door, and tried to usher her out.

She didn't budge. "He's not okay, Frankie. He's had two rounds of chemo, the second more intense than the first, since last fall...and he works too much."

"So tell me again why you live with Charlotte and not back home," he said.

Breathe. "It's closer to my job. It saves gas and driving time." *Lord, how many times have I repeated that over the past year? Twenty? Thirty, at least.*

"How important is this job to you?" Frankie asked.

"More important than anything or...*anyone* here, it seems."

"It's a job and I need a job," Tessa answered. "Anyway, I've had that job since before he got sick...before he started treatment."

She didn't tell him that the campus where she worked was magical, that it was a place of such beauty it transcended her out of the ordinary world and into a new realm. It absorbed her into its beauty and made her real. Trying to explain tree-lined walking paths and park benches and buildings with dark hardwood floors and hundred-year-old windows that overtook her height by nearly double would be lost on Frankie. Trying to tell him about the arched stone footbridge at the entrance of the campus where she liked to sit with her coffee on misty mornings would be ludicrous. So she kept it to herself to avoid his comments, his judgment.

"It's just that it's been a year already with that job. You haven't been over my place since Thanksgiving," he said. "You wanna decorate? Put curtains or whatever up in my apartment. I don't care. I told you that. No flower print stuff, though. That's where I put my foot down."

"And it's going to be another year...at least. That's what I need to tell you," she blurted, pausing to get her bearings.

She was still in the passenger seat of Frankie's truck; he was standing between the open door and Tessa, with his hand on the headrest.

"She making you sign a contract or something?"

Tessa looked down at the dark gray gravel of the parking lot and gathered up the words she needed to say. After five years with Frankie, she would finally tell him what she wanted.

"I've decided to be celibate for a year," she stated, "this year."

"What?"

"I've decided to be celibate for a year," she repeated. "Starting now. Oh, and I'm giving up beer too."

Those were the two variables she needed to remove from her life for now—sex and beer. Maybe it was silly and wouldn't prove anything, but it seemed the most logical thing to do. Too many beers—this meant more than one for Tessa—invariably led to the familiar easiness with Frankie and forgotten condoms, which led to the family planning aisle at CVS. She didn't want to face the day where there might be two blue lines and a lifetime of closed doors that would largely be spent with Frankie on top of her.

"What's this some kind of New Year's resolution? Last year, you moved away. Now you don't want me at all anymore." He was looking straight at her.

"It's just too complicated right now. My father. My job. All the driving. I think I need a return to simplicity." Yes, that's what she craved. *Simplicity. Less to worry about.* She hoped she had articulated that.

"You need to cut yourself off from me? What the fuck, Tessie. I've been waiting for you to come back here, you know, to stay. Get a job around here so we can be together again, properly, and not this back and forth on the weekend shit that you've been doing," he said. "Anyway, I'm doing okay. Business is good. Damn good, actually. It's why I can't drive up there...to Charlotte's. I'm working every night until eight o'clock sometimes later." He paused. "You could take your time finding a job."

"We've known each other a long time, Frankie. It's just..."

"Just what? Not what you want anymore? Obviously."

"It's just...well, I like my job," she said softer than she'd wanted to say it.

"You like your job? Oh please. You make what...ten dollars an hour or something like that? You could do that anywhere. Hell, I could use a secretary at the garage and pay you more than you make now."

Breathe. Just breathe. She looked down at the gravel to

avoid him.

"Are you fucking some other guy? Is that what this is about?"

"No, Frankie. I just told you I want celibacy. No sex, period. Not with anyone."

"Kind of extreme, isn't it, after all these years?"

"I'm hoping it will help me see more clearly."

"What you see is what you get with me, Tessie. I don't get any clearer."

"Not you—me." She instantly hated that she'd pulled that line on him. "I'm a bit lost right now, traveling in this big triangle every week. Work. Charlotte's. Here. Over and over again. I don't get many breaks."

"I told you what you could do about that. If you just listened to me it would be so much easier. There'd be no more exhaustion. No more killing your car with all the back and forth."

"Frankie, I need to figure things out. I think without...sex, I'll be able to concentrate better."

"It makes no sense. So what are we supposed to do? Go bowling and stuff? Talk more?"

"We can talk more if you want," she said, glancing up at his face. He had averted his eyes. "Or not."

"What else is there to talk about? If you don't want me, you don't want me. It's not like we were doing it all that much lately anyway. Hell, I haven't touched you since...since..."

"Thanksgiving weekend," Tessa said, filling in his blank.

"Yeah."

"It's for the best, Frankie. Right now. For me."

He walked away.

The truth was that she felt very little. She felt like a shadow and didn't want to feel that way anymore.

"Come upstairs, Tessa. I still want to give you your

Christmas present," he said, taking her hand to pull her out of the truck. "Then we'll go see your father."

They had to walk around the back of the garage and up a long flight of stairs to get to Frankie's apartment. The stairs always reminded Tessa of a fire escape. Inside looked the same: kitchen table, fold out couch, big screen TV attached to his game console and DVD player.

He dropped his keys on the table and headed down the hall to his bedroom. Tessa stayed put in the kitchen area. He returned a minute later with a big, gift wrapped package done up with shiny red paper and a silver bow. "Come into the living room and sit down," he said.

She followed him to the couch. He placed the box down and told her to open it.

As soon as she'd gotten the top of the box off, it was obvious what was inside. The scent gave it away before she even peeled back the sparkly tissue paper.

"Take it out so you can try it on," he urged.

"No, Frankie. It's too much. I can't."

"Take it out and look at it. Then try it on, Tessie."

She went robotic, listening, and did as he said.

"I went to a lot of stores looking for this. Then I had to find a sales girl around your size to try it on so I wouldn't get something too big for you. Then they only had it in black in your size, so I had to special order it in light brown because you don't like to wear black."

Damn, it's true. She looked like a corpse in black, a petite, pale corpse. Of all the things for him to remember it had to be that she felt like a dead body if she wore black—always had. The high school goth phase had proven short lived after a few weeks of caked on white face powder, black lipstick and heavy eyeliner. Vampire chick just didn't suit her.

He took the leather jacket out of the box and held it up to her unzipped so she could slip right into it. It was gorgeous, something she'd admire on someone else and buy for herself if she could afford it. She touched it with light fingers. It was the perfect kind of soft and supple leather, the color of caramelized onions with the same buttery sheen.

"Put it on. I want to see how it looks on you."

She did. It fit nicely, as if it had been tailor made for her.

"It's too much, Frankie. Did you keep the receipt?" she asked, shaking her head at the thought of keeping it.

"I can afford it. I told you the garage is doing good. Real good."

"Frankie..."

"It looks awesome on you, Tessie baby. You're keeping it," he said, standing a half step away from her, then moving closer and zipping it up over her belly and chest. "Wear it when you're at work. Maybe it will help you concentrate more...you know, figure things out."

They drove quietly to Tremblay's Place, Tessa still wearing the new, special ordered leather jacket. Frankie seemed pleased with himself. She should've known he wouldn't play by the rules.

FOUR

Taking slow, meandering walks around the campus was Tessa's favorite thing to do during her lunch hour. Even in winter, she pulled her snow boots on every day at 1:00 PM, zipped herself into her old woolen coat and set off down one of the paths where she could get away from the academic and administrative buildings and between-class activity for a little while. One Wednesday toward the end of February, she found a new path that was neither shoveled nor plowed, but worn down from others who'd apparently walked it enough to create a jagged, foot-printed indentation in the snow. It wound around a few bare trees and curved a bit before ending at a wide clearing. A glass building all by itself, a greenhouse, sat within the clearing. She walked around it and found its door, pulled the handle, and stuck her head in. The warm, misty air and sudden burst of scent and color greeted her. *What a treasure! How could I have missed this place until now?* The inside was set up in rows, with several large plants taking up entire corners: a banana tree, a couple palm trees, a few flowering tropical trees that she couldn't identify.

She felt like she'd been dropped down into an oasis as she puttered through, fingering big, shiny leaves and sticking her nose into sweet red flowers.

She didn't see the stone bench or the man sitting on it until she turned to leave. She startled slightly and hoped she hadn't been talking to herself or humming a song that might've been caught in her head.

He looked up from the sandwich and newspaper that had been occupying him and nodded at her. "Hello," he said.

"Hello," she returned his greeting.

"Are you a student here?" he asked.

Tessa reached up and pulled the hood of her coat off her head so she could see him better. "No, I was just walking and I came across...I came across this place. I had no idea it was here," she answered.

"It is. It's definitely here." He wore a dark suit, a necktie that looked like one of Charlotte's stained glass creations and black leather shoes that weren't very snow worthy, but definitely looked as though they could've made the tamped down path to the greenhouse.

"So it is. Sorry to disturb you," Tessa said, giving the man a small wave and turning to make her way back to the door. But she hesitated, then started talking—not sure if she was talking to him or just talking. "These trees...I've never seen trees like these in person." She turned to face him again. "That one next to you...do you know what it's called?" she asked him of the plant with the big red leaves just to his left.

"No idea. I just like to sit next to it. It's become my friend, I suppose," the man said.

"What's your name?" she asked.

"Andrew."

"We could just call it an Andrew tree."

"Sounds good. And you are?"

"Heading back out so I'm not late. It was nice meeting

you...Andrew."

He stood up, gathered his newspaper and sandwich remnants, and said, "I meant, who are you? What brings you here today?"

"I work in the admissions office. It's my lunch hour. I like to take walks...in the snow...anytime really. I find it peaceful. Oh, I'm Tessa, Tessa Tremblay."

"Andrew," he repeated his name, "but I think we've already covered that. Andrew Hartigan." He stuck out his right hand. She shook it for a second. "I work at the main library, third floor reference desk, mostly."

They were both quiet as they stepped out of the greenhouse and found their way back to the snow-cleared walkway.

"Well, I'm going this way," Tessa said, turning toward the building that housed the admissions office.

"The snow won't last much longer. Once we get into March, it'll turn to puddles and mud," he said. "You should keep your boots handy for that."

"Yeah." She wanted to say something else, but couldn't think of anything.

Andrew gave her another nod and wave as he turned to walk the rest of the way to the main library. She noticed that he slipped his hands into his coat pockets as he walked. The newspaper he'd been reading in the greenhouse was folded lengthwise and tucked neatly under his left arm. She brought her own hands to her face and lightly touched the jagged line that still remained.

Tessa was relieved when the snow finally melted in early March, making "puddle and mud" month a reality. She kept her boots in the office at all times and continued to slip into them every lunch hour for her daily meanderings around campus. Since finding the greenhouse, she'd found a pond on the far side of the campus, surrounded by a wooded area with a crooked little creek. There was a big oak tree with a swing attached to it. One day during Spring Break when the campus was nearly deserted, she sat on it and pretended to be a kid again. There was also a chapel, a few lazy minutes past the dorms and resident cafeteria. It was a small, simple building with straight wooden benches and an organ in the corner. Between weekends and phone calls home, Tessa popped into the chapel a few times a week to say a quick prayer for her father, never staying long for fear of being discovered. Her faith was shaky at best and she didn't feel like explaining her presence to anyone.

Her lunch hours were the only times she explored. She gave herself that one hour a day—Monday through Friday—to breathe, and those five hours a week were the only time she got to feel a sense of peace and serenity. She even left her cell phone in her desk so there would be no interruptions—especially the ping of a new, pestering text from Frankie.

The campus was big and rural, tucked into the back pocket of the town, nothing like the concrete monstrosity she'd attended a few years ago. When she left the admissions office, she walked into the campus not out of it, as she used to in the beginning. Walking in led her to some magical places. Walking out led her to a busy street with businesses and traffic and pedestrians hurrying in and out of coffee shops and gift boutiques. At lunch hour, this is what people did. They buzzed about doing errands with paper take-out cups in hand. Tessa had tried this at first, tried doing her banking or a grocery run for some item she'd forgotten on the weekend—usually tea or some spice her grandmother wanted to try. But she quickly burned out, getting back to the office with no time to spare and a stomachache from a hastily eaten sandwich. By day's end, she'd felt mechanical, like a wired and battery operated thing. So she started walking inward, to where she could sit and look at tall trees and eat slowly and peacefully.

Mostly, she was alone, but since meeting Andrew, they sometimes bumped into each other on campus and ate lunch together. She had a tendency to casually look for him as though she wasn't looking, and wondered if he did the same. Eventually, they just started planning it. "Lunch at one tomorrow," they'd say when they parted, or "How's your Wednesday look this week? No afternoon meetings?" By the time the trees were blossoming at the end of April, Tessa and Andrew were meeting two or three times a week.

"You can hear them, but if you sit quietly and look at the trees, just sit peacefully and look at the trees, they're invisible. I like to think of the birds. So many birds are in these trees, yet we don't see them. I imagine them sitting, feeding, preening, doing their bird things. Singing. Then after a while, they all fly out, circle around a bit in the sky and land back in the tree. Or maybe a different tree. We don't always see them, but we know they're among us." Sometimes, Tessa forgot when she was thinking and when she was talking. Usually, Andrew was fairly quiet, so she could easily ramble on with no interruption and forget her thoughts were being said aloud.

"If we think about it. If we pay attention. Most people don't," he said.

"No. I like to, though. I like to tune out all the human noise, all the chattering, all the negative talk, the background stuff that seeps in and creates chaos in my head," she said, looking over at Andrew leaning against a tree trunk. "You know what I mean. You do it, too, I think. In the greenhouse. You do it, too."

"Yeah, I suppose." His legs were stretched out in front of him, one foot crossed over the other.

"I don't always like to talk," she said, leaning her back against the adjacent tree trunk. For now, she would allow herself to be quiet.

"Me neither. We should do this more often," Andrew said after a few minutes. "This bird listening. I like it."

They sat quietly with their sandwiches for a long moment.

"I mean, it's kind of overrated, isn't it? Talking? I'm not much good at it," he said.

"I don't believe you."

"You don't believe me? What don't you believe?" he asked with a small, contained laugh.

"I think you're pretending not to be a good conversationalist."

"Oh yeah, and why's that?" he asked.

"Because any guy who wears such cool neckties has built-in conversation skills," she said, glancing over at the geometric patterned tie he was wearing. "It's a given." She was completely making this up, but it sounded good.

"It's only a given that I've been to a few museum gift shops and bought some ties."

After a few minutes, they got up and headed back to where they each needed to be by 2:00 PM.

"I have to say, it's kind of intriguing," Tessa said, as they stepped out of the wooded area and back onto the main path that ran through the center quad.

"I've lost the flow here. What's intriguing?"

"The mystery of...of...you, I guess."

"Not much mystery to me," he said quickly.

"I disagree. One day, if I don't drive you nuts before, you'll tell me a story...about yourself." She'd already told him a few stories about herself. Nothing serious. Nothing major. Nothing life altering. She'd told him of her brief stint as a kindergarten teacher and her disappointment with it. She'd told him she liked to drive and explore. She'd even told him that this campus where they both worked was the most magical place she'd ever seen—and she'd meant it.

"I've learned to be careful about that over the years," he said, as they walked. "About telling personal stories."

"Hmm, I know what you mean, though. It's kind of like open heart surgery."

"Meaning?"

"You hand the tools to someone and you don't know if they'll be the one to open you up or stitch you back together," Tessa said, unsure where this thought had come from. *The birdsongs, maybe.* "Perhaps both."

"You're very wise for a young person," Andrew said.

"You say that as though you're old."

"Older than you, that's for sure."

"A little, I guess."

"More than a little."

"Thanks, though, for calling me wise. I'm not, really. I'm just making it all up as I go."

"It has to come from somewhere, Tessa," Andrew said.

Yeah, the great unknown somewhere.

FIVE

The path got a little narrower as they approached the old, wooden bridge. It was a Friday at the end of May. Tessa stepped over some tree roots that were popping out of the soft ground around the creek. It had been one of their quieter walks, one of their bird listening days, and she got the feeling her companion was too lost in his thoughts to pay attention to his footsteps. Even though the idea of pulling him up and dusting him off would be fun, she doubted Andrew would appreciate getting wet or dirty during his lunch hour. So she gave him a warning. "Pay attention. You might trip and fall and get all mucky-mucky."

"Thanks, yes. You're right. My mind was elsewhere," he said.

"We've got more than a half hour left. Stop thinking about work, will you?" He'd told her of a late afternoon staff meeting that he was dreading. She'd attempted humor to get his mind off it, but they ended up spending the first half of lunch hour eating quietly instead.

"Work? No. Actually, I was just thinking about...your

legs in that little skirt you're wearing today," he said. "Oh God, my thoughts just came out my mouth. I'm sorry. Not trying to be a creep," he quickly backpedaled, then paused. "I didn't really meant to say that out loud. Scratch that, please. Actually, I was just thinking about work, really."

"No way, not scratching it. Too late. And are you going to tell me about these...thoughts?" Tessa asked without looking back at him from her position two or three steps ahead of him on the rickety bridge. She imagined him squeezing his eyes shut and lowering his head, as he sometimes did when he said something unplanned.

"No."

"Well, maybe you'll show me...sometime then," she replied and kept walking.

"Yes...maybe," he said, "sometime."

"Today, perhaps. Later," she suggested, turning around as they stepped off the last creaky, wooden board and onto the dirt path again.

"You want me to show you my thoughts...about...your legs?"

"Well, if you're not going to tell me, then showing me is really the only way to go. Unless, of course, you want to write your thoughts down and let me read them." Tessa knew she was just teasing him, but was curious to see where it would lead. This was how Charlotte and Marcus talked to each other. *Just play. No harm. No hearts.*

"Or maybe you could just read my mind. Maybe we should leave it at that for now," he said, as they passed under a canopy of newly leafed maple trees.

She lightly jabbed her elbow into his side. "Maybe I should've let you fall in the mud."

"That probably would've been less embarrassing," Andrew said, turning his head so she couldn't see his face.

"Really, Andrew. You started it with your comment about my legs and my...what was it? My little skirt," she said, tilting her head at him and then lowering her eyes to the ground. "It's something to talk about anyway."

Perhaps it was the late May sunshine that had gotten into her. Temperatures had approached the mid-seventies all week and she felt silly and flirtatious in this place with its new leaves, all curly and light green hovering over them.

"Okay. It's a nice little skirt," Andrew said quickly. "I rather like it."

She was wearing a simple, dark denim straight cut skirt that ended a couple inches above her knees. It was nothing extraordinary.

"What is it about it that you like?" She was having fun now with this bit of banter, feeling like she didn't need to pull conversation out of the air if she wanted conversation. They could just be silly.

"Well, I don't know. I guess I like the way it fits you. I like how it's...a bit snug there in the back." He paused, then added, "Snug in a good way, of course, in a flattering way." He averted his eyes for a moment.

"So we're not just talking about my legs anymore?"

"Yeah, I guess," he answered and kept walking.

"Maybe we can talk about *your* legs. Hmm?"

"*My legs,*" he said, surprised, as though the suggestion was ridiculous. "No, that wouldn't be very interesting to talk about."

"According to you, maybe. There are two of us here talking about...legs. I might have an opinion on yours," she said, shifting her eyes from his face to his black suit pants, then to his shiny leather shoes and back up to his face again. The museum gift shop neckties and black-rimmed glasses gave him an academic look and the dark suits he wore everyday gave him an instant and constant formality. She was curious to see whether he would switch to beige and light gray suits, and more casual shoes, now that summer was approaching.

She snuck a glance at his hands. On the day she'd met him in the greenhouse, she'd had to look away just to keep her composure. He had the most beautiful hands she'd ever seen on a man—medium-sized and well-groomed—with no straggly hangnails or hairy knuckles. They were the hands of someone who paid attention to things, who noticed things. Most days, she was actually grateful when he put them in his pockets as they walked. But they were talking about legs today. Her mind had wandered and she'd lost track for a moment. *Yes, the sunshine is getting to me.*

"Well, maybe we should be talking about something else," Andrew said.

"Oh, not now. Are you going to spoil this by getting all serious on me? Come on, Andrew, I'm just having fun with you. Being silly." It had taken her a while to gain the ability to talk this way. She'd never been like this back home. Here, she felt more free.

"I was just thinking that maybe we've exhausted the topic."

"Exhausted the topic? Oh, that's hilarious. Maybe I just make you uncomfortable. Is that it, Mr. Dignified Man? And I'm a silly girl, a silly girl who wears snug, little skirts and wants to know your thoughts." *Where is this coming from? A year ago, I never would've talked to a man this way.* She shrugged. *No harm. No hearts.*

As they walked past the lake, they slowed down a little to look at the family of ducks waddling at the shoreline. She threw a few crumbs from her sandwich at them. They flocked to her feet and pecked at the ground.

"Is that how you want me to see you...as a silly girl?" he asked, turning back into his serious self.

"No, not really," she replied after a few seconds of contemplation. *Just playing to my assets, I guess.* Even though she was a bit old to be confused for a typical college student, she knew she could pull it off, could pass for a few years younger with the right outfit and mood. Her stature was that of a teenager. Besides that, where she came from, women were referred to as girls until they were old ladies. Men called women girls. Women called each other girls. Andrew, she could already tell, was not the sort of man who would refer to her as *a girl*.

"Good, because I don't...see you that way at all. I mean, you *can* be silly, like now...and funny...and cute in your miniskirt. Definitely. But it's not primarily how I see you."

"Okay. Something else to talk about then?" She was a bit thrown off, a lot thrown off.

"So now you're the one who's wanting to change the topic?" Andrew asked.

"No, I can talk any topic you want to talk." She was making this up.

"Any topic?"

"Yeah, any topic. If you want to give me a summary of *NBC Nightly News* from last evening, I can fire back my thoughts and opinions. Go for it," Tessa prodded.

"Actually, I missed the news last night. I was working late. You remember. You were there for a little while, wandering around in the stacks." She'd been looking for a book or two to take home over the weekend and had only waved at him as she left the library. He'd been busy helping students. "You had a longer skirt on. It was blue with a swirl sort of pattern. I couldn't see your legs," he teased.

"Ah, so we are back to legs again. I was hoping you'd mention Brian Williams. Now there's a man who probably has killer legs, but we'll never see them in his suits. Besides that, he's always sitting behind that desk. He's more of a torso, I guess. And a face. Nice sexy voice, too. His hair's a bit plastic, though, and over done."

"Brian Williams? You're thinking about Brian Williams now? How did we get here?"

"Just the flow of thoughts in my head, I guess." Tessa's

father often watched *Nightly News* on Friday evenings when she arrived. Or if it was over, he'd give her a recap. Solar flare. Earthquake in New Zealand. Bin Laden was dead. Ebola outbreak in West Africa. ISIS beheadings. Brian Williams reported it all; Brian Williams in a well-cut suit and a purple necktie. "Anyhow, I'm not thinking about Brian Williams."

"You're not?"

"Nope, not even a little," she said.

"You could've fooled me," Andrew said, raising both eyebrows at her as he threw the last of his own crumbs at the hungry ducks.

"No, I couldn't fool you. Wouldn't want to anyway," Tessa said. They crumbled their sandwich wrappers and empty coffee cups, and tossed them into a trash barrel on their way out of the wooded area of the campus. Lunch hour was nearly over and it was a good ten minutes walk from the lake back to the main part of the campus. "You know, you should really talk more. Your voice is very red. Dark red," she said, as they picked up their pace a little.

"What do you mean?"

"Dark red," she repeated. "Warm, deep, like a canyon at sunrise. Well, I guess a canyon's not warm at sunrise. Maybe with the right blanket it would be. Deep, though. See, you've got me putting my foot in my mouth now. I just meant you have a nice voice. Makes me think of the color red. Dark red."

"Okay," he said slowly, emphasizing each syllable. "Dark. Red. So, you don't associate red with anger? Or stop lights?"

"Not at all. It's a strong color."

"Well, thank you. Seems like a compliment then."

"It is."

"Do you hear colors in everyone's voice?"

"No, some are just flat or gray. Or nothing."

Color, Tessa was discovering, was not only in voices, but in everything. She was slowly coming around to this way of seeing the world since she'd been living with Charlotte. She woke up to shelves of glazed pottery over her bed and works in progress scattered about the cottage—even drops of paint that landed on the hardwood floors or table tops and never quite got properly cleaned up.

"Brian Williams? What color is his voice?"

"Hmm...now you're teasing me," she said. "Well, I've only ever heard it on TV and he's never spoken directly to me. Actually, isn't he kind of quiet these days? After his helicopter scandal and all?" It had been weeks since she'd heard his voice as the evening anchor. "Let me think a minute. I guess I'd have to say...purple."

"Purple?"

"Yeah, sort of a medium shade of purple, like his neckties. He has to try to be neutral—half red, half blue. Blended. And definitely not yellow. Yellow is weak."

"Good stuff to know," Andrew said, almost chuckling, but not quite. "I'm not neutral. Or weak, according to your color theory."

"No. You're dark red. I told you that."

They walked a few more steps, quietly—bird listening.

"Want to know what you are?" Andrew asked.

"Yeah. What am I?" *Please don't say pink.*

"Turquoise."

"Cool. I like turquoise."

"Like the ocean. That's kind of dorky and predictable, that I'd say that, right?"

"No," she said. "So my voice is turquoise?"

He paused.

"Oh yes, voices. I think I meant eyes. I guess my mind took voices and turned it into faces...and such. Well, eyes."

"You wouldn't want dark red then...for eyes."

"I suppose not. Is this why I should talk more, so I can

say silly things and look ridiculous?" he asked, his face becoming noticeably pinker.

"Oh stop it, Mr. Dark Red Dignified Man. And I'll take turquoise, thank you."

"You have a very interesting way of seeing things, Tessa. Never bland. Never gray."

That was what she was trying to do this year. She wanted to discover all her colors, her modes of processing and ways of being in the world. She ultimately wished to take the filters off and be authentic. This funny sort of conversation with Andrew was like a little test that let her say what she wanted to say—mostly. *No harm. No hearts.*

"So, what do a silly girl like me and a dignified man like you do on a Friday evening...after work?" This was a bit risky and unprecedented, but she was in the mood for it.

He didn't answer right away.

"We could come back here, hang out with the ducks and the birds again. Drink some sweet tea or something?" He turned to look briefly at her face before continuing on the path that led back to the main campus road.

"Sweet tea?"

"Yeah, sweet tea...in the greenhouse...or on the hillside."

"Bare feet?"

"If you want," he said.

"Or, we could have glasses of merlot on a café terrace in town. That posh little place over on Main Street. What do you think?" she said in her serious voice.

"That sounds very dignified," he said.

"Which will it be then?" Tessa asked, curious to see how this would play out.

"Hmm...dignified or silly?" Andrew pondered aloud. "Well, it's Friday. It's late spring. It's warm. I'd have to say sweet tea on the hillside. Sound good?"

"Yup, sounds good. Maybe I'll change to a longer skirt,

though. Put a little more dignified into my silly. Balance, you know."

He paused for a minute before responding.

"Please don't...balance anything out, I mean. And besides, do you keep a spare skirt handy at work?"

"I went to the laundromat before work this morning. I've got half my clothes in my car right now."

"Good to know," Andrew said, his eyes cast on the walking path and their feet. "Tessa, really, please keep this skirt on for the sweet tea and...bare feet. I was thinking about telling you my thoughts. You know, regarding this..." He swept his hands about wildly, gesturing at her outfit. "I couldn't do that if you had a longer skirt on. The effect would be gone."

"Alrighty then, snug and short it is, Mr. Dignified Man," she said. By this point, she could feel the heat rising into her face.

"Why do you call me that?" Andrew asked.

"Isn't that the image you try to project? In general, I mean?" she asked. "It's your public face, your public persona."

"Well, that's a good thing, right, to have a dignified public image? Why would I not want that?"

"I'm not saying you shouldn't want it, and yeah, it really works for you. I admire it, in fact."

He was always in a suit and tie and good shoes—every day. He never let his hair grow past his collar or missed a day of shaving. He spoke in a manner that projected a sense of inner calm—minus his occasional, yet endearing little stumbles.

"Thank you. Your admiration means a lot to me," he said, putting his hand behind her shoulders as they crossed the entrance to one of the busier campus parking lots.

"We're almost back, Mr. D. Guess I have to put my serious face back on for the next few hours," she said,

winking elaborately and making a final funny face before
putting it away until later.

"Not too serious, please. It will clash with the real
you...and you don't want that. You really don't."

"No?" she replied. There was no real Tessa yet, just her
often clumsy, occasionally graceful attempts at becoming
real.

"No, not when what you've got is...brilliance...and I
mean that in every sense of the word," Andrew said.

Brilliance? She took in the word, *brilliance*, but decided
not to comment. It made her think of intelligence first, then
splendor. A glow. A hint of sparkle, maybe. Nobody had
ever used that word in reference to Tessa. It was almost
funny—almost. She didn't want to wonder what he meant
by it, so she just tucked it away. If he ever said it again, she'd
ask for clarification. "See you later then, Mr. Dignified Man.
Meet you on the hillside at six o'clock."

"Six o'clock, Tessa. I'll bring the sweet tea."

"And I'll bring the merlot...just in case."

"Have you got that in your car, too?"

"Of course. You never know when you might need it."
She, as a general life rule, didn't need it. Since she'd given up
beer back in January, she'd only had the occasional sip of
wine, never more than a half glass worth. The wine in the
car was not for her.

"Glasses?" he asked.

"Glasses? No. I may have a lot in my car, but not wine
glasses. I'll pull some Solo cups from the office. Red ones."

"Perfect. Corkscrew?"

"Nah, I know a trick that involves men's dress shoes.
No corkscrew needed."

"You're going to open a bottle of wine with my shoes?"
"You'll see."

"I can hardly wait," he said.

"Me too...and just to make it fair, I'll take mine off,

too."

"Your shoes, you mean?"

"Isn't that what we were talking about? You know, bare feet?"

"Indeed. Guess my mind must've wandered a bit for a moment," he said.

"Yeah, you seem to be good at that today," Tessa said, pulling at the hem of her skirt to smooth it down.

"So, six o'clock. Hillside. No shoes."

"No necktie either. You can't be barefooted with a Solo cup full of...something and be wearing a necktie. It's incongruous," Tessa teased.

"I suppose it would be...incongruous. Definitely."

They agreed to meet after work. She turned left for the admissions office and he turned right for the main library.

Just before 5:30, Tessa opened her email and found a message from her walking companion.

3:51 PM
Tessa,
Were you serious about the sweet tea and the hillside? I'd hate to show up and wait for you only to find out you were joking, or being "silly" as you say.

~Andrew

5:32 PM
Never mind the sweet tea. I don't like the way all the sugar sits at the bottom! Anyway, I put the bottle of merlot in the fridge at 2:30. Should be nice and cold by now.

~Tessa

5:35 PM
Which hillside will you be on? I don't think we established

that.

5:37 PM
Whichever one you're on.

5:38 PM
North. South. East. Or West, my dear? I am a bit confused and easily distracted, in case you hadn't noticed that by now.

5:41 PM
You'll find me. I'm leaving ten minutes ago so I can get a head start on you. Therefore, I am running late. Catch you in a few. By the way, make sure you don't take your shoes off until you find me. That rickety bridge will give you killer splinters.

~Tessa

5:43 PM
Thanks for the tip. I'm leaving ten minutes ago, too.

~Andrew

Tessa shut down her computer and grabbed her big canvas tote bag from under her desk. The merlot was sideways in the little staff fridge, wrapped in a grocery bag. She pulled it out, slipped it into her tote and headed out. When she stopped in the ladies room at the end of the hall, she only glanced briefly into the mirror. Running her hands over her face, she pressed her eyes closed for a second. Upon opening them, she could see that her morning make-up job was now ten hours old. She blotted her face with a paper towel and decided not to reapply anything. *Maybe I can just be natural. Yes. That'll work.* Andrew seemed like a nice guy, vulnerable in a way she couldn't quite put her finger on, and definitely not too young; definitely a good distance past his twenties. *Breathe,* she reminded herself, *and just be.* It felt good to have a friend who didn't know her life outside of this soft, green place.

It took less than fifteen minutes to walk from the admissions office to the wooded part of the campus. Once she was away from the dorms and classroom buildings and heading toward the quiet, hilly area, she scanned the different paths to see if Andrew was wandering around looking for her. *No sign. Good.* She made it out ahead of him as she hoped she would. *Maybe he got caught up with a last minute phone call, or some essential task that needed handling?*

The hills were everywhere on the campus and she hoped that her clue about the rickety bridge had been sufficient for him to find her. They could've easily met up and walked over together, but that wouldn't have been nearly as much fun. She crossed the old, creaky footbridge that she'd crossed with him a few hours ago, spread out the beach towel she'd brought along and settled on the grass to wait for him.

She listened for birds.

"You had a towel on you, too?" Andrew asked when he approached. "Are you some kind of nomad who wanders around with half your closet, bottles of wine and...towels? Planning to take a bath in the stream later?"

A nomad. "No, I'm not planning to take a bath in the stream later. I had it in the trunk of my car and brought it to sit on. Don't you keep supplies and such in your car in case of...emergencies or whatever?" she asked. "Just a little something I picked up from my dad," she added softly.

"A wise man, then, with a wise and prepared daughter. Is this what constitutes an emergency, though?"

"Most situations are unpredictable enough. Can't hurt to be prepared in some way, no?" She looked up at him from her spot on the towel.

"More words from Dad?"

More like Mum, she thought, but didn't say anything. She didn't want her mum in her thoughts at that moment, but she showed up anyway—unwelcome. Her mother had always, in Tessa's memory, been the sort of person who tried, and usually failed, to control everything. Perhaps her departure all those years ago had been her way of controlling herself, at least. Tessa didn't know and often wondered if she'd ever know her mother's true motivations. "Anyway, you strike me as a former boy scout. 'Be prepared.' Isn't that the motto?" She scooted over a bit to make room for Andrew on the towel and tried to shake the dust of her mother out of her head.

"Yes, be prepared. Something I'm essentially not very good at."

"Are you kidding me? I've been in your office. I've seen you dealing with disgruntled people. You always know what to say to make things right. You can pull anything out of your hat, it seems to me." This was part of the reason she liked to call him 'Mr. Dignified Man.' She liked to imagine his brain as an archival retrieval system. She'd observed him a few times while he was working. When asked a question, Andrew went into a quiet, thoughtful processing mode, then his answers were spot on.

"Not always," Andrew said softly.

"And besides, you probably have your closet arranged by days of the week and your socks and underwear lined up by color in your top drawer."

Andrew laughed at this. "That's more of an organizational thing than a preparedness thing, wouldn't you say?"

"Oh nitpicky, nitpicky. Yes, I suppose so. But coming from a girl who considers keeping a beach towel and a bottle of wine in the trunk of her car as being prepared, then I guess it's easy to mix the two up. What I'm prepared for, I couldn't tell you...sitting on towels and drinking wine when I feel like it, perhaps." *Yeah, right. How far from reality that is for me.*

"Seems like the best kind of things to be prepared for," Andrew said, "And thank you for not changing into a different skirt."

"Yeah, no problem. You made your point about liking this one."

"Probably a bit too much. I'm sorry if I overdid it with that."

"No worries, Andrew. Now let's open this wine before it gets too late," she said.

"See, this is where I'm unprepared. A true former boy scout would have a corkscrew for such an occasion...or at least a Swiss army knife. I've got nothing, not even a sturdy paperclip."

"I told you I know a trick."

"Is this the part where I have to take off my shoes so you can wow me with your bottle opening skills?" Andrew asked.

"Yes indeedy. Go for it. And anyway, I want to see your feet. I bet you've got super cute feet."

"You're cracking me up, Tessa. I guarantee you, they're not that cute."

"Come on, Mr. Librarian Man. We haven't got all night here. Do you want some of this wine or not?"

"I do. Yes," he said.

"Then I need your shoes," Tessa said. "Both of them."

Tessa sat on the towel, hugging her knees and rocking back and forth while she watched Andrew untie his black shoestrings and slide his feet out of his leather dress shoes.

"Here you go. This better be good," he said, handing them over.

She pulled the merlot out of her tote bag, peeled the foil down from the neck and slipped the base of the bottle into one of Andrew's shoes. They were size 10.5 and stiff enough in the sole to get the job done—hopefully. She held the entire unit at a forty-five degree angle and tapped the heel of the shoe that contained the bottle with the heel of the other shoe. More than a dozen vigorous taps later, nothing was happening.

She tried not to imagine how silly she looked.

"And this is why corkscrews are important. Although I have to say this is rather entertaining," Andrew said, giggling at her.

"It's my first attempt. I've seen this done, but haven't actually tried it until now." She let her mind travel back to the evening in her cousin's cottage when the corkscrew had gone missing and Charlotte had pulled one of Marcus' shoes off and demonstrated a technique she'd learned on YouTube. She ended up needing the wall.

With no walls in sight, Tessa made her way to the bridge and gave one of the supports a little shake to test its stability. It seemed like it could handle the force, so she put all her energy into slamming the shoe encased wine bottle into the bridge rail until she had success.

"Perhaps it's not too late for the sweet tea. Or, we could walk into town and get a corkscrew somewhere?"

"There will be no sweet tea, Andrew. I will open this wine...with your shoes. Now let me focus, please."

"All right, I'm zipping it. This is better than *Saturday Night Live*, I have to say."

She didn't respond. Her balance was precarious and she didn't want to end up in the stream with a broken wine bottle. She tried to remember how Charlotte had done it. She visualized it and then, once she had the picture in her mind, she made sure the bottle was snug within the shoe, wrapped both hands tightly around it and put every ounce of strength she possessed in her five feet one inch tall body into opening that bottle. *Slam. Slam. Slam.* Into the bridge rail. It was so loud. She was certain she'd scared all the birds away forever.

Finally, after a good several minutes, she felt the cork slip up a tiny bit. A few more taps and it was nearly halfway out. At this point, Tessa climbed off the bridge and made her way back to the towel and her tote bag. She reached inside for her keys. Once she'd inserted the sharpest and skinniest key into the partially popped up cork and gave it a couple twists and a tug, she was able to slide the cork right out. *Yay! It worked.* She silently thanked Charlotte before looking over at Andrew.

"I am truly impressed," Andrew said.

Smiling broadly at him, she bowed graciously in his direction just for effect.

"Looks like an old sorority house trick, perhaps."

"Nope. I was never a sorority girl."

"No?"

"No. Does that surprise you?"

"Maybe a little."

"Secondhand YouTube knowledge," she admitted.

"Guess it's good for something, then," he said.

She pulled the Solo cups from her tote, poured half a cup's worth and handed it to Andrew, then poured herself a bit less—just a splash into the bottom inch or so of her cup—and stuck the cork loosely back in. She wedged the bottle between a few rocks to keep it from tipping over and rolling away.

"To you, Tessa, for your brilliance in opening this wine with my shoes," Andrew said, holding his cup out to hers for a toast.

That word again. Brilliance. She tucked it away. "Let's not forget the bridge. We should be toasting the bridge. It's the bridge that's brilliant," she said. "And to your shoes, and your feet, Andrew, even though I can't see them under those socks with the green stripe around the toes, but which I'm sure are very cute."

"You're something else, you know that, Tessa. You really are." He was gazing straight at her with a look of deep concentration on his face.

"And are those your...thoughts from earlier that you were planning to tell me?"

He paused for a moment before answering. "No, those are my thoughts from right now."

The grassy area where Tessa and Andrew sat with their wine and bare feet was quiet and deserted, except for the two of them. Most of the campus had slowed down since spring semester had ended and the dorm students had gone home until late August. Summer classes didn't start for another three weeks, so there was that little bit of breathing room that let the campus blossom into June. No trampling feet or evening Frisbee fests, just a couple university employees soaking up the serenity with a bit of wine and a view of the crooked, gurgling stream below their feet.

Tessa lingered over the bit of wine in her plastic cup, enjoying the non-verbal moment and trying to make it last a little longer. She would not have more. That was definite. She'd offer to let Andrew keep it and, if he refused, she'd push the cork deeply back in and pop it into the trunk of her car to take home with her.

The air was starting to pick up its early evening briskness when Tessa put her cup down on the grass, stretched her legs out in front of her and tilted her head back to catch the last of the day's sunshine. She felt Andrew slide a bit closer to her on the towel. The sleeve of his white shirt grazed her arm. He smelled like new pine needles and Tide.

"Do you...mind if I do this?" he asked, as his right hand hovered over Tessa's left knee—nearly touching, but not quite.

"No," she said. "I don't mind." *I don't mind at all.*

As soon as she answered his question, Andrew's fingers

fell gracefully down onto the bare skin of her leg as though they were being slowly released from a state of waiting. His hand simply rested there quietly as they sat on the hillside, the moisture from his palm created a slight stickiness. It must have been a full five minutes before she felt his fingertips grazing her, then sliding around to lightly rub the back side of her knee. Neither of them said anything. She closed her eyes for a moment and took a long, slow breath in and then out—and then another.

"Anyway...these are my...thoughts from earlier. You said maybe I could show you."

"Nice, very nice," Tessa said, swallowing hard. She didn't dare look at his face because she knew her own face had taken on a pinkness that she wanted to conceal if possible. Instead, she sneaked a discreet glance at his hand. "Thank you for showing me your thoughts." She was taken aback by Andrew's sudden touch, not so much surprised that he did it, but by her own response. "Very classy. Very...dignified...see, there's that word again. And, and gentle. I like your thoughts, Andrew." She was almost stuttering. *Oh hell,* she thought, *I'm definitely stuttering. Pull yourself together. It's just a hand on your leg. Hand. Leg. That's it.* Maybe it was slightly more than friendly, but she wouldn't let her mind go there—not yet.

"It feels good. Your skin, I mean. It's nice to touch," he said, barely audibly and without looking at her face. He looked, instead, at his own hand on her leg.

"Yeah," was the only utterance she was capable of in that moment.

Oh Lord, she liked his thoughts more than she expected she would. After the initial weight and sweatiness of his touch for those first minutes, his hand became a feather on her skin, or more accurately, five feathers all playing harmoniously with each other and with her.

Powder blue. His touch is powder blue.

If Tessa didn't get up soon, she would have trouble leaving—distinct trouble. *One more minute,* she told herself. She would allow one more minute before getting up to pack her bag. She started counting slowly in her head, planning to get up when she got to sixty seconds. By the time she reached twenty seconds, Andrew's fingers were inching upward toward the hem of her snug, little skirt. *Enough,* she told herself. *Enough with this counting.* Another forty seconds wasn't possible. She wouldn't be able to account for anything, if she let him touch her for another forty seconds.

"Andrew, maybe we should get going now," she said.

"Get going?"

"Yes...going," she repeated and stood, slid her shoes on and handed his to him.

He sat up straight, putting his shoes back on. "Are you hungry, then? Shall we go out for dinner?" he asked, visibly switching gears.

"No, I'm not hungry. And anyway, I need to go," she quickly replied as they started walking toward the staff parking lot.

"Go? But where? We'd only just gotten there, drank a bit of wine and now you want to go. I didn't mean to upset you. Didn't think I had."

"Andrew, no. It's good. You didn't upset me...at all. Everything's fine. I just have to go."

"Are you meeting up with someone? Friends? Do you have other...better plans?" he implored. "I'm sorry, Tessa. I don't mean to sound so...so, I don't know...confused. It's just that we were sitting so close together and well, I got overwhelmed and couldn't resist. I won't touch you again, if you don't want me to. And really, I wasn't trying to be a creep...at all. I hope you don't think that. It's fine if you don't see me in that way. I just thought...I don't know...that maybe you did."

"Nothing to be confused about, Andrew. Really. It's

fine." She wanted to say that she liked it, but worried that her face would turn red. "I wanted to hang out with you a little tonight and I did. We did. I don't have better plans, believe me. I just have a long drive now and it's getting late."

"How long?"

"A hundred and fifty-five miles," she answered.

"A hundred and fifty-five miles? To where?"

"Home," she said. "I just need to go home now."

SIX

The moon was high in the night sky when Tessa pulled into the gravel driveway of her childhood home in Fairhaven. The salt-misted air and the calls of nearby seagulls came through her open windows. Though she was too far from the beach to hear the crashing waves, she felt them in her bones. Home was on one side of Route 6; Tremblay's Place was on the other.

The dashboard clock told her it was 10:17. Her grandmother had left the porch light on for her. Tessa was glad for the yoga pants and t-shirt she'd changed into at a rest stop on Route 495. She grabbed her tote off the floor and walked up the front yard and into the house. The grass was getting longer now that the weather was warm. *I'll have to cut it in the morning.*

The institutional scent of bleach and cooking oil that had dominated her senses every Friday evening for the past few months hit Tessa the instant she opened the door. By morning, she'd be accustomed to it—even contributing to it.

"Tessa, you made it. I was getting worried about you,"

her grandmother said when Tessa closed the door behind her and slid the deadbolt. "Why so late tonight?"

Usually, she made it home before 8:30 on Friday nights and she hadn't bothered to call to say she'd be late. There were designated times when Tessa called home. Her grandmother didn't seem to understand that long distance charges didn't apply the same way to cell phones as they did to land lines. She'd explained about her calling plan, but Mémère just shook her head as though it was ridiculous.

"I got caught up a little at work at the end of the day, so I got a late start. That's all."

"Your car running okay? Such a long drive," she said, sighing loudly.

"Running fine, Mémère. You know these Toyotas. They're excellent pieces of machinery," Tessa said, finally dropping her bag to the kitchen floor.

"I couldn't sleep 'til you got here. I get so nervous worrying about you with all those nuts on the road. But now that you're home, I'm gonna go to bed now."

"Okay, Mem. See you in the morning. Will it be too disturbing if I take a quick shower now?"

"Go ahead. He's been sleeping on and off for a few hours. Kind of rattling around. Kept telling me to leave him be," Mémère said, mostly to herself. "We'll talk about stuff in the morning. Early, okay. You know me. Always up with the birds...especially now." She tapped Tessa on the shoulder and lumbered off slowly down the hall, her breath trailing slightly behind her heavy footsteps.

Tessa quickly showered and slipped into one of the nightgowns she kept in the bathroom closet. Totally exhausted, she felt like she could easily sleep for days, but knew she only had until about 5:00 AM. *There's much to do tomorrow*, she thought. *Too much.*

The floral printed quilt she kept on her childhood bed was thick and safe and held her quietly as she lay and listened for breaths and rumbling sounds from down the hall. Just as she was dozing off, she rested her hand on her knee, and caressed it lightly with soft fingertips.

Powder blue.

❧

Her father's bedroom door was open ajar, just the way he'd always kept it since Tessa's mother had left. She quietly peeked in to see if he was awake, but she couldn't tell. His eyes were closed, as they often were now, but she detected a little rustling from under his quilt.

"Dad," she called gently to him. "Dad, are you sleeping?"

She padded over to his bedside and bent over him to feel his chest. Rise. Fall. Rise. Fall. *Good.* She'd heard this is what new mothers did when their babies slept for longer than usual, just to make sure everything was still functioning. Her father's chest was still functioning.

"Tessie baby. Sit. Sit, honey. I've been awake for a while. Just don't wanna move. When did you get home?"

"Last night, around ten," she answered.

"I worry about you driving all that way in the dark. How's the car been? Any problems?"

"Fine, Dad. It's a good car."

"Listen, I want you to take it over to Frankie's later. Let him have a look at it."

"Come on, Dad. I don't want to take it to Frankie. He'll keep it all day and then I'm stuck. I can't go to the store for you and Mem. It'll suck hours out of my day." She didn't like to drive her father's truck. She was too short to feel comfortable in the driver's seat. It wasn't worth the trouble of seat and mirror adjustments and the pillow behind her back so she could reach the gas and brake pedals.

"He's a good man, Tessie. He'll take care of you," her

father said, taking slow, labored breaths. "Anyway, better to be stuck here than on the side of Route 495, or worse, one of those old country roads you take sometimes."

After a few minutes of going back and forth about the car and her long drives, Tessa could see that her father was getting tired and upset, two things she didn't want. "Okay, Dad...okay. I'll call and see if I can get an appointment for a tune up."

"No need to call, baby. He can take you anytime," her father said. "He told me."

"He told you?"

"Yup, he comes by on Wednesday nights after work. Puts the trash out on the curb for us. He's been good to me, Tessie, since I've been...unable to do it myself."

"Yes, that's nice of him. You do know that Frankie and I aren't...um, going out with each other right now," Tessa said. "I mean, anymore."

"No, baby. I didn't know. He's still a good guy," Dad said. "You sure he's on the same page about that?"

"Mmm...anyway, Dad, how are you feeling this week?"

"I'm hanging in there, Tessie. I saw the doctor the other day. Wednesday, I guess it was."

He hadn't mentioned his appointment when she'd called on Thursday.

"And? What did he say?" She always asked if his numbers had stabilized yet. That's what they were hoping would be the outcome of his most recent treatment—that his white blood cells would start outnumbering the cancer cells. But she already knew what he was going to say. It had been too long.

"Listen, baby. I closed the restaurant this week."

"What? Why didn't you tell me sooner?"

"What for? You've got your life. Your job. I'm not gonna drag you down."

"Not what I meant, Dad. Anyway, I could've taken a

few sick days to help you. Keep Tremblay's up and running. Be here for you."

"It's better that I just close the door for now. I paid my staff anyway. Maybe now that you're here for the weekend, you can run down there later and make sure the place is still standing. Okay?"

He sunk his head back down into his old, shapeless pillow. Tessa noticed the cold patina of his skin, the worn out look of him. *How did this happen so fast?*

"Tell me what your doctor said."

"Ugh...they did more goddamn tests on me. Blood work. Scans. All that shit. Looks like the treatments they've been pumping into me didn't do much good," he said, turning his head away from his daughter toward the wall on the opposite side of the room.

"Well, surely there are other treatments they can try, Dad."

"Tessie, baby. Listen to me," he said, facing her and pushing himself up on his elbows. "I've been sick for a while now..."

"A while, Dad? It's not even a year that you've been sick."

He closed his eyes to her and turned his head away again.

"How long have you been sick?"

"Probably years. I don't know. It's too late."

She reached out, put his chin in her hand and turned his head toward her. She'd always caught glimpses of the sky in her father's light blue eyes. It was a grounding thing that she used to do when she was little. She looked at his eye color, then up at the sky. On a mostly sunny day, the two colors matched. On a rainy day, the blueness of his eyes served as a reminder that it would be sunny again soon. But that was a long time ago. It was coming back to her now— even after years of hardly looking at his eyes, years when they worked side-by-side and lived in the same house, just the two of them. It was early morning now, before sunrise. When she looked at his eyes, she noticed that the color had faded a bit since the last time she'd really paid attention.

"Dad, you're still young. You're barely over fifty. Why don't you let me take you into Boston? The doctors there are better." She had tried this early on, right after he'd told her of his diagnosis, but he'd refused. He'd wanted to keep his treatment local and not miss too much work in the process.

"They're not better, Tessie, just further away."

"So...what's happening then?" She wanted him to say the words.

"Tessa, look at me," he started.

"I am."

She scooted herself in from the edge of his bed and looked more closely at her father. She wanted to hear his voice, see his bony face that had never regained the plumpness and days of stubble that was his trademark during her childhood. They'd called his unshaven cheeks and chin porcupine quills when his kisses scratched her little face.

"I'm not getting better. I'm getting worse," he said, putting his hand atop hers on the bed.

"The numbers are up again?"

"The numbers, Tessa, we're not looking at those kind of numbers anymore. Those numbers are off the charts. The numbers we're talking now are months, not cells."

"No, Dad. Let me call your doctor. I'll stay here through Monday. I'll get him on the phone and we'll talk about your options. There must be something else you can try."

"Tessa, listen to me. It got me. I didn't choose it. I have it everywhere now." He kept his gaze on her as he spoke. "Listen, baby, they gave me the option...the doctor, I mean. I could go to a nursing home or I could stay home. Your Mémère can't take care of me alone and even with you here on the weekends, I need more."

"Slow down, Dad. What are you talking about?"

"I don't want to go to a nursing home. They'd suck my remaining assets out of me. I'd lose the restaurant. My house. Kate will be here in a little while. We've hired her to come in every day. It's better this way."

She felt like she'd just been punched in the gut.

"I'm making sense, Tessa. I have it everywhere now. It got me."

"Well, *I'll* help you, of course. You don't need to hire people."

"No, baby, I can't allow that."

"Can't allow it? Please, Dad. I've been helping you with Tremblay's since...since I was a kid." *Since Mum left,* she thought. "Since forever."

"That's not the kind of help I need anymore. Anyway, it's too much. You're doing well at your job, right? You like it there. I know you do and you're getting closer to finding your own place. I'm not gonna throw a monkey wrench into that now."

Throw a monkey wrench? First, he had a tumor in his tubes and now he didn't want to throw monkey wrenches into her plans. She couldn't stand his flippancy, and yet, that was her father. He was the guy who minded his own business, the guy who'd rather close the door than call his daughter to ask for a hand. But then she thought that maybe her hands weren't enough for him. Or maybe her hands were not the hands he wanted.

"I'm dying and I need help."

She put her arm around him and leaned her head onto his shoulder. He was warm and sweaty, just like she was. How could he be dying when they were both warm and sweaty and sitting together in his bedroom, in his house, their house, that they had shared and grown in all these years? There was no logic to it. And even with his words, it was still not concrete to Tessa. She would not resign herself to it—not yet. "No, Dad. Even if you have it everywhere, it couldn't take you over."

He released himself from her arm and found his pillow again. "Okay, that's enough talking for now. Go check in with Mémère. See if she needs anything."

She reluctantly obeyed and stood up from his bedside.

"I'm going to make some breakfast for you. What would you like?"

She knew all of his old favorites. They could both whip up his diner staples with their eyes closed: scrambled eggs with diced tomatoes and parmesan cheese, sweet bread Portuguese muffins with big, fat raisins embedded in them, cinnamon French toast spread with honey and sprinkled with powdered sugar, with a side of fresh raspberries. She'd been making such breakfasts with him since she was a little girl, but especially in the last year when she'd worked alongside him every weekend at Tremblay's Place.

"Just a dry toast, baby. That's all. Maybe a little tea," he answered.

"All right, I'll let you know when I've got it ready for you," she said, walking over to both windows in his room and raising the shades to let the early morning sunshine filter in. Within minutes, it would be daylight and she wanted him to see that.

"Just bring it to me. I'll have it in here," he replied, letting his arm collapse from under him. Then he was horizontal in his bed again, his face staring at the ceiling, but with his eyes closed. "You're a good girl, Tessie. Promise me you'll take the car over to Frankie's this afternoon."

"I promise," she said and pressed the heels of both her hands into her eyes hard enough to push the tears back in. She headed to the kitchen to make toast and tea.

Mullens Motorworks was only a ten minute drive from Tessa's childhood home. Frankie's father and Tessa's father were old friends. Now Frankie and his father were business partners. As she wove through the town, she scanned for other options, but knew she wouldn't find any other mechanic who would give her the kind of price that Frankie and his dad would give her. Her passenger seat held a container of chicken vegetable soup and a loaf of banana bread Mémère had made and insisted Tessa bring along, claiming that such a nice young man needed to eat well—"especially if he had to work on a Saturday." She pulled into the back lot where the overhead garage doors stood open during business hours. She knew she would find him quickly here without having to wander through the office.

"Tessie, baby. Long time no see," Frankie called out to her from a work bench.

She walked toward him without responding. When she got close enough to his work bench, she said, "Hey Frank, my father insisted I bring my car in for you to look at. He said you could take it this afternoon."

"I can take you anytime, Tessie baby."

"Please don't call me that. Only my Dad calls me that."

"So, it's *formal* given names only, then? You're calling me Frank, not Frankie, which by the way I prefer, Frankie, I mean, coming from you. And you are officially Tessa and not Tessie baby?"

"Sounds fine to me. So...I don't think anything's wrong with my car, but like I said, my father, you know, he worries. Could I leave it for you to take a look at later when you've got a chance?" She wanted out of his garage—*now*.

"I'll do more than look at it. I'll give it whatever it needs. You shouldn't neglect your car. Take care of it and it'll take care of you," he said, wiping his hands on a rag that he'd pulled from the back pocket of his faded blue Dickies.

"Okay. Thank you, Frankie. I'll leave it here and give a

call later," Tessa said, turning toward the door.

He stepped in front of her and blocked her way. "You don't have to go. Anyway, what are you gonna do...walk home?"

"I guess so, yeah."

"Tessa, it's five or six miles and it's hot out. Come on, if you wanna go home, I'll drive you. Then I'll come back here and work on your car."

"And then you'll have to come back and get me when my car's done?"

"I don't mind."

"Seems like a lot of back and forth to me. I'll just sit in the waiting room," Tessa said. She always had a paperback or two in her tote, along with her MP3 player. She'd be fine sitting and waiting with a wall and a heavy door between herself and Frankie's work area. "How long do you figure it'll be for my car?"

"Don't know 'til I get it up on the jack and have a look under it," Frankie replied.

"Really, Frankie, as far as I know there's nothing wrong with it. Wasn't it just this winter I had it in here and you gave it...what did you call it...all the bells and whistles?"

"All the bells and whistles, Tessie, yes."

"All right, then. What could it need now?" She was losing her patience.

"Well..." Frankie started. "You drive it back and forth from your cousin's to work every day. And that's...how far? And then wherever you go after work these days. Then you drive it a hundred some odd miles from your work back here every Friday and back again on Mondays. Then you run your grandmother's errands and your father's errands and basically drive it into the ground while you're here. So, let's see...that means you put a good five hundred miles a week on this car, maybe more. At the very least, it's way overdue for an oil change, probably more than that. I'm sure your Dad wants me to check your brakes and tires too. So, let me take you home. It might be a couple hours. I've got other jobs here today, as you can see. I'll come back and get you when I'm done. We can go for a beer."

"Well, you certainly seem to know all my comings and goings," Tessa said, frustrated.

"That's my job, Tessa."

"Not really, Frankie. It's not really your job."

"Much as you say that, someone's got to keep track of you," Frankie said, slapping her on the hip with a greasy hand. "Let's go, my truck's unlocked."

She was exasperated by Frankie and actually wanted to go home to see her father and talk to Mémère about the healthcare worker they'd hired. *At least I got to the grocery store early. If I go home now, I can help make dinner and get a load or three of laundry in and out and folded.* Laundry was one of her primary jobs when she went to her father's house on weekends. The washer and dryer were in the basement and Mémère—at her age and size—couldn't manage the steps anymore. It wasn't as bad now as when Dad had been in the throes of chemo, with all the vomiting. But still, it was a week's worth of dirty clothes and bed sheets and towels. She did her own laundry at a Laundromat near Charlotte's cottage or near work before driving home, so she could devote her time to her dad's and Mémère's needs—every weekend.

When her father had first started treatment, this schedule had a goal attached to it. It was a temporary bandage. She wanted to take over the household chores so her father could focus on his health and his business. Her days were straight out: opening up Tremblay's with him, errands on the way home, housework. By Sunday night, she needed a pot of coffee just to make the drive back to Charlotte's, or else she was up a couple hours before dawn to get an early start on her one hundred fifty-five miles.

Frankie's truck looked and smelled the same as ever, with the latest issue of *Car and Driver* on the front seat, a cardboard pine tree hanging from the rearview mirror, and a Tom Petty and the Heartbreakers CD sticking out of the player. She hoped he wouldn't pop it in and play it. She was so not in the mood for "Here Comes My Girl."

"So what kind of beer do you drink these days, Tessa?" he asked, slowly and clearly pronouncing her name as he pulled out of the garage's back parking lot and swung left onto the main road. "You still like Sam Adams? Or are you into more *sophisticated* beverages now?"

"Stop it, Frankie. You know I still like Sam Adams. Haven't I always? I'm just not drinking it now?"

"How's that going? You're abstinence thing? You still holding onto that?"

"Yeah, it's going fine."

"Seems like it's been a year already."

"No, it's the end of May. It's not even half a year."

"Seems like it, though. You haven't stayed over at my place since...since...oh, hell if I can even remember at this point, Tessie."

"November," she reminded him.

"You won't find anyone else who can look past it like I can, you know," he said, turning his gaze away from the road and onto her face for an extended second.

Her hand went instinctively to the jagged scar. As old as it was by now, she could feel it burning and itching at Frankie's words. She turned to look out the passenger's side window. "I don't care about it anymore," she lied, covering it completely with her hand.

"I can still help you, you know. I have money saved."

He'd told her years ago that he would pay for her to have it corrected by a plastic surgeon. She'd told him she would think about it, but knew she wouldn't use his funds if she ever decided to do it. The last thing she wanted was to be indebted to Frankie. She'd be even less real to him because everything would get erased with that plastic surgery.

"I'm good for now. It's fine."

"Yeah, well...the offer's there if you want it," he said. "You sure it's only been a few months since you cut me off, baby?"

"Mmm hmm." *I'm sure.*

"Well, time sure is a funny thing," he said, glancing at her for a long second as they approached the last red light before Tessa's street.

Time. Yes.

The light turned. Frankie punched the gas pedal as he sometimes did when he didn't like what was happening. Once he was back to looking at the road, Tessa looked down at her abdomen. *Time is a funny thing, indeed.* Had she gotten two lines on the test back in December, she'd be six months along by now. She took a deep breath and exhaled it as quietly as possible.

"Yeah, it is," she agreed as Frankie turned the truck into the driveway of her childhood home.

SEVEN

Tessa didn't get back to work until Tuesday afternoon. She'd used Monday to confer with her father's various doctors. They were sorry. They had done what they could. "If only it had been caught sooner, he might have recovered," they said. "The best thing to do now is honor your father's wishes and be there for him." *Bullshit.* She couldn't abide the indifference of it. There had to be a way to make Dad see into the future—to see he still had life in him.

It was mid lunch hour when she got to her desk and saw the pile of work that was starting to accumulate. She booted up her computer and opened her email, which was filled mostly with work related requests, scheduling stuff, and various meetings she needed to attend later in the week. Toward the end of the new messages, there was one from Andrew from three days ago.

> *Saturday, 1:31 AM*
> *Dear Tessa,*
> *I haven't fallen asleep yet. I'm wondering if*

*you're okay and also hoping that you are not upset with me.
Please let me know if you'll allow me to share my 'thoughts'
with you again. Maybe you could even share yours with me.
Any skirt is fine. (Was going for humor there).*

~Andrew

She immediately replied.

*Tuesday, 1:22 PM
Dear Andrew,
You are probably out at lunch now. I just got to work! Bad
weekend. Will not go back home until Friday again. Lunch
and walk tomorrow? Yes, please, to our 'thoughts.' The non-
verbal kind would work best for me now. No words today.
Hope to see you soon.*

~Tessa

On Wednesday afternoon, they met on the main walking
path that ran between the admissions office and the library,
and walked—mostly quietly—to the bridge where they'd sat
with the merlot a few days before.

"So you commute a hundred and fifty-five miles back
and forth from here?" Andrew asked after several minutes.

"Yeah, I do. Each way...on the weekends. I'm used to
it."

"Where do you live during the week?"

She told him about Charlotte's cottage in Hubbardston,
which was thirty-seven miles from work. "It's still a bit of a
drive, but I like driving so I don't mind. It works for now
until I get my act together and find my own place," she said.
Finding her own place had been her focus for several

months, but now that her father wasn't getting better her priority would have to shift. She'd have to tolerate living in Charlotte's walk-in closet a bit longer.

"And what's at home that you go back for every weekend? Do you have commitments there?" Andrew asked. "Family?"

"Yeah, family," she replied, as they walked past the trail that led to the greenhouse. "Well, my father and grandmother live there. They need my help. They're both...disabled in some way. I go and cut the grass, go to the grocery store, do laundry, give my grandmother a break from the cooking and so forth. And visit, of course. Hang out with them, well, with my dad mainly. They're cool people. They really are." *Cool people.* Well, how else could she describe them in the current context? She'd leave it at that. *Cool people, cool disabled people who need me. Yeah, that's a good way to put it, and mostly true.*

"How long have you been doing that...every weekend?" Andrew asked, as they approached a random bench towards the far edge of the campus. They sat and opened their sandwiches.

"A while."

"Well, it's good of you to help them. Is it just you or do you have siblings that you rotate with...or...?"

"No siblings, but it looks like it's not just me anymore. They've hired someone," Tessa answered. "Kate."

"Well, that must be a relief for you. Does it free you up a bit?" he asked.

"No, I still have to go. Want to go," she said. "I need to go, really."

"You're certainly a busy woman, Tessa. May I come straight to the point then?" he asked.

"Yeah."

"Let's say I wanted to hang out with you, take you out, perhaps...drink merlot on the hill, stick our feet in the stream, or something. Are there any evenings when I, when we, might have a chance at that?" He was looking down, not at her.

"Monday. Tuesday. Wednesday. And Thursday. I'm here more than I'm there." *It just doesn't feel that way. It feels like two lives—the actual one and the make-believe one.* This job, this sitting on benches and hillsides with Andrew and sandwiches and wine was the make-believe life. It was a nice indulgence, though, an escape from the reality of her exhausting weekends opening and closing Tremblay's Place with her father, while trying to avoid Frankie as much as possible. There was no balance between the actual and the make-believe—no fulcrum. She tried to think of Charlotte's cottage and her little closet room as the fulcrum that balanced her two worlds, but it seemed more like its own separate entity.

"Okay, good to know," Andrew said before taking a bite of his sandwich.

"Could we possibly get to the non-verbal thoughts now, please?" Tessa asked, reaching out her hand to touch the sleeve of Andrew's white dress shirt. "I'm kind of in a bird listening mood today."

"Yeah," he said, "me too, I guess."

He looked good. Crisp. Perfectly shaven, as usual. His necktie was silk, patterned with dark red dragonflies. She couldn't remember ever seeing him wear it before and wondered if it was new. *Did he buy it over the weekend, hoping I'd notice it? Probably not. Only girls think that way.*

"Sorry I don't have any strong beverages or clever ways of opening them on me today."

"Guess that's more of a Friday thing, right?"

It was more of an anomaly than anything. Her father liked an occasional glass of red wine on the weekends and she'd bought it for him. "Sometimes," Tessa decided to say.

"Quite all right," Andrew replied. "I've got an Arizona

iced tea big enough to share," he said, lifting the oversized can in Tessa's direction. It couldn't have been more than a minute before he spoke again. "That little scar above your lip, is there a story behind that?" he asked.

Tessa moved her hand to the back of Andrew's shirt collar and tilted her head toward him. She bit her bottom lip to stop herself from reacting to his question. "I thought we were doing non-verbal today," she answered. "That's what I feel like, please." *No words today. No words.* "I'm just in a quiet mood."

Tessa had never thought of it as a 'little scar,' as it was over three inches long, thicker in width than a nickel and ran in a jagged curve from the left side of her nose to the center of her upper lip. It was pinkish white now, no longer crimson, but still noticeable. It would always be noticeable.

"Non-verbal, okay," he said. "Sorry I asked. I seem to be the talker today. I'm just curious. I noticed it a while ago. But we can save it for another day, if you want...or not."

"Yes, please, another day," she said, her voice breaking a bit. *Non-verbal, please.* She wondered how badly Andrew needed his glasses and what his eyesight was like without them, but resisted the sudden urge to pull them from his face and make herself a blur to him. She did not say this little scar had given her years of grief. *Don't ask again,* she silently wished. She would be okay in this quiet place, here among the trees and bridges and hills of the campus. There was no need to talk about the night she'd gotten it, but was beginning to wonder if maybe she should put it out in the open as her mother's legacy to her.

Another day. Onward. New place. New Tessa.

Instead of reaching for his glasses to remove them, Tessa moved her fingers up from the stiffness of his collar, onto the skin of his neck and up into his hairline at the nape. He took a quick, sharp breath in and relaxed his shoulders a little.

"This going back and forth to help your family seems to be taking a toll on you. I'm glad you have more help now. Maybe you'll be able to rest more after your long drives, sleep in a little on Saturdays," Andrew said, laying his hand on her arm just above the elbow. She didn't reply. His fingers seemed tentative, quivery.

Non-verbal. Non-verbal. Non-verbal. Please.

Her light and silly bantering style of communicating with Andrew was gone—for today anyway. *How can I go from an extended conversation about legs and feet and creative ways of uncorking a wine bottle to saying my father just told me he's dying?* Just as wearing a necktie with bare feet was incongruous, so too was her shift from the previous Friday to today. Last week her father had been sick. *Sick, goddamn it, but getting treatment, trying at least to become not sick anymore—trying to get back to his former self. Now he's dying.* He seemed to believe he was dying, but not if she had anything to say about it. She had to convince herself that she had plenty to say about it. *Just not now.* Her head was too full for words.

And then Andrew had a hand on her arm and was sliding it upwards toward her shoulder. The shirt she was wearing had loose little sleeves that were easy to reach into and she felt that same feather lightness on her skin that she'd felt a few days ago. *Powder blue.* She closed her eyes and focused on nothing but that feeling, that sense that he was somehow even writing a message on her skin, each finger making a different letter. The early June breeze was warm and gentle enough that the only word she needed was *serenity* and the only feeling she needed was that she actually existed in this place, this magical place of flowers and birdsongs and meandering walking paths.

Just before 2:00 PM, they got up and walked alongside each other and back to their respective jobs.

"Thank you for the non-verbal today, Andrew."

"Anytime, Tessa," he replied, "anytime."

"I think it helped me somewhat," she said.

"I think it helped me, too."

They kept the same pace until the path split and they had to turn in opposite directions.

"Anyway, my birthday is on Sunday," she started. "I'll be at my father's house, of course, but I was wondering if maybe you and I could do something fun one day next week. Maybe after work on Monday or Tuesday. What do you think?"

EIGHT

On Saturday evening, there was enough of a breeze outside to cool Tessa off after a hot, nearly ninety-degree day in which she'd completed all her usual chores and errands. There weren't even mosquitoes, thanks to the bats and the pond full of frogs on the side of the house. Their repetitive noises didn't bother her as they once bothered her mother. "Those goddamn frogs. I can't sleep with them chirping and croaking all night," she used to say. "They eat the mosquitoes," was her father's defense. Tessa tended to agree with her father on this one. In fact, she kind of liked them. It was as though the frogs were talking to each other and to Tessa. "This is small town life in early summer. Keep it simple," they seemed to say from over her shoulder and just beyond the row of shrubs separating her from them. If not for the frogs and bats that ate the mosquitoes, she wouldn't be able to sit out on the front steps at 10:00 PM in June.

Her father had been well enough to attend Mass earlier without any fainting or pulling over along the way so he could vomit on the curb, as he had done a few times during

72

his chemo treatments. He seemed to feel better, if only spiritually, with the body of Christ in him, and the Eucharistic Ministers were good about coming to his pew so he didn't have to walk up the aisle on shaky legs.

A crunching of tires over gravel interrupted the serenity of the frog songs. Tessa had been staring up at the starry sky, but averted her eyes from the constellations to the driveway at the disruption. Frankie jumped out the driver's side of his pickup truck with a twelve pack of Sam Adams in his hand.

"We never got to that beer last weekend, Tessa," Frankie said, as he popped one open and handed it to her, then did the same for himself.

"No thanks, Frankie. I'm all set."

"Come on, Tessa. One beer. It's already open," he said, plopping himself down on the porch step next to her. "How's your car been?" he asked after a few swallows of his beer.

"Good. Fine. Trying to cut down on unnecessary driving during the week to spare it a little wear and tear," she said. *And too frequent visits to Mullens Motorworks for more tune-ups,* she thought.

He finished off his beer and popped himself another. "Am I drinking alone here, Tessa?"

Her own can remained untouched. "How many did you have before stopping here, Frankie?"

"Maybe two."

Maybe two means at least three. "So that puts you on your fourth now. Slow down. I'm tired and I don't feel like driving you home," she warned.

"You won't have to, Tessie baby. I'll be fine. Just relaxing a little with you."

"Well, Frankie, if you're too *relaxed* to walk a straight line, then I'll have to drive you home, won't I?"

"Or you could just take it easy, babe, and just let me be."

Tessa did not want to spend her Saturday evening with Frankie, and certainly not her Saturday night. All she wanted was to sit on her front steps and feel the evening air, listen to the pond sounds and watch the bats flittering above her. She wanted to think about her father, quiet and resting in the house, bringing oxygen into his body. And after, when some serenity took over her mind, if even for a moment, she wanted to imagine herself sitting on a bench with Andrew, surrounded by flowering trees. Maybe she'd even call his cell phone later to say goodnight.

There wasn't room for Frankie in this string of quiet moments that she was trying to put together, but Frankie had a way of appearing and Tessa had trouble sending him away. She lacked something unnamable, some inability to be bluntly direct, but at least she wasn't going home with him anymore. That was over and done with. No more backpedaling her way out. She was done with Frankie. *Damn it, will I ever be done with Frankie?*

"Why are you here on a Saturday night? I thought you had buddies to hang out with."

"Tessie baby, I'm twenty-nine years old. All my buddies are married or engaged by now. I'm the only one left that isn't. It kind of sucks to always be the third wheel or the fifth wheel," he said, halfway through his current beer. "Take a sip of yours, Tessie. Don't be so afraid of me. I've never hurt you and I never will."

"Please, Frankie. I'm anything but afraid of you," she replied. She was more afraid of herself. A twelve pack of Sam Adams and a Saturday night with Frankie had not proven to be the smartest combination over the years. On several occasions, one beer just led to another and another and then familiarity took over. There had been a few too many Sunday mornings she'd spent berating herself for getting sucked back in—again.

Last November, when her father began another round

of chemo and Tessa started coming home to help every weekend, she'd had her last beer and last Saturday night with Frankie Mullens Jr.

Her can was still on the steps between them, creating a ring of condensation beneath it. He tapped it with his fingernails, then slid it a bit closer to her.

"I'm all set, Frankie."

"Here," he said, picking it up and taking a swallow. "I'll share it with you. You won't do anything stupid on half a beer, if that's what you're so worried about."

When he handed it back to her, she relented and took a couple swallows of it. It had been months since she'd tasted beer and she found that she still liked it, though not as much anymore. It was a little bitter to her now, but the familiar smell pulled her in and she ended up drinking the rest of the can.

"See, that didn't kill you did it, Tessie?"

"Why do you do this to me, Frankie?"

"Do what, babe?"

"Show up here?" she asked.

"Is it so bad that I show up here? It's not like you were busy or anything," he said. "You were just sitting here."

"My father's very sick, you know. They say he's down to months. Maybe weeks. He's got this woman coming in every day now. This health worker." She wouldn't say the words *hospice* or *palliative care*, because Tessa had neither determined which it was or figured out the difference between the two.

"Tessa, I knew that before you did."

"Since when?"

"Your grandmother calls me. Tells me stuff," Frankie said, setting the empty can down on the concrete step.

Tessa just breathed and let herself absorb this. "It's nice of you to come by on Wednesdays to take care of the trash for them. They appreciate it," she said.

"Yeah, I know they do. It's no big deal. I drive right by on my way home anyway."

"Frankie, you live upstairs from your garage," she said. "Or did you move since..." *Since what?* she thought. *Since the last time we had a beer or twelve together? Since the last time I went home with you on a Saturday night? Since I decided I was done with you? Really done.*

"I do towing and jumpstarts. Emergency assistance. Takes me all over town," he said. He then stood up and walked a few steps to the driveway, kicking up the gravel. "You don't miss me, do you, Tessa?"

"I appreciate what you do to help them during the week when I can't be here," she said.

"Not what I asked," he replied and walked toward her, bouncing a stone in his hand.

"Frankie, stop. You're going to get us into a situation. I can't do this right now. I need to think about my father." This was true, but she also needed to not think about Frankie. This was never an issue unless he appeared on her doorstep and wanted to reminisce with her. It was harder when he was full of beer.

He got in her face. "You can't think about your father and me at the same time?" he asked.

"Not really. Worrying about him...his health...sucks everything out of me when I'm here on the weekends."

"Yeah, on the weekends for you. Why do you have to work so far away? It's not exactly practical, is it? And it's not like it's some great job. You could've found an office job around here."

She took a deep breath. "I've had that job for almost two years. I like it. And no, it's not some great job, but it's a job and jobs aren't exactly easy to come by nowadays. I'm lucky to have what I have. Really, Frankie you're starting to piss me off with your...comments."

"Not trying to piss you off, Tessie. But if it was my

father dying, I think I'd be around more. Just trying to see your perspective, I guess."

He stumbled and grabbed at the porch railing.

"Here's my perspective, then," she said, raising one hand up at the sky. "They are both asleep right now. I have a precious little while to sit here and breathe. That's what I came out here to do."

"Can I breathe with you? Just for now?" He sat down very close to her on the step before she could answer. His left leg brushed against her right one for a few seconds before she scooted back a little away from him. She bent both her knees up to her chest and hugged them to her so as to be self-contained, a capsule unto herself. *Maybe then he'll go away.* All these defenses were tiring.

"I was thinking of making some coffee. Do you want some?" she asked without immediately moving.

"Not yet, Tessie. Let's breathe first. It's a nice night," Frankie replied, suddenly calmer. Or maybe he was numb from the beer.

"Yeah, it is. That's why I'm out here," she said.

They sat until the moon rose over the treetops, which was only a short time—a half hour at the most—and she told him she wanted to go in and relax on the couch with a book. She offered him coffee again, but he declined.

"You think maybe I can use the bathroom before I go? All that beer, you know."

"We're in the woods here, Frankie. Go for it. I'll close my eyes."

"No need, it's not like you haven't seen it before," he said, "Really though, I couldn't do that to your grandmother's rose bush."

It had been her mother's rose bush, but she didn't mention this to Frankie. She and Tessa had planted it so many years ago, back when Tessa was little more than a toddler. She remembered pricking her finger on one of the thorns, as they transferred the bush into the ground. Her mother had said, "you have to be careful with roses," and told her to stick her finger in her mouth to stop the bleeding. She still remembered the metallic taste.

"All right, use the one off the kitchen so you don't wake anyone up."

"After you," Frankie said, holding the screen door open for her.

She was standing by the kitchen door, ready to usher him out when he emerged from the bathroom.

"You never answered me when I asked you if you miss me, Tessa," he said, lingering in the doorjamb with newly minty breath.

"You're familiar, Frankie. We go back a long way," she said.

"That's all it is, then...I guess...for you, anyway," he said. "Is that the book you're reading?" he asked of the vegan cookbook on the table.

"Yes," she answered, "I'm trying to learn some new recipes."

"Tremblay's will lose all its good customers if you start putting that vegetarian stuff on your father's menu."

She only sighed. "It's for his health. I'm reading up on foods that would benefit him right now."

"Believe me, though," Frankie said. "No red-blooded American guy wants to eat sprouts and mushrooms and pretend it's a burger."

"Are you okay to drive yourself home?"

"Yup, I'm good, Tessie baby, just fine," he said, kissing her cheek as he stepped out the back door with his keys in hand.

She left the porch light on, so Frankie wouldn't trip on the gravel and fall on his face in the driveway.

Tessa grabbed the cookbook from the table and sunk into the couch. From her position, she could see the driveway where Frankie's truck sat cold and dark. He must've passed out in the driver's seat.

Tessa woke up when she heard her father tossing around in his bed sheets. She discreetly peeked her head around the corner of his door, in case he didn't want to be seen yet. His shoulders were shaking under his pajama shirt. He rocked back and forth, facing the wall opposite the door. She tiptoed away and went to put the kettle on and figure out what she could make him to eat before his health worker arrived.

It's Sunday. Is Kate coming today or is it her day off? She couldn't remember the conversation with Mémère. It had been such an onslaught of information, full of schedules and booklets to read and lists of his pain medications. The only thing she could remember was Kate telling them to let Ben eat whatever he wanted, whatever he could hold down. *Eating just anything will not benefit him.* Even Tessa knew that and she made a mental note to sit down with Kate soon and explain how she felt.

It was 5:00 AM. She'd woken up stiff and achy, her book crushed between her arm and the back of the couch. After twisting her hair up into a messy bun and grabbing her keys, she quietly let herself out the back door to go check on Tremblay's Place. It had been nearly a month since she'd worked beside her father. She didn't miss the place itself, just the idea of it. All his good pans were there and probably lots of stuff in the freezer that she could take home little by little to feed him. Whenever he had leftover produce, he froze it to use in his pies. When she was a little girl, she scoffed at his spinach and feta pie and told him it was gross to put spinach in a pie. But when he gave her a slice, she just melted right into it. *That's what I'll make him today; spinach and feta pie.* She was sure he'd still have all the ingredients at the restaurant.

Clutching her keys in her hand, she rounded the corner of the house and headed for the driveway. She saw that Frankie's truck—with a sleeping Frankie in the driver's seat—was still parked behind her car, blocking her.

"Frankie," she said, tapping at the window. "C'mon Frankie, I need to get out of here. I need you to move your truck." She noticed the rest of his twelve pack was empty on the passenger's seat.

He didn't budge and was actually snoring. *Damn it.*

"Tessa," her grandmother called from the living room window. Mémère was breathing hard, as though the day had already knocked the air from her lungs.

"What's the matter, Mem?" she asked, turning around to see if Frankie had backed up yet. *Nothing,* she thought. *His truck is dormant and so is its driver.*

"You crazy? It's five in the morning. Get in the house before the neighbors see what's happening."

"The only thing happening is that I'm trying to back my car up and Frankie is blocking my way. He's sleeping."

"Why in the world is he sleeping in his truck out there?"

"He fell asleep, I guess."

"When?"

"Last night. Ten or eleven, I guess."

"Really, Tessa. You certainly could've offered him the couch, if he was too tired..."

"He was too drunk, Mem, not too tired. I didn't want to deal with him in the house waking up you and Dad."

"That would've been better than him sleeping in his truck, don't you think? Good Lord, we'll look like crazy people around here," she said. "Come inside the house, Tessa. I'm not talking out the window anymore. It's ridiculous."

Tessa walked around the house, keys in hand, no longer

careful to keep them from jingling, and went in through the back door.

"You left the tea kettle on," Mémère said, "that's what woke me up."

It was late afternoon by the time Tessa got to Tremblay's Place. Her father had fallen asleep after lunch and the bit of birthday cake Mémère had served. The Sunday health aide—not Kate—had come and gone already. Tessa figured she had maybe an hour to get what she needed, get home to make the spinach and feta pie for him, then be on her way back to Charlotte's house for the coming week.

"What the hell, Frankie. You scared the shit out of me," Tessa yelped when she heard footsteps in the kitchen. She was in the walk-in freezer with the door propped open when she noticed him.

He only laughed. "The door was open."

She hadn't locked it behind her, as she knew she'd be in and out quickly.

"What are you doing here?" she asked.

"Came to see you. Talk to you."

"I need to be quick, Frankie. It's getting late," she said, stepping out of the freezer.

"Late for what?"

"Just late. I'm getting some of my father's good pans and..." she started to tell him, but then stopped. *No need to explain to him,* she decided.

"And?"

"I want to make him a healthy dinner and some meals for the week before I go."

"Mmm...for the week, huh?"

"Yes, Frankie, it's Sunday. I need to go back soon and I don't want him just eating anything. He needs good nutrition now."

"Hmm...don't know about that, Tessie. He probably needs something else."

"Excuse me, please," she said, as she tried to maneuver her way around him and out of the freezer. "I need to pass by. I really just need to pass by, Frankie."

He didn't move.

"I really just need...I don't know, Frankie...peace in my head, I guess."

"Peace in your head? Seems to me all your comings and goings, all your back and forth are not helping you get peace in your head," Frankie said, air quoting her. "I mean, really, you've said it wears you out," he added.

"I don't mind driving." Tessa usually felt the most at peace when she was driving. It meant music of her own choosing and a stretch of road in which she had serenity and solitude, with nobody asking her for anything. From work to her father's house took just over two hours without stopping. Before her father was in chemo, she used to meander off the road and stop at antique shops to browse and fantasize about how she'd decorate her own place when she finally had one. Or she'd pop into little coffee places along the way. Nowadays, there wasn't leisure time for stopping and lingering. Still, it was two hours with nobody asking her for anything or telling her the right way to do something. *It's suspended time.*

"It's just that you don't seem to understand what's practical, Tessa."

"Practical? I've been practical all my life." She thought of the path that led her to the present moment. Through her late teens and into her twenties, she'd lived peacefully with her father, worked with him at his little restaurant and gone to college. She was focused on a plan that hadn't worked out—a plan to be an independent woman with an education and a meaningful career.

"I don't know, Tessa. You're not being very practical

now. Not at all, if you ask me. Wouldn't being in one place give you more peace?"

"Frankie, please, I can't keep having this conversation. It's not helping. I'm trying to take things as they come. I'm helping my dad the best way I can right now." Most of her non-work time was going toward her father in some way. She called him almost every night and either talked to him or her grandmother. She was working on accepting Kate's role, was even working on being grateful for her presence. *And if I can just get these good pans and enough spinach to make a pie, or three or four spinach pies, I can leave for the week with a sense of peace—a little anyway.*

"Living with him, or at least in the same town, would be best," Frankie said, "if you *really* wanted to help him."

"Frankie, enough! I need to go. I'm working tomorrow and it's late now," Tessa said, reaching into her bag for her keys. "And I have stuff to do before I go." The laundry was in the dryer and she still needed to pick up Mémère's blood pressure prescription before the pharmacy closed.

He leaned over her and grabbed her around the waist with one arm. "What time do you start work in the morning? Nine?"

"Eight."

"I'm up by five on Mondays. Mondays are busy at the garage. I start early. Stay with me tonight. I'll wake you up in plenty of time to get you to work by eight. I'll even make you a cup of coffee for the road." His grip was tight. His mouth was on her. Then his leg was pressed onto her crotch, trying to wedge itself in. "Come on, Tessie, it's been a long time. Let's stop this bullshit. I miss you."

"There's no bullshit, Frankie. I can't get peace in my head, if you're always...always..."

"Always what?" he interrupted.

She took a breath and attempted to collect herself, as well as the right words.

"Always at me," she said, her eyes closed.

"At you? Always at you? He's your father and I do more for him than you do."

"What are you talking about? The trash? The midweek grocery runs if they run out of eggs or milk?"

"If you were here all week, you'd see what I do."

"Is that all you're going to say?"

"Go, Tessa. Go drive for two hours and clear your head. I'll deal with your father and grandmother. It's fine. They trust me," he said, letting go of her and reaching into his pocket for his own keys. "See you next weekend," he called back to her, as he opened the door of his truck.

As soon as he drove away, Tessa flipped the lock on the door of Tremblay's Place and went back into the kitchen. She lined up the three bags of frozen spinach, a dozen eggs, a carton of feta cheese and her father's pie crust, which he made in batches and froze to use whenever the urge to bake a pie struck him. She pulled spices down from the rack and a large mixing bowl from under the counter. *The big oven takes too long to warm up, so I'll use the smaller one.* She clicked the knob to 375 degrees and got to work. Once she'd made four spinach and feta pies, she wrapped them, shut everything down and drove back to her father's house to finish up the weekend.

I hate Frankie. All the way to Charlotte's cottage, she hated him. She drove and drove, his words still in her head, his breath on her face, his insinuations that still made her feel so small and inconsequential. Still, she couldn't help but wonder if he was right, and didn't want to face Frankie being right. *Of course I should live with Dad. I should be there 24/7. I should do everything I can. I shouldn't walk out every Sunday night and drive away. I should insist.* But Tessa didn't insist with her father. She was the child and he was the parent, the adult.

She arrived to a dark cottage and went straight to bed, but couldn't sleep. Charlotte was home and alone. *No Marcus tonight?* At least her cousin was asleep. Tessa had the place to herself in that sense. It was a small relief to be in a place that allowed for a little bit of breathing room.

When Charlotte slept, she slept deeply. When she was awake at night, which was often, she was not a quiet roommate. It was the mark of an artist to be aware and present and occupy the space around her. Charlotte liked to see, feel, be tactile and create. To her, the world was texture and color. It was all about bringing the raw material into some kind of life. Clay became pottery. Cloth became eclectic tote bags. Color became personal attributes. Tessa loved this about her cousin. The world was vivid to Charlotte, much more so than Tessa ever imagined or believed possible. She was starting to feel it, too—sometimes slowly, sometimes in bursts.

Tonight as Charlotte slept, Tessa padded about the little house and stared out windows at the hazy moon glow on the water, the tiny, breeze-driven waves on the shoreline. In the living room, there was a heavy wooden table that was used for just about everything from eating to mixing paint colors. Tessa reached under it and into the stash of miscellaneous scraps that Charlotte kept there. She pulled out a little stack of scrap paper and mentally put *buy sketch pad* on her list of things to do for the coming week.

Tessa had never learned to draw for real. She could only trace or use templates and had no concept of how to create a vanishing point or of which colors complemented or contrasted with each other. *Yellow and purple, is it? Yellow and purple seem like good opposites.* Tessa opened a drawer on the side of the table and fished around until she found a box with a few colored pencils in it.

By 2:00 AM, the moon was low, nearly gone from the window. She stood with the scrap paper and pencils, drawing the moon as she saw it—nearly gone.

Her drawing had a cartoon quality to it, something a child might produce. She even contemplated giving it a face, but decided against it. She felt eight years old again. There was no fatigue. No voices telling her anything. Just a dim room and a colored pencil in her hand. *Surely this is what keeps Charlotte awake at night too. Only Charlotte's a real artist. I'm only playing at it.* When she had filled the paper with her purple and yellow fantasy moon, she went to bed, tossed about on her mattress for a while, then finally fell asleep after remembering that is was no longer her birthday, but the day after.

NINE

It was raining on Monday, the day after Tessa's birthday. She'd given up the idea of finding Andrew on the footpath and taking a walk with him, assuming she'd just have lunch at her desk. Perhaps when the torrents slowed to a drizzle she'd dodge puddles for a hot tea and a bowl of the cafeteria's soup of the day. But when she opened her email toward the end of the morning, there was a new message from Andrew.

> *Monday, 11:11 AM*
> *Tessa,*
> *Did you bring an umbrella today? Let me know.*
>
> *~Andrew*
>
> *Monday, 11:32 AM*
> *Yes, Andrew. I always have one in the trunk of my car. Be prepared, you know! Do you need to borrow it?*

~*Tessa*

Monday, 11:36 AM
No, I don't need to borrow it. I have my own. Just wondering if you were up for a walk to the greenhouse for lunch?

~*A*

Monday, 11:42 AM
Dear Mr. Williams,
Sounds perfect. It's a good thing I'm wearing a very dignified and classy outfit today (with not too much leg showing). No cameras though, please. My friend Andrew would be so jealous! Can't wait. Does 1:00 PM work for you?

Sincerely,
~*Tessa Tremblay*

P.S. Are you wearing one of your purple neckties? Please, please!!!

Monday, 11:51 AM
Dear Ms. Tremblay, I regret to inform you that Mr. Williams will be unable to meet with you, but am glad you seem more yourself today and gracefully ask to join you in his absence. Your silliness appears to have returned. Must be riding your birthday vibes from yesterday. Looking forward to a wet walk to the greenhouse later. Yes, 1:00 PM is perfect. See you then. And I don't have any purple ties. You must stop confusing me with your celebrity crush!

~*Andrew Hartigan (NOT Brian Williams)*

Yes, Tessa had an umbrella. No, she did not have proper shoes that covered her feet. She was strictly a sandals girl in the warmer months, with the exception of a pair of sneakers for her runs and her crazy busy weekends when she needed to rush off to church and the grocery store and mow the lawn without fear of losing a toe. She'd packed her boots away once mud and puddle month was over, and her sneakers were not in her car today. *I must've forgotten them on Dad's back porch last night. Oh, well. Wet feet won't kill me.*

At 12:55, Tessa grabbed a yogurt and a banana out of the staff kitchen, tossed them in her tote and headed out the door. She popped her umbrella open against the deluge and made a dash for the greenhouse, all the while shaking her head at Andrew's silliness to be out in this weather.

When she arrived ten minutes later, Andrew was already there, shaking the drops off his own umbrella, then propping it against the glass wall to dry out a bit.

"Well, yes. That looks like a very dignified outfit today, Ms. Tremblay," he said with a laugh.

"As dignified as a drowned rat. Pardon the cliché. My brain must be wet, too."

"Where did your legs go?" he teased. "Did you retire that snug little skirt after...after the last time I saw you wearing it?"

"Retire it? Hah! It's raining frogs and dogs out there, Andrew. My snug little skirt would look like a funny swimsuit on a day like this. But thanks for asking. I haven't forgotten how much you like it," she replied. "Nice and warm in here, though. I'm taking off this jacket and these wet sandals." Tessa peeled her rain jacket away from her skin and spread it out on one of the benches. She then bent to unfasten her sandal straps so she could sit on the bench with her feet under her.

"Anyway, happy birthday a day late. Is it okay to ask how many years you've been gracing our planet here?"

Andrew asked, between bites of his sandwich.

"Gracing our planet here?" She laughed at his choice of words. "Twenty-five. Prior to that, I lived in a big, sturdy nest on a far away colony with a family of pre-historic birds. I don't know why they sent me here, really, but I'm slowly getting used to it."

"I love your quick humor, Tessa. You're very funny."

It must be my rain soaked brain that's making me funny. "Thank you and how many years have you been...gracing this planet here, Andrew Hartigan?"

"A decade longer than you have. More like a decade and a half. I'm...thirty-nine, closing in on forty, actually, in a few months. Not looking forward to that."

"You look younger. I would've guessed thirty-four. Thirty-five, tops," she said honestly.

"Well, that's good to know. You sure you're not just flattering me?"

"Oh yeah, I'm just flattering you. Why would I need to flatter you? Really?" Tessa asked. "Anyway, my father asked me who my friends are these days...who I spend time with when I'm here."

"And what did you tell him?" Andrew asked.

"I told him I have a friend at work who is cuter than Brian Williams and has nicer legs too."

Andrew just snorted. "And how would you know that...about the legs? You've never seen mine. Or Brian Williams' legs. You said so yourself. He's more of a torso and a face...and what was it? A nice, sexy voice?"

"Something like that. You're much younger anyway and you've got far better hair."

"Probably not that much younger, but thanks about the hair," he said, chuckling. "So, do you dream about Brian Williams when you're back home on weekends tending to your family?"

"Really, Andrew. I couldn't give two figs about Brian

Williams," Tessa said.

"Couldn't give two figs?" He laughed.

"Guess my rain-soaked brain couldn't come up with anything better. It's one of my grandmother's old expressions."

"Of course. My grandmother used to say that, too," Andrew laughed. "Have you ever eaten a fig?"

"Oddly enough, I don't think so. They're hard to find around here, aren't they?"

"I suppose. They're very good for you, though. And sweet. You'd like them."

"I'll have to put that on my to-do list," Tessa remarked. "Eat figs."

"Sounds good. It's too bad there isn't a fig tree here in the greenhouse. We could just pluck them and eat them right now."

"Yes indeedy, Mr. Cuter than Brian Williams Man."

"Brian Williams again? Maybe we can move on from the whole Brian Williams thing now. I think it's run its course. You clearly have a huge crush on the man and it's becoming sort of annoying. You know...all these comparisons."

"Two figs, Andrew. Two. Figs!" Tessa laughed. "Besides that, who always comes up more favorable?"

"I suppose."

"I just like to tease you," she said. "It's fun."

"I'm glad you're feeling better today than you were last week. Was it a better weekend at home than the previous one?" he asked.

"My grandmother made me a cake, one of her specialties. She used to run a bakery back in her day. And my father felt well enough to sit on the deck with us and have a piece. We even finished off that bottle of merlot," she smiled. "Well, my father and grandmother finished it. I only had my usual half glass." This happened late on Sunday, after they'd eaten one of the spinach and feta pies.

"Sounds like a good birthday. Do you still want to do something with me?"

"Of course I do," she answered, sticking her elbow lightly into his side.

"What'd you have in mind, Tessa? Dinner out?" He paused for a moment. "A little skydiving, perhaps?"

"Oh skydiving, yes please. I had no idea you were that adventurous, Andrew."

"I'm not. I was joking."

"Good. So was I. I can't even tolerate roller coasters."

"Really? That surprises me about you," he said, tilting his head a little in her direction. "I'll have to scratch that off my list of ideas then."

"Yeah, definitely. Just something simple works for me. How about tomorrow after work...I mean, if you're free tomorrow after work. Oh, and no gifts please," she added, instantly feeling silly for assuming he'd get her a gift. "I'm too old for birthday gifts."

"You're never too old for birthday gifts."

"Really, Andrew. Something simple. No gifts," she said.

"No skydiving or roller coasters, either. Sounds easy enough," he said. "You know, you never told me what your father's disability is. Do you mind if I ask?"

Why this? Why now? Oh, not when we're having such a light and fun lunch in the greenhouse, she thought, while the rain battered the windows all around them and created a wavy world of color as it dripped down. She slid closer to him, rested her head on his shoulder and closed her eyes. *It's good to have a friend here.*

He seemed to understand immediately. "It's okay, Tessa. You don't have to tell me," he said in a soft voice as he put his arm around her shoulder. "I have to learn to shut my dumb inquisitive mouth sometimes."

She was non-verbal for several minutes before deciding

to tell him about her father's illness.

"I will, though...tell you, I mean," she started. "It's not so much just a disability. He's full of cancer and he's dying. He's only fifty-one. Probably won't make it until the end of the year. That's what he says anyway. I haven't quite wrapped my head around it just yet." *Oh God, did I really say it out loud? Can I somehow retract it?* Her gaze went instantly to the greenhouse's damp concrete floor.

Andrew pulled her closer to him and ran his fingers up and down her arm in a soothing way. It was different than his usual light and feathery touch. This touch was more intentional, more assertive, more understanding.

"God, Tessa. I didn't realize it was that. When you said he was disabled, I assumed an injured veteran or a guy who hurt his back and was out of work, recuperating." He paused. "Come here. Come *here,* Tessa."

He stood and spread his arms to her. She fell into him. He hugged her tightly, pressing his hands onto her lower back as he pulled her even closer toward him. She let herself meld into him as her tears dripped onto his shirt.

"I'm glad you're my friend," she said after a minute or two.

"Yeah, me too," he replied.

Oh God, Andrew. Non-verbal. Non-verbal. Non-verbal, please.

TEN

Tessa had been back at the cottage, tossing around in her little closet room for some time. Her mind wandered from her father to Andrew and back again in cycles. She'd called home after work and had gotten Mémère, who'd told her that her father was sleeping—which may or may not have been true. *Perhaps she just didn't feel like getting up to deliver the phone to him. Perhaps she, too, is exhausted from caring for him, her only son, and only wants to get into her bed and stay there.*

Charlotte was not a quiet insomniac—not at all. Tessa's cousin had been in a phase of late night productivity for several nights now, excluding the deep sleep on Sunday. Tessa could sense a frenzied mode to it.

She opened her bedroom door, stretched from side-to-side and padded over to Charlotte's pottery wheel. "Channeling?" she asked over the noise of the wheel. Charlotte was deep in her zone and deep in her clay.

"Hard few days. Yes, channeling. See how it works?" Charlotte nodded at the shelf that held her newest creations in process, but kept her hands moving. "Sorry I woke you up."

"It's okay. I've got a lot in my head anyway," Tessa said. "Tell me what happened."

Charlotte was silent, her hands caked in wet clay. She rubbed and pinched the lump of gray, as it spun around and around on the wheel. She was transforming it, putting her heart in. Tessa knew this piece would be brilliant. She also knew Charlotte wouldn't sell it. She never sold the ones she stayed up all night to create.

"Nothing extraordinary. Got my heart broken a couple years ago. Happens to us all sometimes." She paused. "But this...this was one of those rare things I didn't even see coming until I was too far gone." She dug her fingertips deeper into the clay, creating a wide groove in the work-in-progress. "Hard anniversary this week. Hence, this," she said, pointing again at all her new projects.

Tessa waited for more.

"We were friends. Polite acquaintances, really, until one day we were alone together and everything between us just burst open. It was like I'd found someone who mirrored my own soul. We could be completely ourselves together. No filter. Complete ease." For a moment, Charlotte closed her eyes and ran a thumb across her own cheek, leaving a smear of gray from her nose to her ear. "It was beautiful while it lasted, but it was...it was too complicated. Right person. Wrong time."

"How long did it last?" Tessa wanted to know, suddenly hungry to feel it vicariously.

"Four and a half months. But it doesn't matter. It could've been one day and I'd still have felt the same. It was the intensity of it. The purity. It was authentic. You know what I'm saying?"

Tessa didn't. *What do I know of intensity and purity and love with such limited reference points of my own?* "What was

95

complicated about it?" She could ask this because she understood complicated.

"We had to meet discreetly—mostly here. It's out of the way here," Charlotte said. "There were others involved, you see. Not on my end, but on hers, and mutual guilt and shame because of that."

"Hers?"

"Yes, hers. She was married and had a family. Husband. Kids. Completely unavailable to me...and yet, I was hers and she was mine for that short time. In the end, she couldn't leave them. Wouldn't. And I never should've asked her to. It was selfish of me to even consider it." Charlotte looked up at Tessa. "Are you shocked? Not what you expected?"

"A little maybe," Tessa admitted. "I'm so sorry."

"It was real, you know. I never felt that way about a person before...or since." She started to cry. "And I probably won't ever again."

"What was her name?"

"Marlene."

"Beautiful."

"Yeah, she is. Deep green eyes. I see the whole world in them."

"Do you still see her?" Tessa asked, surprised by Charlotte's present tense response.

"No. Just picturing her in my mind right now. Is. Was. It's all the same, anyway."

They let a little time pass before resuming the conversation. Tessa wanted to perk Charlotte up, bring her back to the moment. "So...why Marcus?" Tessa had noticed that Marcus was also beautiful, with his thick wavy hair that had a tendency to fall over one eye.

"It's easy to pretend with him. It's like theater. We play roles with each other. We understand each other. He's not in love with me. It's mutual there. And, really, we're great friends. So why the hell not?"

Tessa knew her face must be betraying her.

"It's a touch thing, Tessa. I'm very tactile, as you obviously know. The mind needs to wander sometimes—often for me—and touch can help that. Have you noticed his hands, how delicate they are? He has an artist's hands. And he's good with them, almost as good as a woman is with her hands," she said, rubbing just her thumbs along the top edge of the clay. Her creation was becoming taller and more symmetrical. It looked like it could become a vase, but Tessa knew that Charlotte could completely reshape it. She hoped it would become a vase, though. Visions of big, red Gerber daisies in it had already formed in Tessa's mind. "Sometimes I even fall asleep with Marcus. And when his hands are wrapped around me...that's when I feel her the most. And then his mouth becomes her mouth. His long thick hair becomes hers. And so on."

Tessa slid to the floor, too tired to stand any longer. She wanted to stick her fingers into the clay on Charlotte's pottery wheel. *Another time, perhaps, I'll ask for a lesson.* Instead, she let Charlotte's story float around in her head.

"I haven't had sex since last November," Tessa said after a while.

"Because...?"

"It's an experiment," she said, "to see if I miss it."

"And do you?"

"Not really, but I think about it quite often."

"Of course you do. That means you miss it. Or...it means you need it."

She told her cousin about Frankie—all of it. It was such a relief to have someone else hear it, validate that she wasn't imagining his overbearance with her.

"There's such a thing as a realm of desire that can't be ignored for very long. It's not the same as love, not for me anyway and not for most guys your age. Believe me. It doesn't need to be complicated. If there's one thing I've learned, it's that. It can just be for fun. For release. For escape," she said, all the while pressing her fingers into the clay. "Marcus has some cute young friends he works with at the theater. I'm sure he could hook you up with someone."

"Um, no...not yet. I don't need it that badly. I want to give myself a year."

"A year? Really? That would never work for me. I'd think about it too much, and Marlene, who I think about anyway, but it's less tragic with that outlet. Don't make yourself loony, Tessa." After a minute or two, she said, "Come here."

Tessa slid up from the floor.

"Put your hands on it...and feel."

Tentatively, slowly, she touched the lump of spinning clay, closed her eyes and imagined it becoming something else.

Eleven

Tuesday, 8:37 AM
Dear Tessa,
I'm using my lunch hour today to figure out your surprise.
Stop by my office at the end of the day. Is 5:30 okay? We'll
go from there.

~Andrew

Tuesday, 9:06 AM
Dear Andrew,
Okey-dokey, Mr. D. See you at 5:30. Looking forward to it.
Remember, no gifts.

~Tessa
P.S. Thank you for understanding yesterday. You give really
good hugs.

Tuesday, 9:14 AM
Dear Tessa,

I do understand. I'm glad the hug helped you for the moment. And, you are unbelievably nice to hug also. See you after work. No roller coasters, I promise.

~Andrew

Tessa tried her best to plow through her day, stopping only for a quick sandwich in the little staff kitchen at 1:30 PM. Her to-do list was getting shorter by the hour. The first week of June was a relatively quiet time to be working in a college admissions office. Her supervisor was off on vacation this week. There were hardly any students popping in to ask questions, just the occasional lost, hopeful newcomer who was looking for the registrar's or bursar's office or directions to the library. She was good at answering that last one. *Follow the path until it splits, turn right, pull heavy glass doors open, walk past main desk and up the stairs. Say hello to quiet, well-dressed librarian who works on the third floor. For best results, wink and make funny faces at him, but do not disturb him between 1:00 and 2:00 PM because he is planning a birthday surprise.*

The phone even rang less frequently as summer approached. From May finals to the upcoming summer session, the campus was in a state of quiet but steady transition. It still rang enough to disrupt her workflow, though, and the more her workflow was interrupted, the more her mind wandered. It wandered to her walk to Andrew's office at 5:30 PM in anticipation of her birthday surprise. More often, it wandered to her father. She wondered if he was up and around today, or if he was stuck in his bed on this warm, sunny day. Tessa hoped, at least, that Kate was encouraging him to sit on the deck and maybe even eat a little lunch there. She tried to picture him in his lounge chair with a cup of soup in his hands and a magazine in his lap, appreciating the breeze and the birdsongs. But she knew this was an unlikely scenario. She could just about get him outside on the weekends and had to promise to tell him a story if he agreed to a bit of sunshine. Mostly, she feared that Kate's presence wasn't a positive thing for her father's state of mind.

At 5:00 PM, Tessa shut down the office and went outside to call Mémère before going to meet Andrew. By the seventh ring, her grandmother finally picked up. As usual, her breath sounded heavy over the miles.

"What's wrong Tessa? Why are you calling here on a Tuesday night?"

"Mem, nothing's wrong. I just wanted to check in. You know, see how things are going with...Kate."

"It's all right. We're adjusting to her being here. You know your father. He's not one to let strangers do for him. He's kind of awkward around her. Tries to send her home early," she said.

"Do you let her go early?" Tessa asked.

"It's only been a few days so far. She's here by seven o'clock. Gives him his medicine and tries to make him comfortable. She talks to him a little bit."

"Is he getting around, Mem?" Tessa asked. "Or does he just lie in bed?"

"No, no sweetheart. He's up and down. He's tired a lot, though. You know all this, Tessa. Watch your phone bill. There's no need to call here on a Tuesday. You take care of yourself. We'll see you Friday, okay?"

Tessa felt dismissed. She wanted to talk to her father, hear his voice if only for a minute or two, but Mémère was trying to cut the call short. "Don't worry about my phone bill, Mem. I have seven hundred minutes a month."

"I don't know what that means."

"It means I can call whenever I want," she replied.

"Still, it's not free to call whenever you want."

"It's fine, Mem, believe me. Let me talk to him for a

minute now."

"He's resting, Tessa. Kate left a while ago and he's worn out. I'll wake him in a little while to eat supper with us," Mémère said, "when Frankie gets here."

Tessa inhaled. "Why is Frankie eating supper with you and Dad?"

"Because he's a single man who works hard and helps us quite a lot."

"Don't let him get too comfortable, Mem," Tessa said.

"Somebody has to make him comfortable, Tessa. Somebody has to cook for him," Mémère said. "Are you done working for today?"

"Yes, I'm done working. I have plans with a friend from work. Belated birthday celebration sort of thing," she said, then worried that using the word 'celebration' may have been over the top.

"Okay, go then. I need to go check the pork chops anyway."

"Don't give Dad too much fried food, Mem, it's..." she started, then heard the phone disconnect. She pressed the end button and squeezed her eyes shut for a few seconds before tossing the phone into her bag. After three deep breaths, she stood, checked the office door to make sure she'd locked it, then headed to the library to meet Andrew.

She wasn't sure if her call to Mémère had helped her state of mind or not.

When Tessa got to the library, she stopped in the ground floor ladies' room for a pee and to check that her eyes were not red or puffy. The mirror revealed that her scar was more prominent today than usual. It was funny how emotions seemed to affect it, making it more visible, even bumpier, when she was worried or sad. Or when she'd just been reminded of Frankie. *Damn it.* After a quick, but concentrated dab with her concealer and a swipe across her lips with a medium pink gloss, she felt slightly better about it. *I haven't hidden it, but at least I've decorated it.* She tried to make it look like a normal part of her face. *At this point, what else can it be?*

Tessa spent another minute or two in front of the mirror, examining the rest of her face before heading upstairs. This was the year she'd decided to become. *Become what?* Become more alive, more of who she felt she was before her life had nearly been stolen from her all those years ago. Finally, she would become the real Tessa. *In this place, I can become the real Tessa.* She couldn't be melancholy or preoccupied today—not for this belated birthday celebration with Andrew—sweet Andrew, who seemed to like her.

It was just before 5:30 PM when she tapped on Andrew's partially open door with her knuckles.

He ushered her in and offered her a chair. "Wait for me here, Tessa. I need to get some things from the fridge. I'll be right back and then we can go," Andrew said, sounding eager. His enthusiasm was a perk.

Within minutes, he was back with a large insulated cooler bag. "Shall we go now, birthday girl?" he asked, extending a hand out to her in a 'let's go' gesture.

"Where are we going?"

"I thought you wanted a surprise."

"Okay, don't tell me, then. I can wait," Tessa said. "Are we walking or driving?"

"Walking. It's not any further than where we usually go...just the other way."

"It's fine. I've got my walking sandals on today, good rubber soles. I can walk forever."

"Good to know, but it's only about ten minutes. Fifteen, maybe. We're not even leaving the campus...unless you want to," Andrew said. "I just need to grab something from my car first, though."

"It's your surprise, Andrew. I'm open to anything...well, except skydiving or roller coasters."

He raised his eyebrows at her. When they got to his car, he popped the trunk and pulled out a picnic basket and a folded blanket. "You know, it's good you wore your walking sandals and comfortable clothes today, Tessa, with where we're going. Although, I have to tell you I rather miss your little skirt."

"Hah, you just had to comment, didn't you?" she teased. "Just felt like more of a pants day today." She laughed.

"I often feel that way myself," he said, smirking a little. "I can hardly blame you. You must get tired of being ogled."

"Ogled! What a funny word. No, I don't mind being...ogled, as you say. Besides that, you're most likely the only one around here ogling me. Anyway, you put up with all my silly Brian Williams comments, so that gives you free rein to ogle me to your heart's content, Mr. Dignified Andrew."

"I'm not so dignified if I'm ogling you, am I?"

"You're always dignified. It's who you are," she said quickly and truthfully. "Anyway, what's there to ogle, if I'm wearing pants today? We'll have to find another topic of conversation," she said, recalling their funny chat from two weeks ago.

"Yes, with your legs covered up...let's see, we'll have to think of another subject matter. But I'm sure we'll come up with something. After all, you can talk any topic, isn't that right?"

"Any topic," she agreed. "Let's not provoke any tears today, though."

"I'm sorry about that. I never meant to provoke tears, believe me."

The tears were almost worth it for the hug I got out of it. She almost said this, but didn't. *Light and easy today.* She would try to keep it light and easy. *Be birthday Tessa.*

"So, is talking about your visits home on the weekends off limits, then?" he asked. "How is your father doing?"

Tessa noticed that Andrew had a way of asking a yes or no question, then continued to pursue the topic before the yes or no answer came. She didn't really mind. It was an improvement over the days when he hardly talked at all.

"I just called home and talked to my grandmother. She wouldn't let me talk to him...said he was resting," Tessa said. "The person I told you they hired, Kate...she's a palliative care nurse." She instantly felt the familiar heaviness starting to build up in her eyes. "Damn it. No tears provoked. Isn't that what we just agreed on, Andrew?"

"Clearly you need to talk about it though, Tessa."

"I'm trying to give it some space. Today, right now, especially. I want to feel like a normal young person, having a normal birthday with...a friend."

"Sounds good, then. Maybe I'll just stop talking altogether. I get into less trouble that way, it seems," he said.

"Or we could talk about you...about your family. Only if you want to, of course," Tessa suggested. "There's so little I know about you. About where you come from." *Your inner landscape,* she wanted to say. *You.* She was still feeling a bit raw from yesterday.

"Okay. Maybe. We're almost there now," he said. "Vermont, by the way."

"Vermont? You're from Vermont?"

"Born and raised. Most of my family is still there."

They were trekking through a wooded part of the campus, down a winding path far from the footbridge.

"There's a clearing over there just past that big rock. I was thinking that's where we'd have your birthday picnic," Andrew said, after a minute or two of silence.

"You're running the show here, Brian Williams. It's your planning. My surprise. It's all good. Here. There. Wherever," Tessa said.

"Okay, Miss Silly. That's the new deal. You call me Brian Williams, I get to call you Miss Silly."

"Is that supposed to bother me?" Tessa asked, teasing.
"Does it?" Andrew asked.

"No, I like it. That you see me as silly is a compliment in a way. I try not to let my situation at home bring me down all week. It's hard for me to think about it all the time...but also hard not to think about it," she said. "Being funny or silly kind of takes the edge off it, if you know what I mean." It also let her try out a new way of being. Being funny or silly with Andrew felt natural to her.

He didn't say anything; just put his arm around her shoulder as they walked toward the edge of campus where tall pine tress stood strong and stable, creating a canopy overhead. When they got to the clearing, he told her to sit down on the rock and close her eyes. She breathed in the scent of pine needles as she sat perched atop the big rock, while she awaited Andrew's surprise. She heard his rustlings, his unpacking of the cooler bag and the picnic basket. The blanket he'd carried tucked under his arm sent a rush of air at her when he snapped it open and fluttered it for a second or two before letting it settle in a clear spot beneath the trees. There was a clanking of glass and metal and the sounds of plastic containers being popped open.

She let her mind wander yet again to her family a hundred fifty-five miles away from this place, this make-believe life. *I wonder if Dad is still resting or if he's now eating supper with Mémère?* She thought of simple food like tomato soup with Ritz crackers crushed into it and tried to visualize him lifting the spoon to her mouth when she was little. *And why the hell is Frankie there, eating with them? It makes no sense that I am here in this pine tree haven and Frankie is there with them.*

Her thoughts were interrupted when Andrew said, "Okay, Miss Tessa. You can open your eyes now. Your birthday surprise is ready. I hope you like it." He was standing close enough for her to smell the starch on his shirt.

"I won't open them until you call me Miss Silly."

"Open your eyes, Miss Silly," he said, kissing her very lightly on her cheekbone, so lightly that it felt more like a breeze than lips touching her cheek.

"Oh, this is a big improvement over my towel and Solo cups," Tessa remarked when she saw the scene before her.

On the blanket, he'd spread the contents of the two containers he'd carried. There was a small platter of shrimp cocktail, a bottle of merlot with proper wine glasses and a corkscrew, a chilled chocolate tart with whipped cream and sliced strawberries on top and a ceramic bowl full of fresh figs. *Figs.* This was the part that blew Tessa's mind. *Figs.*

"Oh my God, Andrew. Look at this. Look at these," she said, jumping down from the rock. She picked up a fig to feel its softness. "Where did you get them?"

"Trader Joe's"

"Really? I've never seen them there," she said.

"I hadn't either, but I figured if any place would have them, it would be them. So I called and asked. They get them shipped in fresh from California twice a week during June. It's the early crop. Another crop comes late summer, early fall. New batch came in this morning. Guess it was my lucky day."

"Mine, too," Tessa said. "This was very sweet of you, Andrew. All of this. It's a perfect surprise. Thank you." *A little too perfect maybe.* All she'd expected was a latte and perhaps a slice of cake at one of the cafés in town.

"You're welcome, Tessa," he said, scanning the blanket and all its contents as though making sure nothing was going to melt or tip over. "So...there's quite a bit of food here. I hope you brought your appetite."

"I did," she replied, watching him open the wine with the corkscrew. "Do you think maybe I could still convince you to take your shoes off for me? If I took off mine, perhaps?" she asked, slipping out of her black, leather sandals. *Might as well get comfortable and enjoy it,* she thought.

"Done," he said, kicking them off. "I'm all set with this tie, too. Don't want to be too...incongruous for you," he said, tugging a little at his collar to loosen it before unknotting it. He slipped it off and placed it on the picnic blanket.

He then handed her a glass of wine, quite fuller than what she would've poured for herself. She took several sips, then found a stable place to set it down so it wouldn't spill.

As they talked and ate, they saved the figs, enjoying the sight of them, bright and drippy in their bowl. Andrew told her he was from a small town thirty miles south of Burlington where he'd lived most of his life. He had one brother and one nephew. His parents still lived in his childhood home on a little dead end street. She realized he was about the same distance from home that she was— *possibly a bit further.*

"What brought you here?" she asked.

"A change of scenery mainly," he said, "a fresh start, I suppose."

Andrew was looking at her, then down at the picnic blanket, then back up at her. She didn't ask any more questions, knowing from experience when someone was reaching the limit of what they wanted to share.

"Me, too," Tessa replied. She didn't add that she hadn't found her fresh start yet, that she was still floundering, still bouncing from one place to another from weekday to weekend and hadn't had an actual home in quite some time. She didn't mention that all she wanted in this life—aside from a miraculous healing of her father—was a place that was absolutely hers and the time and resources to find it and decorate it, then inhabit it fully. Her place. *Someday. Soon.*

"Your turn to close your eyes, Andrew," she said.

He did as she asked and she moved closer and sat next to him, side-by-side, their hips nearly touching.

"How is it possible...really...*how*...is it possible that you're single when you do things like this for your female friends on their birthdays?" she asked, putting her hand atop his and weaving their fingers together. It was the first time she'd directly touched his hand. It felt smooth and warm and just slightly reluctant.

He hesitated for a few seconds before answering. "It's fairly recent that I've been single...and I...haven't done a thing like this in quite a while," he replied, curling his hand into hers and closing the gap between their fingers.

She reached over to his eyelids with her free hand and touched them lightly with her fingertips to make sure they were closed. Then she slid herself onto his lap, put his head in her hands and kissed him in a way that she'd never kissed any other man in her life—from his cheeks, along the edge of his face at his jawbone and then on his mouth for a long time. A good, long time. His tongue was the perfect kind of sweet. Andrew's reciprocation said way too much and she picked up the glass of wine he'd poured her and drank the rest of it down in one gulp.

Both of Andrew's hands slipped beneath Tessa's long hair, his fingers weaved in and around the strands as though he was trying to loosely braid it. She leaned her head back and let the sensation of his fingers sink into her. The slight tugging at her scalp was shooting another kind of non-verbal urge straight through her body. *Oh God, what was that New Year's oath again? What had Charlotte said last night about realms or something?* "Andrew, I...I want...," she started, then stopped talking, unsure what she even wanted to say.

"Tell me what you want, Tessa," he said softly, mostly with his mouth on her jawbone. "I'm pretty sure it's what I want, too."

She opened her eyes, looked over at the picnic he'd created for her and was astounded at all the thought that had gone into it.

"I want to...I really want to...eat one of these figs," she said, slipping off his lap. "That's mostly what I want...right now."

"Yeah. That's exactly what I was thinking you might want. That's why I got them for you."

There was a hint of sarcasm in his response, but it was mostly teasing she detected, as though he clearly knew she wasn't done expressing her wants quite yet.

Tessa reached into the bowl and picked one up. They were small and soft and lightly fragrant. The really ripe ones had a clear, sticky juice dripping from them which gave them an instant lusciousness.

"You can just bite into it, you know. It doesn't need to be peeled...or prepared in any way," he said, looking at her.

"Okay. Aren't you going to have one, too?" she asked.

"Yeah, I am," he said, picking one up and biting into it. She did the same.

"Oh God, Andrew. These are awesome. Let's eat all of them."

"Yes, let's," he replied. "The thing about figs is that they're only fresh for about a day or two, not much longer. They are delicate and sweet and perfect, but you can't wait very long to enjoy them or...you'll miss your chance."

"Sort of an instant gratification thing, then, these figs...these beautiful, sweet figs," Tessa said, biting into the second one Andrew offered her, then licking the bit of pulp from his fingers.

"Or...a seizing-the-moment sort-of-thing," he replied, putting his lips to her ear. "Come home with me, Tessa. Please. Come home with me tonight."

"Let's go," she said without any further thought.

TWELVE

The drive to Andrew's apartment was a short one, ten minutes at the most. Tessa left her car on campus and went with him in his. It was not quite dark yet, as they passed through the center of town, past the Main Street cafés and businesses, the clothing shops and hair salons. Andrew took several rights, then a left onto a small side street. He parked in the building's resident lot and popped the trunk, so he could bring the rest of their picnic indoors to either enjoy or save for later.

"One small favor to ask you, Tessa," he said, as they rode the elevator up to the fourth floor.

"You're not going to ask me to wear a costume or anything, are you? 'Cause I'm not into that kinky stuff...really, I'm not," she said, sliding her hand into his waistband and brushing the skin of his hip for a second or two, distinctly aware, yet not caring, that her New Year's resolution would not make it into the next day. *Hell, it probably won't make it into the next half hour. It's June, anyway. Isn't six months of a resolution enough?*

He grabbed her and pulled her toward him.

"No, Tessa. No costumes," he said, as the door opened and they stepped out onto the fourth floor hallway.

"What is it then, Mr. Librarian Man?" she implored, as they approached his door and he unlocked it. "Speak up."

"I was just going to say that...you know...you may not call me Brian Williams when you are in my bed with me."

"Oh, aren't you fairly confident that I will be in your bed with you. What makes you think I'm not just coming over to play Scrabble?" she teased.

"Tessa." He said her name and then paused. "You just put your hand in my underwear, I'm thinking that playing Scrabble is not exactly what you had in mind. Besides, you don't stand a chance of beating me at Scrabble. I'm a Scrabble master."

"I bet you are. But I could still kick your ass at it. I'd need to see it first, though."

"My Scrabble board?"

"No, Brian Williams. I need to see your ass first. Then I need to sink my fingers into it just to gauge how hard I can kick it, of course, when we play Scrabble," she teased. "Sometime."

"Not too hard, I hope. I do like sitting down without pain," he said, gripping her wrist tightly in his hand.

"Oh, no worries there. I would kiss it all better afterwards...massage it, too, for as long as it took to heal your pain."

"Really, Tessa. Your humor is very arousing," he said. "Seriously, though, can we cut the Brian Williams references for the rest of the night? I don't think my ego is up to it."

"Anyway, Andrew, I wouldn't dream of it. You are Andrew. Andrew Hartigan. I know who you are. Besides, who the hell is Brian Williams? Really? Just a torso and a face," she said, kissing him.

"And a nice, sexy voice," he added.

"Oh, get over it. Yours is far sexier, believe me. There's no comparison. I'll take dark red over purple any day. And since the subject is open, no calling me Silly Girl when I'm in your bed, either."

"Definitely not. That would be totally incongruous," he said, pressing her against the wall outside his bedroom and running his fingertips up and down her bare arms.

"Highly incongruous," she retorted, stumbling for the doorway into the room.

"Deal. Shall we shake on it?"

"Really, Andrew? Shake on it? I think we can come up with something a little better than a handshake. Now let's go, Mr. Williams. We're not in your bed yet."

"My car is still at the campus. At some point, you'll have to drive me there so I can go home...well, back to Charlotte's house," Tessa said into Andrew's ear after collapsing on top of him—again.

"Unfortunately, yes. You wouldn't happen to have half your closet in your car today, would you?"

"No, I usually save my laundry for Fridays. So, looks like we missed my traveling wardrobe by a few days."

"Pity. I was just thinking it would solve your 'what to wear for work tomorrow' question if you wanted to stay here...with me tonight."

"Oh Andrew, how very tempting. This whole evening has been such a beautiful surprise. Really. All of it...from the figs to the wine to...this," she said, rubbing his belly lightly with her knuckles and letting her fingertips linger over his hips. "Best birthday ever. I have to say, though, I wasn't expecting to end up here...like this."

"Really?" he asked.

"Yes, really. I was expecting a latte and a slice of cake," she admitted. "If I'd expected this, I would've put some spare clothes in the trunk of my car."

"Ah, not keeping up with Mum's advice about unexpected situations," he said. "That was your Mum's advice, yes?"

"Yes," she replied sternly. "Why'd you have to bring that up? Let's not ruin the evening, please."

"Sorry. Didn't know I was hitting a sensitive spot there," he said, raising both his hands in his own defense.

"I know, I shouldn't have snapped at you like that. I'm sorry, Andrew," Tessa said, kissing him softly on the mouth and putting her fingers into his wavy, dark hair and twirling it a little. Without his glasses on, Tessa could see the tiny lines that were just starting to form on the outer corners of Andrew's eyes. *This man is more beautiful than I deserve,* she thought.

"It's okay. Now I know. I'll be more careful."

"You shouldn't have to be careful about what you say to me. I like the way we communicate with each other. Being silly and spontaneous, saying whatever we want," Tessa said.

"Yes, we seem to have gotten better with the non-verbal stuff, too," he said, rolling on top of her again.

"Andrew, it's almost midnight. I should go. I've loved this night. It's been perfect and...well, more than I expected, if you know what I mean," Tessa said.

"I think I do," he replied.

"Thank you. Those figs were almost too good for words."

"Too good for words, yes. The figs. And Tessa, really, you don't have to keep thanking me. It's not as though I'm not enjoying it, too...this night, I mean. I'm enjoying it, too...quite obviously," Andrew said, pressing his mouth onto her neck and breathing a warm, slow breath onto her skin.

"I'm not going to get home tonight, if you keep doing that," she said, tilting her head to the side to give him better access to the spot on her neck that he was exploring.

"That's the idea," he whispered. "Your skin, Tessa...oh, God, I love your skin. It's incredible to touch. I can't seem to stop."

His fingers skimmed her eyelashes, her mouth, then her scar.

She flinched a tiny bit, hoping he wouldn't notice, but continued to let him touch it. She was quiet and considered brushing his hand away, but couldn't move as Andrew's fingers slowly traced her scar from one end to the other. Her eyes stung for a second when she noticed his fingers quivering, as though he wasn't sure if he should be touching this part of her, as if it was too intimate. She blinked off the forthcoming tear like it was nothing, though it wasn't, and let him continue for several minutes. An unfamiliar feeling, not quite nervousness and not quite contentment, formed in her stomach.

"Does it hurt," he asked after a while.

"Not anymore," she answered. *Not too much,* she thought, looking closely at his blue-gray eyes and the midnight stubble on his face before sinking deeper into his pillow. "I've had it since I was a kid. I was in an accident when I was fourteen."

"What kind of accident?" Andrew asked.

"Car."

"Were you badly hurt...otherwise?" he asked, pulling the bedspread up over her shoulder.

"What do you mean?" she asked, feeling the thickness and new warmth of Andrew's bedspread on her bare skin.

"In the car accident? Were you hurt beyond this?" His fingers were still on her face.

She said nothing and just closed her eyes, leaned her head onto his shoulder, and traced his lips with her fingers to stop his talking. She needed to feel and not think. Not thinking too much at this moment was critical—she knew. *Critical.* All she wanted was to feel pleasure of the body, the skin. She didn't want to talk or think or mentally dissect this night. There was no point in it, especially when Andrew had already proven himself to be a very suitable provider of physical pleasure.

"Stay, Tessa," he said, then slid the tip of his tongue over the scar on her face, as though he was trying to memorize it with more than just his fingers. "Please? We'll wake up early and I'll drive you to your cousin's place so you can change your clothes. Then we can go for breakfast before work. What do you say?"

What can I say? His fingers and tongue had already answered his own question. Any response of hers would be irrelevant. "Are there any of those figs left? I'd love another one later...or in the morning," she decided to say.

"Maybe one or two. Hopefully two. One for each of us," he said.

"If not, we could share the last one."

"Definitely. And we won't use a knife to slice it. Just teeth," he said.

❧

"Well, it looks like my celibacy oath just went out the window. You seem to have that effect on me, my dear friend," Tessa said when she woke up with her head pressed into Andrew's chest.

He kissed the top of her head, then lifted her hair and rubbed the back of her neck with his fingertips. "Celibacy oath, Tessa. Really? You're too funny for this hour of the morning."

"Four times in one night, Andrew. It's good I didn't swear on a Bible or anything."

"Yes, that would've been a shame...if you'd sworn to celibacy on a Bible, Tessa," he said, laughing. "Can't say I'm sorry that your oath is over, though. And if I may ask, why would someone like you take an oath of celibacy? Assuming you're serious, of course."

"Someone like me?" she asked.

"Yeah, someone like you," he repeated. "Someone fun and interesting and sexy and...well, like you."

"Simplicity," she answered, knowing it was enough for now.

"Simplicity," he repeated. "Good answer. My own...celibacy, I guess you could call it, for lack of a better word, though certainly not an oath, has been more out of fear."

"Fear of what?" Tessa asked, unsure if she really wanted to know the answer.

"Just fear," he said, closing his eyes for a moment.

She rolled off his chest and onto her back. "You're not going to be weird with me now, are you? We're still friends, I hope," Tessa said.

"We're still friends, Tessa. Yes, yes. Good friends. Why wouldn't we be?" He touched her face and closed his eyes again. "The best of...I hope."

Four times in one night. She kind of wanted to bask in it for a while, but she didn't have the sort of girlfriends with whom she could share this and had never been the sort of girl who had these types of conversations. Whenever she happened to overhear one, she always felt a sort of misplaced intimacy, like she was trapped in someone's bedroom closet. Instead, she opened her purple butterfly journal—that she'd been keeping on and off for the past year and a half—and spilled it all to the white-lined pages. *I won't even tell Charlotte later when I get back to the cottage. I'll keep this to myself.*

The first time with Andrew had been full of urgency, quick and intense without even time to work up a sweat.

They'd crashed into each other without even bothering to turn down the comforter or pull the shades in his bedroom. Wordlessly, they gave each other what they needed, that sweet release that had been building in both of them for months. There was only a minute or so of awkwardness afterward when she had to pee and didn't want to walk to the bathroom naked, but didn't want to get completely re-dressed either. So she'd grabbed his white shirt from the corner of the bed and slipped it on. It was long enough to cover her bum and the tops of her thighs. When she'd gotten back to the bedroom, he'd said, 'Keep it on. It looks good on you.' She climbed on top of him and let her mouth wander everywhere. She especially liked the sides of his neck, just below his earlobes, and quickly discovered that he was exquisitely sensitive to even the slightest bit of pressure there. His preference were hands, and he'd promised her that before she got out of his bed again, he'd touch every millimeter of her body. Every millimeter. This had begun their long and slow second time. The third go around was a half asleep, way after midnight frenzy, as if they needed to prove that they wanted each other over and over again. Then they'd slept a little and, when they woke up, Tessa was halfway on top of Andrew, her head crushed into his chest and his right arm wrapped all the way around her waist. The fourth time, well, that fourth time was staying strictly in her memory. *Not even my journal needs to know the details.*

They were both dreadfully late for work on Wednesday. There had been no time to go back to Charlotte's house to change her clothes. She ended up wearing the same pants she'd worn the day before, while borrowing a pale blue polo shirt from Andrew. It was somewhat big for her but made her feel really sexy all day. *I'll have to skip my lunch hour to make up the time,* she thought, when she arrived at the office mid-morning.

Thirteen

Wednesday, 3:17 PM
Dear Tessa,
I enjoyed your birthday very much. I hope you did as well.

~Andrew

Wednesday, 4:39 PM
Indeed, Mr. Dignified Man. It was awesome. Great figs. Thank you for such an introduction to them. They are beautiful and sweet and did you know they are actually inverted flowers? Dorky me, I did a Google search on the little darlings. Couldn't resist. Did you know they fight cancer, along with lots of other foods, too? Yes, I'm sure you probably knew this. Anyway, I'm going to bring some home for my father this weekend. Don't know where my head has been this past year as he's struggled with conventional medicine to heal him. Time for something natural, maybe. Thank you for opening my eyes to some other hope for him.

~*Tessa*

Wednesday, 4:53 PM
Dear Tessa,
You are most welcome for the figs. They are indeed beautiful and sweet. I don't know how effective they'll be on your father's health, though, as you've said his cancer is quite advanced. Just don't want to see you disappointed over a situation that is probably beyond your control. Worth a try, though. Couldn't do any harm.

~*Andrew*

P.S. Short staffed tonight. I need to stay until closing. Could you stop by and see me before you leave campus? Please.

Wednesday, 5:02 PM
Dear Andrew,
Brian Williams would never doubt the magical healing power of FIGS. He has an open mind! I am not delusional. Really! Just trying to perk up before going to my Dad's this weekend. If I can get him outside a little, it would be good for him. I don't think he sees the sunshine much during the week. If I can pump him full of figs and eradicate his cancer, I will be ecstatic. Again, not delusional, just carrying a sliver of hope in my little heart.

~*Tessa*

Wednesday, 5:13 PM
Dear Tessa,
I can give you Brian Williams' email address at NBC News if you'd like to open an exchange with him regarding his opinion on figs or any other matter. If not, you're stuck with my opinion, which is the following: Your father is a

lucky man to have you taking care of him. I'm sure he sees more sunshine on the weekends. Slivers of hope are good to have, but sometimes releasing hope is more realistic. Last but not least, your heart is not little. It's exactly the right size for you.

~Andrew

P.S. Are you stopping by before you leave or not? I need to see your face. I need to touch you.

Wednesday, 5:21 PM
Stopping by, yes! Had an influx of online applications to sort through today. Weird for June. Some of these personal essays are a hoot and some are so devastatingly beautiful they made me cry. See you soon.

~Tessa

Wednesday, 5:27 PM
I've heard a good remedy for crying while reading students' personal essays is to always have a supply of figs in your desk. See you soon.

~xo Andrew

First thing Thursday morning, Tessa stopped at Trader Joe's before heading into work and bought the entire fresh fig display. When she got to the office, she put them all in the staff fridge in hopes of keeping them fresh until the weekend.

Thursday, 8:47 AM

Dear Andrew,
I need to do some library research today. Thinking of using
lunch hour and might need an expert's help. Will you be
there from 1–2?

~Tessa

Thursday, 8:54 AM
Dear Tessa,
Yes, I'll be here. Of course I'll help you. What are you
researching?

~Andrew

Thursday, 9:03 AM
Holistic and nutritional methods of slowing down, dare I
say reversing, advanced cancer in a patient who's already
had surgery to remove tumors, chemotherapy and radiation
over a nearly two-year time frame. I am excited by what
I've read so far about figs and other super foods, but if I'm
going to get him started on a serious regimen, I need as much
information as I can get.

~Tessa

Thursday, 9:16 AM
Dear Tessa,
Is your father on board for this regimen? Have you talked
about it with him?

~A

Thursday, 9:22 AM
He's had a team of doctors tell him he probably won't live
the rest of the year. He's down to months.

~Tessa

She closed there. *Down to months.* She could've said she wasn't ready to lose him yet or that she wanted to put some quality back into his life. She could've said she hated that there was a palliative care nurse coming in daily to give him opiates, as needed. She could've told Andrew that she needed to keep her father, that he was the thread that connected her to the larger world. But she kept all that in and only said the basics. Andrew was here in her magical place. Her father was home, fighting or acquiescing to his body's deterioration, as the case may be. She could bring home the magic of this place, but there was no need to mix them. No need to create that chaos in her heart.

Thursday, 9:25 AM
Come by at 1:00. I'll help you as much as I can.

~A

Thursday, 9:31 AM
Thank you, Mr. Librarian Man. You're awesome! Must get out of email now and do some work or there won't be a lunch hour. See you later.

~xo Tessa

Just after 1:00 PM, Tessa arrived at Andrew's office on the third floor of the university library. He showed her in and flipped the lock on the door, so there would be no interruptions for an hour. Before turning businesslike, he kissed her briefly with her face in his hands.

"I went down to the cafeteria and got us some salads and tea. We can still have lunch while we work," he said, pulling a folder from the corner of his desk and handing it to her. "I had a little time this morning, so I got started for you. I found you several books, as well."

"You're like an information angel," she said, kissing his cheeks. She opened the folder and found a stack of pages filled with alternative cancer therapies, case studies, nutritional advice from raw food plans to juicing to organic veganism—all from reputable sources. He found her names and contact information for a half dozen holistic practitioners from central Massachusetts, across the Boston area, and down to the tip of Cape Cod. There was a good chunk of information on the detrimental effects of traditional medical treatment of cancer. She stopped scanning the pages and focused on this bit.

"It wipes out the immune system. The damn chemo wipes out the immune system. Of course." She couldn't remember hearing this, though knew it must've been said at some point and she must've tuned it out, failed to ask questions. "I went with him a few times in the beginning. I insisted on going. They never said it wouldn't work, only that he had to have it. Why wouldn't we believe them? It will make him nauseated, they said. He will be tired, they said, and lose his hair and become gaunt, they said. Blah, blah. How stupid of me. How young and stupid." She started to cry.

"Tessa, don't blame yourself. Believe me, that does no good. I know. It's very easy to get pissed off at the doctors, the nurses, anyone. Yourself, especially. Most people don't question the experts in these situations. They just trust," he said, "and really, they're just doing the job they've been trained to do. Most think they have all the answers because they have letters at the end of their names."

"Once the immune system has been compromised by numerous chemotherapy sessions and/or radiation, the body of the cancer patient becomes quite weak, making alternative (holistic) treatment approaches more challenging," she read aloud from another page. "In some cases, especially with older cancer patients, a holistic approach may not be possible." And further on, "Successful eradication of disease or even a period of remission is dependent on the patient's total mental, physical and spiritual belief in curing himself/herself and total commitment to the implementation of a naturopathic lifestyle."

Oh Lord, what a load of horse shit. Mental, physical and spiritual belief in curing himself. This would take a lot. If only her father would just believe in the physical aspect of it, Tessa could take on the mental stuff. She could research with Andrew's help. She could put together a program and persuasively present it to him. As for the spiritual side of it, well, Mémère was always talking to the Virgin Mary and Saint Anthony and above all, Jesus. If anyone was cut out for spiritual healing help, it was Tessa's grandmother. But then, hadn't she always talked to the Virgin Mary and Saint Anthony and rubbed the crucifix around her neck all the time? She carried her rosary beads around in her housecoat pocket, so she could sneak in a few Hail Mary's in her spare moments. *What good has that done so far?*

She stood, put the folder on Andrew's desk and turned to look out the window. June was in full swing. A border of bright orange tiger lilies was blooming along the edge of the sidewalk. Summer session students were sitting on the grass with textbooks and laptops in front of them, studying and sipping iced coffees from tall, plastic Dunkin Donuts or Starbucks cups. Tessa lowered her gaze to the vent below Andrew's windowsill where the air conditioning came through. She put her fingers on it to feel the cool air on her skin. Andrew came up behind her and slipped his arms beneath her arms and then tightly around her waist. He smelled good, like Irish Spring soap and a clean shirt. She had no words and only wanted to feel him embracing her.

"Thank you for finding all this for me, Andrew. This would've taken me all day...at least. All week probably," she said after several minutes.

"No problem. Do you think any of it will be helpful?" he asked.

"Maybe. Maybe not. I'll look through the list of practitioners you put together and contact one or two of them. See what they can suggest for him." There was a Dr. Berenger, a naturopath who had been in practice for nearly twenty years, on the upper section of Route 128 whom she would call. *Or email first,* she thought, *just to get a feel.* She would need a week or two off from work to get started on this.

"There's a lot of other stuff out there, Tessa. This is just the tip of the iceberg. This is what comes up in an initial search. I haven't even tapped the academic databases yet, and there are many. But I'm digging deeper, finding other things we can try," he said into the back of her head, as they both looked at the procession of summer students who were getting up from their benches and spots beneath trees and heading off to their afternoon classes. "Don't give up."

FOURTEEN

"Where did you learn that?" she asked him breathlessly. "That...way of touching a woman's body that's so...so..." She didn't want to say *arousing* or *gentle* or *erotic* or *mesmerizing*, although it was all of these, so she settled, blandly, on *nice*. Then she felt silly for asking. He was fourteen years older and obviously more experienced. *He had a wife once,* she thought, *and who knows how many lovers prior to or since that. He had someone to sleep with every night, to make love with, for years probably.* Tessa realized she still didn't know any of the details and she wondered what had happened.

"Where, Tessa? Well...inside me, I guess. It's a response."

"A response?"

"Yes. To you. To your skin. Your body. Your essence. Well, you, in general."

She smiled and was grateful for the answer he gave.

"You have the kind of skin that begs to be touched like this," he said, trailing his fingertips softly over her bare shoulders and then down to her chest.

"Begs?" She couldn't help laughing. "My skin is begging?"

"You don't like that word?"

"I don't like to beg." It sounded so desperate to beg. Like begging for forgiveness. Begging for attention. Begging for her father to get well. Begging for her mother to come back before he died and knowing this would not happen. *No, Tessa Tremblay does not beg—not for anything or anyone.*

"Okay, how about *asks nicely?* Your skin is asking nicely to be touched like this...by me. *By me,*" he repeated, as if he was verifying it to himself and to her. "Maybe it's my hands that are begging." His thumb ran across her bottom lip.

She let his fingers wander into her mouth for a few seconds and sucked them tightly one by one with her lips, before releasing them and fixing her gaze on his face.

"Good God, Tessa. The things you do," he said, exhaling.

"No begging now, Andrew," she said, playing with the word.

"No begging, just asking nicely," he said, tilting his head in her direction. "Please?"

They were on his couch with plates of their take-out dinner and glasses of the sweet white wine she'd brought over strewn on his coffee table. She decided to kiss him straight on the mouth with her hands on either side of his face. His lips and tongue were salty and sweet at the same time.

"I like this...thing...this connection we seem to have," Tessa said. "There's a simplicity to it."

"Simplicity? You think so?" he asked, his gaze embedded in her face.

"Yeah, I think so. I *want* you. Your hands, your touch, the feel of you on me...in me. You seem to want me, too. You...satisfy me. Lord knows that, and probably your neighbors know it, too," she said, slightly embarrassed. "Do

I...satisfy you?"

"Yeah, I'll say," he quickly responded, "more than you can imagine, in fact."

"There's no begging. No imbalance, I guess. Simplicity," she said again. "And, my God, Andrew, these hands. This way of touching me like you are tracing something. It's almost as though you're writing words on my body." *I love it,* she almost said, but didn't.

"Writing words?"

"It feels that way," she said, a little embarrassed. "Sometimes."

"I am, although I never consciously thought of it as words," he admitted. "It's a story I'm telling you...non-verbally."

"A story?"

"My story. It has to be told gently and slowly and without words, without spoken words...for now. And you have allowed me to tell it to you. I'm very grateful for that."

They were both quiet for several minutes. She looked closely at him, at his hands, arms, the small crinkles at the corners of his eyes and mouth when he smiled a little, and she wondered at his story. He was more beautiful than she deserved. She'd felt this way from the very first time they'd touched.

"Do you think you'll ever tell me...in spoken words?" she asked after finishing the bit of wine that remained in her glass. Andrew had learned to only pour her half a glass.

"I will, but not yet. Please. I'm not quite there yet." He pulled her shirt over her head and let his hands take over. She kept her eyes open, leaned back onto the armrest of his couch and let his unspoken words dance across her skin and then deep inside her. "God, Tessa. Please. Please."

When they woke up together the next morning, Tessa and Andrew lingered in his bed until nearly 8:00 AM. His apartment was five miles from the university, a good thirty miles closer than Charlotte's house was to campus. If Tessa could find a place to live that was this close to her job, it would be a dream.

"I'm going to miss you when you're away for a week. More than a week," he said. "What will I do with these hands that touch you so...*nicely?*" he teased.

"Oh, don't torture me or anything, Andrew. Promise me you won't find your hands begging to touch anyone else. No cute, young summer student who wears snug little skirts and wants to open a bottle of wine with your shoes." She instantly hated that she sounded jealous.

He laughed. "As if, Tessa...as if," was all he said. He then sat in bed and swung his legs over the side to get up.

She grabbed him around the waist, a bit tighter than she ever had, and put her mouth on the back of his neck. "Maybe I can get away for a night and we can meet halfway somewhere. Park in the woods of a state forest and go a little crazy in your backseat. What do you think?"

"Like a couple of teenagers, eh?"

"Yeah, sweet cheeks...like a couple of teenagers." She felt her face blush. "Sorry I just called you sweet cheeks. That was silly."

"It's okay, my little fig. I told you I like you silly," he said. "Balances me out."

The depth of his voice, just the sound of it, did something to her. She was starting to hear his voice everywhere, even starting to hear it when she read his emails and when she felt his touch. *That voice. That dark red voice.* And yet her mother's words and voice were there, too, always reverberating that one lesson that stuck so stubbornly in Tessa's mind. *Don't fall in love. You're too young. Just turn your heart off and have fun.* Love was complicated—this, she knew. There was a simplicity to her relationship with Andrew. This thing with Andrew was too simple to be love. She knew this, too.

As she sat with her coffee before leaving his apartment, Tessa looked at Andrew as he stood at the counter waiting for the toast to pop up. Her eyes then scanned the photos on his fridge. There were only a few: One of himself and a big dog, hiking. One of a man who looked somewhat like what Andrew would look like with a beard and a few gray hairs. This one had a young smiling boy in it who was wearing a swimsuit and bright orange arm floaties. "My brother and nephew," he told her, when he noticed her eyes skimming the snapshots. There were various shots of mountains and forests and the ocean. A postcard of Van Gogh's sunflowers.

"Do you want jam or cream cheese?" he asked when the toast was ready.

It seemed like a simple enough question. "Honey," she answered.

"Excuse me?"

"Honey," she repeated. Her father always kept a jar on every table at Tremblay's. "Do you have any honey? For the toast?"

"No. I'm sorry. I don't tend to keep it around. I'll pick some up, though, for you...for next time. For today, though, all I can offer you is jam or cream cheese."

"You should try it. Honey, I mean. It's really the best thing on toast. Pretty good in coffee, too."

"We'll try it together, then...the next time you're here," he said, as he pulled out a chair to sit.

She felt a strangeness and realized it was the first time they'd ever sat at a table together. His hands were occupied with his breakfast, the fingers of his right hand wrapped around his coffee mug, while the fingers of his left held his toast. There was a little smear of cream cheese on his thumb.

"Jam, then, please. But I'll do it myself," she said,

reaching for the jar and the knife. She couldn't bear to watch him spread jam on toast for her. It was too much, too intimate. Even after the birthday picnic, the figs, the nights in his bed over the past few weeks, spreading jam on toast was too intimate. *I'm not ready for that.* She would've cried for sure and she didn't want to cry now. Then he'd ask her why she was crying and she'd have nothing to say. She could justify crying over her father's illness, but over her lover holding a piece of toast in his hands—spreading it with jam and then handing it to her with a little smile on his face— was too much. She imagined it nonetheless.

She glanced away from him and back at the photographs on the fridge. A little information—just a little—was what she needed. Andrew was halfway into his toast, when she couldn't stand wondering any longer. "Andrew? Can I ask you something?" she asked, keeping her gaze on the photographs, not on him.

"Okay," he replied, putting his toast down.

"Did she...die?"

"Did who die?" he asked.

"Your wife? I'm not trying to upset you. I just got that feeling and, well, you know, I've had it on my mind quite a bit lately. Death, I mean. Illness. You know, with my dad and all. The end...of things. Of good, normal things. Oh, stop me, please. I'm babbling. I'm nervous. I'm weirdly nervous and really uncomfortable in this moment right now. I'm sorry I asked. It's just that I am, well, curious. Don't be mad or...I don't know, sad, I guess, that I asked," she said, her heart thumping ridiculously and the warmth from her red cheeks spreading over her whole face. She looked down into her cooling coffee to avoid his eyes.

She listened to his breathing. One deep breath and an exhale—mild.

Then he answered her. "No. My wife...my former wife, that is, didn't die. She's perfectly healthy as far as I know," he said, then paused for a moment before finishing his answer. "She left me. She...divorced me."

Tessa didn't attempt to decipher his tone of voice. As far as she was concerned, it was neutral. *Just neutral. Just relaying the facts.* He was only providing the answer she was seeking. *Nothing more.* After his statement, he was quiet and more reserved than usual during conversation that had suddenly turned serious.

"Oh." She thought about saying she was sorry, but she really wasn't and didn't want to pry any more. She didn't ask how long ago or why, but instead bit into her toast and tried to think about going to work, and then to her father's house for the next eleven days to get him started on some way of curing him that didn't involve chemo or radiation or hospital stays.

Damn it. Why did I ask? Why leave on a glum note? And why did I think his wife had died? It surfaced in her then that Andrew had a reticence about him and a sense of reserved loneliness that made her think he may have been a young widower. Also, he didn't seem like the sort of guy a woman would leave.

"I'll tell you more about it another time. We need to get going soon. It's almost quarter to nine," he said, getting up to put the dishes in the sink.

She went up to him from behind and put her arms around his waist. He leaned into her, tilted his head so the back of his neck rested lightly on her mouth. This was enough for now. She could both smell him and taste him. *Simple. Enough.*

When she opened her email that morning, Tessa had a response from Dr. Berenger's office. Yes, they had appointments available for the following week, but there were only a few left. The doctor would need to see her father as soon as possible, given the history she described, and do a comprehensive blood work to determine his receptivity to a natural treatment plan. No, unfortunately, they didn't accept her father's insurance plan. She wouldn't mention that to him when she told him about this doctor, but just discreetly pay the bill. *A consultation and lab fees can't be more than a few hundred dollars,* she figured. She'd use some of her savings. An apartment of her own could wait a bit longer.

She sent off a brief thank you email to the doctor's office for their quick response and stated that she would be calling soon to set up an appointment for her father. That done, she went about her day, working straight through her usual lunch hour—no walk with Andrew or little getaway to the greenhouse. By 3:30 PM, she wrapped up her day, bought a sandwich in the cafeteria and ate it while she walked over to the library to say goodbye to Andrew. She promised to call him if the urge for a mid-week rendezvous hit her. She doubted she'd make it very long without this urge, but thought she'd played it cool enough to make him think she was fine. They walked over to his office, where he locked the door for a few minutes, kissed her long and sweet on her lips and on her scar. She was getting used to his fondness of it and didn't flinch as much anymore. He put his hands on her face, ran his fingers over it and told her he would miss her.

Am I real to you? What do your fingers feel when they touch me, when they skim over my skin? My face? When they are in my mouth surrounded by my lips, my teeth, my wet tongue, do I feel real? Her mind raced and she wasn't sure what she had merely thought and what she may have said aloud.

"I need to get going. Keep this up and you're going to have to physically peel me off you about thirty minutes from now."

"I've had worse tasks to perform. That wouldn't be so terrible, Tessa," he teased. "But you need to get going. I

know. I know. And I'm supposed to be working right now."
He kissed her again, lightly, and then stepped back. "Drive
carefully, please. Say hello to your father for me. I hope
you're able to make use of the information we found."

"You found it all, Andrew, and yes, I think it will be
helpful. I've already contacted one of the naturopaths. I'm
hoping we can visit him next week and see what can be
done. And I'm bringing home all those books you found and
those articles and different therapies you printed out for me.
Looks like some good stuff. I can sit and read when he's
sleeping or when...the nurse is with him."

"Call me with updates...only if you want to, I mean," he
said.

She hugged him and let her hands slip into the
waistband of his black pants just enough to get a little closer
to his skin without actually touching it. She didn't want to
untuck his shirt and make him disheveled while he was
working. "I'll call you with updates, Andrew. I'll call you just
to say goodnight. I'll call you when I need that mid-week
rendezvous in your backseat, sweet cheeks," she said,
winking at him as she had that first day he touched her leg.

"I'm thinking a hotel room would work better. I'm a
little old for the backseat, my luscious fig."

"Deal. You can get anything you want from me, if you
call me your *luscious fig*."

"Good to know, Tessa. Now go please. My mind is
starting to wander inappropriately in the context we're in
here," he said, gesturing toward his office door, which they
both knew could get knocked upon at any moment. It was
late afternoon; his busy time—after day classes ended and
before the evening ones started.

She only laughed. His dignity was one of the coolest
things about him.

FIFTEEN

"I have some vacation time, so I'm here for the next week and a half," Tessa said, when she walked into the kitchen early Friday evening.

Her father was sitting at the table with a fried egg and cup of orange juice in front of him, and Mémère was pulling something sweet out of the oven. "Just in time, Tessa. I'll cut you the first slice," she said, placing the baked item on the counter top. "When it cools a bit, I'll wrap up half of it for you to bring to Frankie."

Tessa had gotten a voicemail and three text messages from Frankie already this week, which she had not answered. He was just checking in, as he liked to say, and wondering if she might be ready for a beer at his place this weekend. "Hasn't it been long enough yet?"

Her grandmother's creation was a cinnamon coffee cake, with a sticky glaze and probably some raisins and walnuts inside it. It was one of Mémère's specialties and Tessa loved it. Her father loved it, too, but she doubted he had the appetite for any of it tonight. He looked worn out.

She decided she wouldn't mention any of her plans until morning.

By 7:30 PM, Tessa told her grandmother to go relax, that she'd wash the dishes and clean up the kitchen. Then she'd sit with the books she'd brought along and try to get some information out of them.

After turning her father's bed down for him, Tessa puttered about in the hallway while he used the bathroom. This part of the day with him always seemed so gray, this feeling that he was not quite an invalid, but not quite capable of taking care of himself either. On many occasions, she'd had to clean up the bathroom after him. She never mentioned this to him, as his dignity was critical.

Just before 5:00 AM, Tessa woke up to the sound of her father shuffling down the hall. The reading lamp was still on, the view out the living room window still black.

"I saw the light on. You're up early, Tessie," her father said, walking slowly into the room.

"Never made it to bed. I was up late, reading."

"Anything good?"

"Recipe books," she replied, not entirely dishonest.

"Recipe books? That was always my domain, baby. Love me a good recipe book. You gonna make me a fabulous breakfast? I could do with one. I'm hungry today."

"I could, yes. Are you in the mood for a veggie omelet? I stopped off at the farmer's market yesterday. Got some nice tomatoes and some other stuff."

"Could you make it now, you think? I don't want to wait until Kate gets here. Then it gets all businesslike and serious around here."

"Just sit here for now. I'm getting up anyway," she said, the couch was still cozy and warm for him. "I'll let you know when it's ready."

"There's a greenhouse on the campus where I work," Tessa said, as they sat at the kitchen table with their breakfast. She hadn't heard any sounds from Mémère's bedroom yet. "I go there sometimes. Your rosebush out front reminded me of it, a little. I wanted to bring some of them in for you." Tessa looked over at the jar on the counter that held the small bunch of roses she'd clipped after her father had gone to bed.

"I didn't know it was blooming already," he said.

"It is. It had seventeen roses on it last night when I snipped these five. Probably has more by now. Lots of little buds. I'll bring you some for your bedroom later," she said.

"Tell me about this greenhouse where you go sometimes," he said.

"Okay," she said, "it's really beautiful there, like an escape, a tropical escape. It's pretty big, almost like a maze on the inside with little paths to follow and so many unusual plants that I'd never seen before. And it smells so good in there. It's warm and misty and, well, just nice, Dad. You'd like it," Tessa said. "It's where I met my friend, Andrew. He was in there one day when I walked in." She'd told her dad about Andrew once when he'd asked if she'd made any new friends at her job. "Maybe I'll take you there one day next week. What do you think?"

"Tell me about this Andrew fella, Tessie."

"What do you want to know about him?"

"What does he do to your heart? That's mainly what I want to know."

"Gee, Dad. Nothing like starting off with the big questions."

"I don't have much time left, Tessa. I need to get straight to the point, baby," he said, laughing a little. "What does he do to your heart?"

All the sitting around the house, pondering stuff, was

making her father sentimental. *When has he ever been sentimental?* He was an elbows deep in work kind of guy. A decent father to her. *Definitely.* He had done his best she always thought, even if there had been big voids along the way. After her mother had left, he'd closed up for a long time. He worked. She worked. They were side-by-side, but not sidekicks. *Never sentimental.*

"What does he do to my heart?" She could feel herself rolling her eyes. "I...I don't want to think about that yet. And anyway, I don't know. We haven't known each other that long, really," she said, pausing to consider something that would satisfy her father's question. "Can I just tell you that he's a nice guy? He's sweet...thoughtful, I mean. He bought me figs for my birthday. That's how I got interested in figs."

"What else?" he asked.

She tried to think of something else about Andrew that would end this silly conversation and move their dialogue toward the real reason she was home for a week and a half.

"Well...he's got really nice...hands. I like his hands," Tessa blurted. *Wrong choice. Damn it!* Tessa sensed that she was turning pink in front of her father and knew she would need to call Andrew later. *I like how his hands make me quiver all over,* she thought, but obviously didn't say out loud. *I like to put his long fingers in my mouth and suck on them until we are both nearly delirious with desire. Oh God, day one of eleven. Day one of eleven.* "Anyway, Dad, I want to talk to you about some research that I've done, we've done, Andrew and I. He helped me. He did most of it, really. It's what he's good at."

"He's good at research? Or good at helping you?" He was teasing her now. Digging.

"Both, I guess. He's a reference librarian. He researches and he helps. It's his job. It's what he's good at, like I said."

"And he's got nice hands, Tessie baby." He was definitely teasing her now. "How long have the two of you been together?"

"We're not *together,* Dad. Not like you're thinking anyway." *What's he thinking?* After all, they were sleeping together, quite frequently and deliciously. But Tessa knew better. She knew that calling a guy her boyfriend was ridiculous and juvenile. Anyway, Andrew was far from a boy—very far.

"No need to get upset, baby. Just curious about the guy my baby girl is so hesitant to tell her old man about," he said, winking at her. "What's he look like? How about that. Nice and easy to answer. Tall. Short. Dark hair. Blonde. Heavy. Slim. Fill in the blank, Tessie. You know I just want you to be happy, baby."

Happy, baby. Yes, she knew her father wanted that.

"He's sort of medium height, I suppose. Maybe on the cusp of tall, but coming from me almost everyone is tall. Thick, dark hair, almost black. A little wavy. Blue eyes, but not as blue as yours. His are more of a cloudy grayish blue. Yours are mostly sunny. Slim, but not too slim. A good size, I guess. Strong arms and back." She was trying too hard to be bland, generic, but lost it, she knew, with the *strong arms and back* bit. She felt like she was ten years younger, at least, fifteen and not twenty-five. She felt like she was in high school again, trying to persuade her father to let her go to an after prom party with some teenage boy, like she was selling his good qualities. *How silly. It's nothing like that. Nothing at all.* "Anyway, Dad, Andrew's nice, very nice, handsome, dignified, well mannered and all that. Great hands...handshake, I mean. You'd like him. Now can we move on, please? I have some ideas I want to tell you about."

"Sounds to me like he's done something to your heart," he said, ignoring her last statement. "Something good."

Why didn't he worry more about my heart when I was younger and without a mother? Or maybe he did and just did so quietly. It was funny how the end of one's life, or thoughts of it, could bring out qualities that were so well concealed during the bulk of a lifetime. It was like cleaning the house in a panic when company was due to arrive any minute. It seemed like that anyway.

No hearts. Please no hearts yet with Andrew. It's a body connection for now. It's a non-verbal, sensory thing. It was skin and touch and scent and his stubbly early morning cheeks and chin which he quickly shaved smooth upon waking. For Tessa, it was half glasses of wine and funny commentary about bare feet and bare knees. It was touch, above all else—his touch. It was his hands that were the bridge from him to her, not anybody's heart.

"Please, Dad. My heart is my heart. Okay. It's not like yours. Not so pure...I guess. My heart is like...hers," she said and paused, unsure how to continue. "Unlucky for me, isn't it, that I should get hers and not yours?"

Tessa's heart had a heaviness and darkness. She knew this. It wasn't a maybe. Like it or not, she was her mother's daughter. She could decorate it, dress it up in silliness and humor, but it had the same absence of color, the same absence of light. Her own heart had all the same incapacities that her mother's heart had.

"Subject dropped then, effective now," he said firmly, then added, "nice hands are a start, I suppose. They're an important thing for a man to have...or so I've been told."

Great. I've upset him. Now I'll have to wait for him to calm down.

Tessa got up to clear the table, just as she heard Mémère's bedroom door creaking open at the end of the hall. She went to the stove, flicked the burner for the kettle and pulled out a mug for her grandmother's tea.

"Dad, I want to tell you about this doctor I discovered the

other day. He's a naturopathic doctor." She'd managed to get him out on the deck by late Saturday afternoon.

"What the hell's a naturo-what's-it doctor?"

"Naturopathic. The whole person, not just the ailment. I mean, he looks at the bigger picture, not just a tumor or the cancer cells. He treats *you*, not just your illness." *Oh God, it isn't coming out right.* "You need to talk to him. He can explain it better than I can."

"Tessa, love. It's too late for me to get some miracle cures. I have Stage IV, inoperable, terminal cancer. I've had second and third opinions already," he said somberly. "What's this natural guy gonna do for me anyway? Give me herbs and such?"

"He'll start with blood work to see what your status is and what your receptivity to a regimen would be." She was using their language. She hated the word regimen. It sounded so strict, so severe.

"Blood work, Tessa. No. No more goddamn blood work. Look at my arms. You see these marks all over me? These purple marks? That's from the last blood work. It's been weeks, but I don't heal easily now. I don't heal, period. They can never get my veins on the first try. They collapse or they roll or whatever the hell they do. I'm sick of being a pincushion."

"I'll go with you. I'll sit with you when they draw your blood. I'll distract you. Talk. You won't even know they're drawing blood."

"Nice try, baby. I've never not known."

"I called already. They have openings next week, but I need to book one for you before they fill up. Please, Dad. What harm can it do? Just go." She almost said, *just do it for me,* but didn't. She didn't want to pester him or lay guilt on him. And she wouldn't beg. "Just talk to the guy. If you don't like him, if he's a quack, we'll never go back. I've read up on this guy. I've emailed his office and talked to them a little bit. What have you got to lose by going?"

"I know what my status is, Tessie. It's too late. Nobody's going to cure me at this point," he said, tilting his gaze upward to the clouds, then back down at Tessa. "I know you're young and you might still have the...the hope in some miracle for me, but I've been through enough. Enough tests. Enough surgeries. Enough treatments that didn't work. Enough hope. I can't do it anymore." His voice broke, fractured actually, before he attempted to recover it. "I'm just living day-to-day now. Do you want to join me in that or pester me?"

"Magical thoughts, Dad. Remember that?" she asked.

"You were a baby, well, a little girl." He was almost crying. She could hear it in his voice. "It was a fairytale I made up for you. It's make believe, Tessa."

"The day before my first day of kindergarten, I was terrified. I didn't want to go. Remember? I wanted to go to the restaurant with you and bake pies all day. I wanted to sit at that long counter in the kitchen and play with the mixing bowls and the flour and sugar and whatever else you'd let me put my fingers into. So, the day before the first day of kindergarten, you took me with you. You put a big, red checkered apron on me. You had to wrap the strings around my waist three times so I wouldn't trip. Then you gave me a pie crust that you'd already made and every sweet spice from the rack. Then blueberries. Chopped apples. Raisins. A peach. Do you remember what you told me to do?"

"Mix it all up and sprinkle it with sweetness," he answered, his eyes cloudy.

"You told me to pretend the fruit was my fear. You told me to mash it up in my hands until it wasn't scary anymore, then sprinkle it with sweetness and scoop it into the pie crust and we'd bake it."

"Yes, and we baked it."

"And it was the best pie ever."

"It was the best pie ever, yes, baby," he said, indulging her memory. "Better than any I'd ever made myself."

"And you said that after you smash your fear and sprinkle it with sweetness and bake it until it was warm and crispy...then you can eat your fear and it won't be fear anymore," Tessa said.

"And you said *how?*" he said through his tears.

"And you told me it was magical thoughts. Sometimes, we just need a few magical thoughts."

"Pretty heavy stuff for a five-year-old, I guess," he said.

"It worked, though. I went to kindergarten the next day full of pie and magical thoughts and told everyone that my dad was more magical than Santa Claus."

"I don't have it anymore, Tessa. I must've given all my magic to you."

"I don't believe you."

"I don't want to go. No more doctors' offices. I've had enough. I decided that already, Tessa. I told you that a couple weeks ago."

"You just want to die then?"

"I'm going to whether I want to or not," he said somewhat softly. "I don't have a fear of it."

Tessa had a fear of it. Her father may not, but she wasn't quite ready to be floating freely in the world with no parent. Even at twenty-five years old, she liked that anchor, she needed it.

"What if this naturopath can help you live longer? Put you into remission?"

"I've had remissions, Tessie. Plenty of them. Remissions don't last."

"Has Kate ever taken your blood?" Tessa asked.

"No, that's not what Kate is here for. What's this got to do with Kate?"

"She could though, right? What if you let Kate take your blood and I can take it to be analyzed. Then we see what this Dr. Berenger says. I could call the office and ask if we could do that. What do you say, Dad?"

"How about if we bake a magical thoughts pie and pretend you're five again?"

"I can't convince you, can I, Dad?"

Tessa Tremblay doesn't beg, she reminded herself. She'd ask again after they'd made and eaten the pie to see if the magic had started working yet. If not, then she might have to change her begging policy just this once.

"Did you bring any more figs with you this time?" he asked, after a few minutes.

"Yeah, got a couple dozen in the fridge. You want some?"

"I'm thinking a fig pie might be pretty magical right about now," he said, laying a hand atop hers and tapping it lightly. "We wouldn't even have to sprinkle too much sweetness onto them. They're pretty sweet already. That Andrew fella of yours knew what he was doing there. That's all I'm going to say about it. Let's go bake, baby."

"Okay, do you have any fig pie recipes, Dad?" she asked, then instantly knew what he was going to say before he said it.

"No, Tessie baby, we'll just make it up as we go. It's up here. All my recipes, all of anything, really, is right up here, he said, tapping his bald head.

Of course.

"Come on then, restaurant man. Let's see if you've still got the magic," she said. She smiled halfheartedly, pulled her father up from his deck chair and guided him back into the house. The kitchen had always been his domain.

When he was engrossed in mixing ingredients for a crust and she was slicing the figs in half lengthwise, Tessa popped one into her mouth. Then she offered one to him.

"They're inverted flowers, Dad. Check 'em out," she said, as she traced the dark pink pulp with her finger. "A

145

female fig wasp tunnels her way inside and lays her eggs. Of course, she never makes it out, but that's okay. It's a symbiotic relationship. The fig wasp needs the fig and most varieties of fig trees cannot be pollinated by anything but these tiny little wasps. They risk everything to get in there and lay their eggs, losing their wings in the process. But it's okay. Their life's purpose is to pollinate fig flowers. You see, when you open one up, it's so pretty. So colorful. The flower doesn't blossom outward. It blossoms inward. That's kind of magical, right, Dad? I mean, what other flower blossoms inward? I can't think of any."

Her dad looked up at her, while continuing to mix. He was sitting at the kitchen table. She was standing at the counter, slicing.

"Let me see one, baby."

She handed two over; one whole, one sliced.

"They're beautiful inside and out, Tessa. But wow, inside. Yup. They're flowers on the inside. Nice discovery." He winked at her.

"They're a super food, you know."

"Super," he said with a little wink of sarcasm. Food had always been important to him, but to him food was food. It was about taste and presentation and being elbow deep in its preparation. He didn't eat anything he didn't like. Nutrition was secondary.

"Really, Dad," she said, treading carefully. "They provide more calcium, potassium and iron than most other fruits. They promote the growth of good bacteria in the large intestine. And they're super sweet." She plopped another one in her mouth.

She'd learned all this after her birthday picnic with Andrew, through a simple online search. It was Andrew who'd dug much deeper with the natural treatment research, but the sweet little fig was the catalyst.

"Grab a pie pan for me, baby. This crust is just about

ready to go."

She pulled one from the cabinet and handed it to him.

He took his rolled-out pie crust off the board, lifted it and spread it into the pan. After pressing the bottom snugly in, he created waves around the edge with his thumbs. "Simple pie, baby. These little figgies are sweet enough. Bring 'em over here and help me spread them out on the crust."

"You must've read about super foods, Dad," Tessa said tentatively. "When you started your treatments, what did they tell you to eat? I don't remember."

"Eat what you can, they said. Whatever you can hold down."

"And now? Will you be able to hold this down? This pie?"

"This pie will be the best pie ever...well...second best. Second only to that fruity concoction you came up with twenty years ago," he said, smiling a little half smile at her. "I can hold stuff down now, so long as it's palatable."

She'd noticed that he didn't vomit much anymore. No chemo. No nausea. "We could do all the super foods as pies, Dad. How about that?"

More spinach pies. Blackberry pie. Dark red cherry pie. Pomegranate pie. Can pomegranates be made into pie?

"I read about a program...a cancer treatment program where you eat fruits and vegetables all day. Organic. Lots and lots. You even juice it and drink it. We could get all your favorites—everything you like. What do you think?" The cost seemed prohibitive when she'd first read about juicing up to twenty pounds of organic vegetables daily, but then she thought about the produce suppliers her father had used over the years for Tremblay's—local farmers who would give her a discount, if not some stuff for free.

"Don't know if that will help me, Tessa, or be much to the old taste buds."

"But we could try. No harm in trying, right? I have a book on this from the library, several books, actually," she said, as she spread the sliced figs on her father's pie crust.

The night before, she'd read a book by a German doctor who advocated this plan. She found it on the couch and set it down on the table next to her father. The cover photo was of the doctor's smiling face surrounded by organic vegetables. He was holding a very tall glass full of watery green liquid.

Her father glanced at the picture, made a face, then looked at Tessa.

"You know, I've had stuff like that and I can make them thicker. I can make them sweet. Gives me energy. Makes me run faster," she said.

"I don't think I'll be beating you in any road races, baby girl."

"No, maybe not. Probably not, but it could power you up a bit," she said. "I'll make you one later."

He said nothing, just handed her the finished pie, assembled and ready to bake.

She slipped it into the waiting oven.

"When she left...that wasn't the first time, you know."

By early evening, they were sitting on the deck again with the remainder of the fig pie—which was proving to be magical after all—on the table. Tessa's father was relaxed and more serene than she'd seen him in a while. He was in a talking mood—a sharing mood.

"I always had that feeling," she said.

"Not long after you were born, you were two months old, she ran off for a night. I went crazy trying to find her, trying to figure out where she might be. She told me she was going out to buy diapers for you. I offered to go, but she insisted, said she needed the fresh air. Hours went by and it got dark. I thought she'd broken down somewhere or been in an accident. I got in my car and started looking for her, going to all the stores where she might buy diapers. My mind was racing, you know. What if she'd been jumped or carjacked in a parking lot. Anything was possible. It all went through my mind," he paused. "Everything but...but where she actually was."

"Where was she?"

"At the beach. She was sitting on the beach in the dark. It was still summertime so it doesn't sound so strange, but it was way after midnight by the time I found her...nearly dawn, in fact."

"How did you know she was there?"

"Default. Nothing but default, I guess. I couldn't think of any more places to look. I had been to the hospital, the police station. I'd called some of her relatives that she talked to on a regular basis. Caused quite a stir, I did, that's for sure. But then it just came to me that she might be there," he said. "She'd always liked it there." He looked away from Tessa and up at the treetops in the backyard.

Tessa thought about her mother, in her early twenties then with a husband and baby at home, sitting alone on the beach in the middle of the night. She wondered if it had been high tide or low, full moon or crescent or some waning or waxing phase in between. She tried to imagine how long her mother sat there and what she had been pondering. Then, an instant later, she knew. Tessa knew what her mother was pondering because she had been there, too—first in her mind and then on that cold, Christmas Eve day last year. It was her place of serenity, where chaos became order. When she looked at the water, any body of water, she was enveloped in the blue-green of it. Blue-green was the color of clarity to Tessa. The beach would've been black when her mother was there. Depending on the moon's phase, it could've glowed a little.

"Was I with you when you found her?"

"No, no. You were a little baby. Mémère came to the house and stayed with you."

"Oh."

"And it was raining. It had started to rain at some point and she was soaked. I just wanted to get her home, so we could all be together."

"So what did she say?" Tessa asked, not sure she truly wanted to know. "Why was she there in the rain...at night?"

"She told me to go home and take care of you. She said she was no good at it, that she didn't know how to be a mother. She said she couldn't think when she was at home."

"With me. She couldn't think when she was with me," Tessa said it as a statement, not a question.

"I only saw her depression that night, never before. She was good at hiding it," he said. "I told her I'd help her or get her help—whatever she needed, it would be okay. Everything would work out fine, I promised her."

"And then?" *Had there been help?* Tessa wondered.

"She said, 'Never mind, Ben. We can't afford any help.' She then threw herself into motherhood for a while, and it seemed to work, but maybe she was just shutting herself down and doing what she had to do. I don't know," he said, looking down at the deck. "And she didn't take off again..."

"She took off all the time when I was a kid. Don't you remember?"

"I was blind to it, Tessa," he said. "I tried to pretend her disappearances were her way of managing her troubles. She said she went to museums and out shopping and on various retreats or whatever she called them. She went for walks on the beach. I never joined her. I didn't help her, after promising I would." As he talked, his breathing got thicker and more labored. "I failed her. I failed at being a husband."

Tessa put her hand on his back. "Dad, you can stop. Really. I think I get it," she said, not wanting him to get too agitated. *But maybe it's helpful for him to say it all—finally.*

He continued. "We were young, too young perhaps. We'd been married for a little while, not even a year. We had nothing back then, just a tiny apartment and each other, of course. That was pretty good, you know, just having each other. She wasn't even working when we found out she was expecting you. She was still taking classes in this or that, trying to figure out what she liked, what she wanted to pursue. And then you were born and I thought, well, let's just focus on this for now, this baby, this little family that we'd made and I told her that. And again, I told her that on the beach that rainy night. Then I made her get in the car with me. We'd pick up her car the next day. And we did. This time, we brought you with us and I held you. I walked along the shore with you, even stuck your bare little feet in the ocean, Tessie. And I told her she could go there with you anytime. She didn't have to be alone. Everything would work out fine."

She needed a partner, Tessa thought, *not a baby to take care of.* "What about her classes, Dad? Did she ever start them back up again after I was born?" *Unlikely,* Tessa thought. *There was no money for that. She just pushed it on me.* "Be well educated and well employed. Remember how she used to always say that to me? And look where I am now. I have a degree I don't use and a simple, common office job."

"Stop it, Tessa. No degree is useless. Your job is just where you are right now. Nothing wrong with that."

Tessa felt silly then. She actually liked her office job for the most part. Even if the salary wasn't enough to get her own place and it didn't challenge her too much—being rather routine and clerical—it was what she could manage in her present situation, her stepping stone out of the mistake of trying to be an elementary school teacher. The lunch time company was pretty sweet, too.

"You want a challenge, Tessa? You want different

work?" her father asked. "Cuz I've got a restaurant, you know. It needs a good dose of creativity and a little TLC. It needs a smart, dedicated person to resurrect it." He let this hang in the air for a minute. "It's yours, Tessa, in my will. It's all yours. Title. Deed. Everything. It's got no more mortgage. In its heyday, it was turning a good profit. Real good. It was my livelihood, my life...for so long..." He paused and looked at her.

And that was that. She had inadvertently changed the subject just when he was beginning a long overdue conversation about her mother. He was moving on to his love of Tremblay's Place, his true marriage.

"You could do whatever you want with it. Breakfast only. Coffee shop. Bakery." He paused before continuing. "Little café with fancy fig pies and cheese tarts and cool live bands on Friday nights."

Little café with fancy fig pies and cheese tarts and cool live bands on Friday nights. He's clearly thought about this a bit.

"I don't know, Dad. It's a lot to consider right now," she replied, her mind swimming in all directions. The fantasy of it intrigued her a little, but the location was far from ideal. It was way down here in Fairhaven, too far from the life she was trying to create.

"Just think about it. You wouldn't need to hire too many people. It's small."

The idea of hiring anyone filled Tessa with fear. She was too young and inexperienced to be the boss. Her father had been the boss. Yes, Benjamin Tremblay, in his day, how she hated that expression, *in his day,* had been an excellent restaurant owner. His little corner of the world, as he'd called it, was a bustling place where he'd spent so much of his time that it became his whole world. And when her mother wasn't around, Tessa had lived in her father's world with him. She'd done her homework in a corner booth and had early dinners there. She went with him on the weekends and helped out. Once she was in her teens, she cleared and set tables, washed dishes, waited tables. She'd even learned to bake.

Through all her time working with Dad, their relationship had a thread of shared experience which she imagined long-term co-workers developed over the years. It wasn't particularly intimate, but close in a camaraderie sort of way. But it was always understood that he was the proprietor and she was the helper.

"You should let me help you get well. Then I could help you with it. Change it up a bit. Every little beachside diner needs some new oomph once in a while."

He didn't respond.

"I could call Dr. Berenger's office right now. C'mon, Dad. One appointment."

"I'm wiped out, baby. All this talking. Help into my bed, will you?"

And that was that—again.

Dismissed. Subject closed. She wondered if her presence in his house for eleven days was even welcome.

By the time she'd fished her phone out of her tote bag that evening, there were four missed calls—all from Frankie—and Tessa knew he would show up soon, if he knew she was home. She moved her car into the carport and parked her father's truck behind it so it wasn't visible from the street. She then turned off every light in the house and went to her bedroom.

Sixteen

After five days at home with her father and grandmother, Tessa and Andrew met at a motel off Route 495. She needed to feel like she existed in another place—her Andrew place. It was a Wednesday, the perfect night for them to spend together because he didn't need to go into work until 2:00 PM the following day. They had each driven a little over seventy-five miles, arrived just before sunset, and could be together until noon on Thursday. Tessa calculated how much time that gave them. *Sixteen hours. Oh, glorious heaven. Sixteen hours with Andrew and his perfect hands after not seeing him for nearly a week.* She'd made a day's worth of green drinks—heavy on the fruit for palatability—arranged an extra aide to be with her father in the morning, promised to keep her phone on and nearby, and hoped for the best.

As soon as they got into the room, she immediately tore into him, needing to release a week's worth of energy, needing to feel real.

"Get inside me, Andrew," Tessa said into his ear before smothering his mouth with her own and unzipping his pants, "now."

Wordless from her mouth on him, he obliged. She pulled him into her and tightened every muscle in her body around him until she melted into his weight.

"Dear God, Tessa. That was quite a how do you do," he said, collapsing on the pillow next to her. "Did you even say hello to me first?"

"Hello, Andrew. Happy Wednesday night. It's good to see you and, yeah, this beats the backseat any day. Good suggestion," she said, running her fingers lightly over the teeth marks she'd made on his shoulder. "Did I hurt you?" she asked, tickling the little indentations on his skin.

"You've never hurt me, Tessa. Quite the opposite, actually."

Her fingers continued down his chest and torso, where she rested them in the space between his belly button and his pelvis. It was one of her favorite spots on his body. With her fingers spread out, her hand fit just right there.

"Any day, any night, Tessa," he said, grabbing her hand and bringing it to his mouth for a long moment and licking each of her fingers, then her palm and upwards to the inner fold of her elbow. "I want you all the time, Tessa. You've done so much for me. Oh God, I missed you this week. I missed this sweet skin of yours. This sweet mouth. Everything. Everything about you. Our funny lunches and walks. The greenhouse. *You.* I've missed *you.*"

"Missed you, too...a lot," she said quick and breezy, casual. "Do you have any words to write on me tonight? I'm in the mood for a good, non-verbal story. 'Dear Tessa,' it should start and you take it from there."

"You want a story or a letter?" Andrew asked.

"Mix it up, Andrew. I'm sure it will be to my liking, no matter what. Maybe you could even throw some foreign words in there. Make it nice and spicy."

"Hmm, non-verbal, foreign words? I'll see what I can

come up with," he teased.

She stretched out and kicked the sheet all the way off.

"Turn around, then. I want your shoulders. Your spine. The backs of your knees, Tessa. My sweet Tessa."

His silent words flowed and flowed from his fingertips, his palms and even the tip of his tongue on her skin.

"Am I real, Andrew? Am I real? Is this real?"

"I hope so," Andrew said.

"You hope what?" Tessa asked.

"That you're real. I'd be awfully disappointed, if you were an illusion. And this, well, I'm here. You're here. I can feel you. You can feel me. Seems real, right?"

She hadn't realized she'd said it out loud. "I'm so silly. Just being silly," she backpedaled. "See what you do to my mind, and you haven't even given me any wine tonight."

He continued his slow exploration of her back.

Maybe I shouldn't talk anymore, just feel. Yes, that's what I should do. Empty my mind and feel. It's what she seemed to do best in Andrew's company.

"Tell me what you feel like when I do this," Andrew said after a few minutes. "I want words, Tessa, actual words from your mouth. *Real* words."

She hesitated. There weren't words for it, at least none readily available. *I drift away and float. I just float and then come back down, but with an unusual grace and lightness that I cannot explain. It's so silly to try to explain. Oh, don't make me explain. I cannot. But these are thoughts, mere thoughts, not real words.* Just abstraction.

"I just like it. It feels so good," she replied after a minute or two. "Your touch is amazing. It just feels good," she said quickly, somewhat embarrassed that he was asking her to describe it.

"Seems like it's more than...more than just that," he said.

"Maybe."

"Yes, maybe, Tessa. Maybe you could close your eyes and tell me what it feels like," he said, as his fingers danced up and down her spine and his tongue painted a scene on her shoulders. "Just try."

Words. Okay. Real words. She closed her eyes and let the sensation speak the words for her without forethought. "I am on a cliff. A big, open meadow at the top of a cliff. There are wild flowers growing here and there. It's a little misty, but not raining. Not raining. It feels like dawn and evening at the same time. It's warm. Summertime. My thoughts go away. All the bad stuff in my head flies away and falls into the sea below. I only feel. I feel you here with me in this place, this cliff with mist and flowers. There's a shaded color about it, sort of green and gray and red with a soft orange glow around the edges. The flowers, they're red. Everything else is green and a soft, hazy gray. There's a small house in the distance, just one, and we can go there if we want to sleep. It feels quiet, mostly. Serenity. It feels like serenity. It's a wonderful place. This feeling that you give me is a place. I want to be the little house in the distance; want to feel what the earth and the air and the sea bring to me. I want to let my bare feet feel the soil and rock as we walk toward the edge and look out at the waves. It's better than...better than love. That's what it is, what it feels like. More than anything else, it's better than anything I thought I'd ever feel."

When she opened her eyes she was staring at the crisp, white motel bed pillow, not at Andrew. *Dear God, not at Andrew.* She felt like she'd been cracked open and the glue was nowhere in sight. Her eyes were wet. She noticed a small tear stain on the pillowcase and pressed her face into it.

"My God. That was well said. Better than love, Tessa?"

"Yes, better. This place that you bring me to with your touch, Andrew, is the best place I've ever been," she said, turning around to face him again. "It's your hands. I love your hands so much. These hands." And yet she felt silly for saying, even thinking, that another person's hands could do all this.

She pressed her own hands onto his and let the hot tears form, release themselves briefly, and then stop as Andrew's thumbs ran gently across her cheeks. *Glue. But no, Andrew cannot be my glue. I need to be my own glue. Or perhaps I just needed to let myself come undone, let myself be unglued.*

Andrew pressed his hands more firmly than he ever had around her hips, lifted her off the bed and slipped into her. And again, she wondered how she could live without this for a week at a time. It was becoming a physiological need. *This. Andrew.* He was sustenance, like scrambled eggs and coffee. *Like oxygen.*

"Your phone rang while you were in the shower," she told Andrew when he came out of the bathroom the following morning, wearing only a pair of khaki pants and rubbing a towel over his wet hair. He looked beyond delicious and she had a sudden fantasy that they were a vacationing couple preparing for a day of sightseeing, followed by an evening of relaxing and going to bed early.

"You should've joined me, then you wouldn't have had to listen to my dorky ring tone," he said, running his hands through his hair and flicking the damp towel at her in jest.

She liked that he had the *Jeopardy* theme song as a ring tone. For her own phone, she used one of the bland pre-programmed ones, something with birds chirping and bells chiming in rotation.

He grabbed his glasses from the bedside table, then his phone, and looked at the missed call number on the screen before dialing into his voice mail.

Tessa watched him pace the floor with the phone to his ear. She got up and used the bathroom then, turning the faucet on full blast to give him privacy.

"Anything important?" she asked when she came out, hoping it wasn't work requesting him to go in early.

"It was Heather."

"Heather?"

"My ex-wife."

"Does she routinely call you this early in the morning?" What she really wanted to know was whether Heather routinely called him—period.

"Not routinely, but sometimes," Andrew replied. "She said she had news."

Tessa could feel a tightness forming in her trachea, like something was stuck there. It was not quite pain, but something approaching pain—like a new splinter that was getting pushed further in the more she tried to pull it out.

"What was the news?" Tessa asked, then backpedaled. "Sorry. Don't mean to step in. It's not really my business, I guess." *Is it my business or not?* She wondered.

"She didn't go into much detail. An offer on the house and something else. She didn't say. Just something else. I don't know."

"The house?"

"Yes. We're trying to sell our house. Our old house. It's taking a while."

"I can leave the room, if you want to call her back." It almost killed Tessa to say this and she definitely realized in that moment that her connection with Andrew was more than physical. It was more than a touch thing or a distraction from her concerns about her father. She looked at his hands sliding the phone into his pocket and her mind wandered mercilessly to Heather. *Heather? Such a name.* She pictured someone with light, smooth hair who wore flouncy skirts and kept flowers on the bedside table. *Heather's lavender, of course. Color, scent and feel. Lavender.*

"No. Stay here," he said. "Anyway, I'm not calling her back now."

The *now* meant that he would call her back later, when he was alone. Tessa took several discreet, or what she hoped where discreet, deep breaths. Then she got dressed. Panties. Bra. t-shirt. Shorts. Even sandals. She felt like taking a walk, getting some air and probably a coffee.

"Are you thinking of checking out already? It's early. There's still some time before we have to be out of here."

She hoped he wasn't trying to entice her. Heather was still in the room with them—in the air and in the cell phone in Andrew's pocket. She felt like all she could do was breathe in and out. "Just getting my stuff together. I thought maybe a coffee and some breakfast might be a good idea. What do you think?" She asked, hoping she sounded nonchalant.

Tessa tried to change the channel in her head, tried to think about her father and how he was doing. *Was Kate getting him out of bed now and giving him a green drink, maybe walking him out onto the deck for some fresh, morning air? Or was she injecting him with meds because he was immobilized by pain?* She thought about calling home, but the thought was taken over by the image of Heather speed dialing Andrew, leaving the voice message and hanging up in frustration when he hadn't answered.

"Alrighty, then," Andrew said.

"It just surprised me, that's all," she said once she was dressed and had her tote bag packed up and slung over her shoulder. "I mean, I know you have an ex-wife. You've told me. I just didn't expect her to call you while you were..."

"...in a motel room with you?"

"Yeah."

"It's nothing to worry about, Tessa. We're done. Heather and I. We've been done for a while now."

"How long were you together?" Tessa asked. "Married?"

"Six years."

"Six years," she said. "How long have you been apart? Divorced?"

"Apart for three years, officially divorced for almost two."

She remembered their conversation of a week ago at his kitchen table. *She left me. She divorced me.* He hadn't said, *it didn't work out* or *we got a divorce.* She'd left him. *She left me.* Tessa's mother popped into her mind at that moment, which was rare in Andrew's company. Usually, being with Andrew kept thoughts of her mother away. *She left me.* Leaving was what one person did to another. It wasn't mutual. Her fingers went instinctively to the jagged line on her face.

"I'm really hungry, Andrew. I want to eat scrambled eggs and sausage and toast and coffee, please. Let's go find a place to eat breakfast." She needed to fill herself up, to nourish herself.

His face was guarded, but still so soft around the edges. Those blue-gray eyes—a little cloudier than usual—glanced at her. She tried to decipher his look, but was failing miserably.

"Okay, Tessa. Let's go, my dear. I'll buy you the best breakfast you've ever had," he said and put his arm behind her shoulders as they left the motel room.

He hadn't called her *my dear* since that day she'd invited him to drink merlot by the stream. It accentuated something about the two of them, the age difference, perhaps. Or maybe it really was a term of endearment but, at that moment, it felt more like a condescension. Tessa doubted that he'd ever called Heather *my dear* and this made her feel very small.

There was no need to even get in the car. The motel where they'd stayed was across the street from a strip mall that contained an IHOP, a Dunkin Donuts and, at the far end of the parking lot, a little family-owned place called Sunrise Café. They steered themselves in its direction and went inside. It reminded Tessa of Tremblay's' Place in its decor, size and menu selections. The waitress, an older lady with fluffy gray-blonde hair who wore a bright pink blouse tucked into a black skirt, even indulged Tessa's request of chopped tomatoes sprinkled with basil and shredded parmesan as a side dish to her eggs. They even had dark, seeded rye bread. She'd told her father years ago that Tremblay's needed dark rye on its menu. People liked it, she told him, and despite his reluctance and fear that it wouldn't sell, he ordered some and offered it to his customers. Before long, it was doing better than the wheat and white breads that had been his diner staples for a decade or more. When she suggested oat bread and multigrain rolls, he added those too, and watched how they brought in customers.

There were four other tables with customers that Thursday morning at Sunrise Café. Tessa and Andrew sat in a back corner of the restaurant, a table that allowed her to notice everything, from the location of the coffee pot to the swinging kitchen door with its circular window at eye level.

While they waited for their breakfasts, Tessa got the nerve to ask Andrew for more about his past. "Tell me your story, Andrew. In words." *In words. Real words. In public, he would have to use real, verbal words and not his tongue on the backs of her shoulders or his fingers on her naked legs.*

"We've had this house on the market for almost two years. It's been very frustrating. No offers—nothing—despite lowering the price every ninety days. We were beginning to think we'd be better off holding onto it, but we can't. We have to sell. It's time to sell. We have to," he rambled on. "Anyway, we've given the broker full access. She can show it whenever, if ever, someone's interested without having to let either of us know first. It was becoming too difficult to know when someone had a showing, only to get no result—too draining. Well, finally we have an offer. It's less than what we agreed to accept, but at this point, we'll most likely take it."

She let him continue without interrupting him.

"I'll need to take a couple days off and go up to Vermont to help her get everything sorted out with the broker. Not sure exactly when yet."

"Why did you and Heather get divorced? Why did she...why did she leave you, Andrew?" This was mainly what Tessa needed to know, not merely information about their soon to be former house.

He looked down at his placemat, adjusting his fork, spoon and butter knife along its edges; then unfolded his napkin and put it on his lap before taking a sip of his coffee.

"She didn't like who I was anymore. We didn't agree on things. Major things."

"What kinds of things?" Tessa asked cautiously. She thought of her mother and all the arguments and silent fights there had been over the years with her father. She'd been too young to understand marriage, but knew her parents' relationship had always been unstable. Her father worked. Her mother cried or ran away.

The waitress approached, smiling, with two steaming plates of eggs.

"Here you go, loves. Enjoy. I'll be around to refill your coffees in a minute or two," she said, as she put their breakfasts in front of them and winked her veteran waitress wink.

"It's too much, Tessa," Andrew said, picking up his fork.

She knew he wasn't talking about the amount of food on his plate.

"It's too much to talk about right now. I can't. C'mon, let's eat. You're starving, right?"

SEVENTEEN

Tessa woke early on Friday morning, on alert for her father's stirrings. There were five full days left before she had to return to work. She wanted to get to him before Kate showed up at 7:00 AM. *A walk,* she was thinking, *a walk on this bright, sunny July morning, possibly even around the big block.* The big block, as they'd called it when Tessa was little and learning to ride a bicycle, was up to the top of their street, a quarter mile stretch on the main road, then back down another two side streets until they were back home. It was a perfect square mile, but even up and down the street for as long as he was able would do him so much good. She had not given up on the power of nutrition and exercise. Even though he wouldn't go to the naturopath, Tessa continued to provide what he would take. She was putting the research to use in her own way, combining approaches and bits and pieces of different programs she'd read about. He wouldn't do coffee enemas or twenty pounds of produce daily, but he'd drink a thick organic smoothie once or twice a day. She'd even managed to order some B17 powder from

Mexico to mix in. And he'd get out and stretch as his body allowed—*which is a little more often than before,* she'd noticed.

And he'd talk. Fill her up with talk.

The digital clock on her bureau said 6:02 AM when Tessa got out of bed and peeked into her father's bedroom. He was sitting on the edge of his bed, his feet on the floor. She looked him up and down, from his bald head to the bony torso and prominent ribcage. His stomach, though, was still swollen—even months after his last chemo treatment. She suspected it was a side effect of the pain medication that Kate gave him. *Or another tumor that's growing.* But this thought went out as fast as it went in. She wouldn't entertain that notion. *Nope. No way.* His legs were covered by his cotton pajama bottoms, but she could tell that underneath the thin fabric he was more skeletal than she wanted to face.

"Hey, Dad," she said from his doorway.

"Good morning, baby. Come here and give me a hand."

Tessa's father's hands were neither too large nor too small for a man's hands. They were medium-sized, with neatly clipped and clean fingernails, like Andrew's hands. She suddenly felt a wave of weirdness for comparing her father's hands to those of her lover. Her face must have flushed at this thought and she quickly attempted to let it flow through and not linger. It was her father's hands that had first taught her the peace be with you handshake, how to mix a batter and now, how to grab hold and pull someone to a standing position. Andrew's had taught her sensual touch and non-verbal communication.

Different, of course. Separate. I must keep them separate.

"Tessa," her father's voice brought her back. "You're way out there, baby. What are you thinking about?"

"Oh nothing, Dad. You need help getting up? Can I get you a shirt? A t-shirt, maybe. Supposed to be hot today. You think you might be up for a little walk today?" She'd woken with the thought of powering themselves up with spinach, kale, and berry smoothies, thick and full of good stuff to invigorate the cells. His cells. Then getting a bit of fresh air into his lungs. She needed to do all this before Mémère started in on the bacon and waffles.

"Easy, easy. One thing at a time, baby. I need to get to the bathroom and take a leak first. Pull me up from this bed. I can do the rest."

"Okay, Dad. Ready?" she asked, taking his hands in hers. "One. Two. Three. Up."

He got to his feet, steadied himself and thanked her. Then he shuffled across the hall to the bathroom. He left the door slightly open in his usual manner. It was his just-in-case mechanism, just like leaving his bedroom door ajar. He'd gotten in the habit of doing that after Tessa's mother left, better to hear Tessa if she needed him, even though she had been a teenager and always kept her own door closed. Now she kept hers open or simply slept on the couch in the living room when she was home.

She opened his second drawer to get him a t-shirt. There were only a couple clean ones left. Since her father was up, Tessa decided to strip his bed and get the sheets and pillowcases into the hamper, too. She pulled the top sheet down and out from between the mattress and box spring, then climbed onto the center of the bed and tugged the corners of the fitted sheet off, rolled the two sheets together and stuffed them into the hamper in the corner of the room. She grabbed each pillow and shook it out of its case. That's when a marble covered, black composition notebook fell out and hit the bare mattress with a gentle thump.

Tessa poked her head out of the bedroom and looked across the hall to see if her father was still in the bathroom and whether he needed help. *He seems okay for the moment,* she thought. Door still ajar, she returned to the mattress and the notebook. She opened it tentatively, hoping beyond logic that it was a list of his medications or a simple chronicle of his days and progress or lack thereof. Blue Paper Mate ink filled about half the undated pages. The rest were blank and smooth. Instead of reading it, she scanned it quickly and non-intrusively.

Poems. Notes and scribbles. Lists of rhyming words in the margins.

She flipped until she found a completed poem a few pages into the notebook. In her father's big, loopy handwriting, she read:

Bodies remember
Even when our minds fail us
The skin feels whispers
Smooth as pale sunbeams
Through stained glass windows

When bodies fail
And minds must complete us
Memory and love become hurried and chaotic
Quick, quick love
Before it's too late

She closed the notebook and laid it in the far, top corner of his bed when she heard the faucet stop running.

"Dad, I have a shirt for you. Want me to bring it in?"

"What'd ya say, Tessie?"

She stepped into the hallway. "How do you feel about a short walk up the street before it gets too hot? I found you a shirt."

"Just leave it on my bed for me. I'm almost done in here."

"Okay, Dad. I'm running downstairs to get an early start on the laundry. I'll put some clean sheets on your bed in a few minutes."

"No need to change my bed. Kate did it yesterday."

By the time her father got his shirt on, Tessa had thrown his sheets, pillowcases and everything else that had been in his hamper into the washing machine. She went into her childhood bedroom, changed into a pair of shorts and a tank top, then returned to his room.

The notebook was gone from the bare mattress. She felt as though she had intruded into his soul, uninvited.

"How much of it did you read?" he asked without looking up at her.

"I just scanned it a little, really," she said, ashamed. "I'm sorry. I shouldn't have. One poem. That's all. Just one."

"Which one?"

"The one about bodies and minds remembering and failing and chaotic love before it's too late."

"Oh baby, you're a better poet than your old man, that's for sure. Those are just the ramblings of a bored guy stuck in his room with nothing to do all day."

"What are you trying to remember before...before your body fails you?"

"Come on, Tessa. Let's take this walk before I zonk out on you mid-step, okay. The last time I did this walk, it took me forty-five minutes," he said, as Tessa knelt on the kitchen floor to tie her father's shoes. "Not too tight, baby. I'm skinny as hell, but my feet are like two water balloons. Go figure."

"I'll be careful, Dad." It was true. His feet were swollen and looked on the verge of splitting open and oozing. "Is it the medication doing that to your feet?"

"Edema. Kate says it could be toxins accumulating. I'll need to soak 'em after or they'll hurt like a son of a bitch."

"Are you sure you can take a walk, Dad? I don't want to make you feel worse."

"Let's go. Nothing hurts too much right now. Kate usually sets up my foot bath as soon as we get back."

"I didn't realize you went out walking with Kate," Tessa

said. "That's good. Does she give you those drinks I make for you?"

"Sometimes."

"Sometimes? Maybe they're helping you. Do you think? A couple weeks ago, you weren't walking forty-five minutes at a time."

"Well, it's only been a couple of times and just around the block was enough to wear me out."

"Don't worry, Dad. I'm not signing you up for the half marathon." She laughed a little. "Just around the block. Do you have it in you?"

"I think I'm gonna give it a shot. Just for you, Tessie. You can hold me up, if I need it. You're small, but strong. You're a powerhouse. I know you are."

Eighteen

By Tuesday night, Tessa and her father had made three days worth of super food recipes, including fruit pies of all sorts: fig, cherry, blueberry. She'd stocked his fridge and freezer with bottles of the green drinks that seemed to be giving him the strength to get little things done. She noticed that he was organizing his closet, often spending hours at a time with his notebooks and file boxes in front of him. Then he would sleep and do a bit more. He talked about going to the restaurant the following weekend to 'settle up' a bit.

When she kissed him goodbye on Wednesday morning before driving herself back to the campus and her job, he told her he'd see her on Friday. She didn't realize how exhausted she was until she sat down at her desk and turned her computer on. Halfway down the long list of new, mostly work-related, emails was one from Andrew. She opened that one first.

Monday, 3:14 AM
Hi Tessa,

So, I've done a bit more research for you. If you, and especially your father, are serious about finding a natural treatment for him, there are options. I've been reading all sorts of information over the weekend. I've cocooned myself in my office, actually. I left you a phone message last night, but I know how silly you are about not checking your phone. I can't wait to see you when you get back, so I can tell you what I've been learning here...and hug and kiss you abundantly, of course.

xo, Andrew

P.S. Please don't wear my favorite little skirt of yours or I will be hopelessly distracted and we won't make it beyond the first page!

She shot him a quick email to thank him, promising she'd be by the library to see him shortly after 5:00 PM. She then immersed herself in work for the rest of the day.

"I'm sorry I can't sit with you right now. I'm on the reference desk until six-thirty," Andrew said when Tessa arrived a few minutes after 5:00 PM. He set her up in his office with the stack of articles and books and a list of websites to check out.

I'll go through the websites first, she decided, *and just throw the rest in my bag to take home.*

She started at the top of his list, even though it was the third website down on the list that was highlighted and asterisked with notes in the margin and the word *THIS* written and circled. She quickly scanned the first and second websites, both of which featured bone-thin women with long dark hair and perfect skin, the first of whom claimed that a fully raw food diet had not only healed all her physical ailments but also had turned her eyes bright green when they had previously been dull hazel-brown. Tessa listened for a minute or two before moving on to the second one. Another ultra thin woman—this one going through various yoga poses while talking—was on the screen. Her focus seemed more on cleaning up the gut and removing toxins by way of an all organic vegan diet and twice weekly coffee enemas. *Oh have mercy.* Her father wasn't going down that path with the enemas. She'd left the book by the German doctor for him to read and he'd only handed it back to her saying he wasn't going to let anyone shoot coffee up his ass in the name of health. And that was that. Tessa could understand. *Why does natural treatment have to be so weird?*

Though intrigued by the obvious glow of the woman and the flexibility of her body, Tessa doubted she'd ever been terminally ill. Maybe she'd had to deal with constipation or acne and had chosen an extreme avenue to achieve her goals. It wasn't something her father could relate to. Andrew had thrown it all in there for her consideration, though. More information. More choice. More details. *Mister detail.* She had to appreciate it, even though some of it was too far-fetched to be doable. At least he'd gotten a laugh out of her. *Maybe that's why he included the first two and highlighted the third.* She moved down the list.

The third website included links to a YouTube channel featuring short segments produced by a thirtyish-year old man who wore a crisp white t-shirt and a pair of Lycra running shorts. He was blond in a way that was almost not blond, but not quite brunette or redhead either. She clicked on the first video and saw him in a kitchen preparing what he called his giant anti-cancer salad. Tessa rested her elbows on Andrew's desk, wrapped her chin with her hands and watched.

His voice was emerald green. His face was very lightly sun-kissed, as though he was just in from his garden and decided to shoot a segment. She listened to him talk about kale and avocadoes, organic sprouts and beans of all sorts. Then he got into cleansing the cells and clearing out the toxins, as he chopped and mixed and squeezed the juice of half a lemon over his creation.

Tessa scrolled down the list of videos on his channel. He also promoted green drinks mixed with wheatgrass. *Fine. That I can manage to get into Dad. The sweeter the better.* She'd discovered when she threw one or two organic pears in with the greens, her father would drink it down without complaint. This emerald green man on the screen had a list of recipes for those with discriminating taste buds.

About halfway down the screen she saw what Andrew had highlighted in his notes. *THIS. Scientists are studying anti-tumor effects of cannabis in cancer patients. Cannabis oil as an effective alternative to chemotherapy. Single father jailed for treating young daughter with cannabis oil. Family of boy with severe seizure disorder relocates to Colorado to legally seek treatment with cannabis oil. Medical marijuana dispensaries in Massachusetts face lengthy licensing process.* The list went on further. Tessa curled her legs under herself in Andrew's desk chair and clicked on as many articles, videos and links to more information as she could. She discovered Leafly.com, Medical Jane and The Holistic Cannabis Summit, which featured interviews with researchers and medical professionals worldwide.

When Andrew popped back into his office after his shift at the reference desk, she was fully engrossed in a story about a Canadian man who had produced a treatment for hundreds of cancer patients in the form of cannabis oil. He'd used it himself and cured his own skin cancer and had given it away free of charge to anyone who needed it. When doctors gave up and patients in his community went home without hope, he said, "Try this." She watched him talk from his back porch about the countless miracles he'd seen. Every few minutes the camera panned out onto his expansive property to show where he'd grown and harvested his medicine. The man in the video became serious and irate when he told the story of his land being raided by police, who dug out and stole all his plants one day when he was away from home.

"I can get some of that for your father," Andrew said from over her shoulder. "That oil."

"Really?" she asked, disbelieving. "How?"

"I meet a lot of people in this place. I'm good at asking questions. Believe me. I could get you some."

"I don't think he'll do it. My father, I mean. He was always very strict about that stuff when I was younger. Always gave me the speech about making good decisions and told me all he had to do was look in my eyes and he could tell. That, and he could smell it a mile away."

"I'm still researching this, Tessa. Keep flipping through these pages I printed. There's a lot more," he said, handing her another stack of articles. "I read these over the weekend. It blew my mind how much sense it all makes."

Andrew went over to the bookshelf behind his desk and pulled down a book by Rick Simpson, the Canadian man who'd made the oil. He also pulled down a book on the endocannabinoid system. *The what system? Endocannabinoid system.* Tessa had aced biology and didn't remember this system. There was the skeletal system. The endocrine and lymphatic systems. The circulatory and nervous systems. The reproductive system. There had never been an endocannabinoid system. She couldn't even pronounce it without tripping over all the syllables.

Next in the video loop was a piece about how to make the oil. They both watched as the man on the screen put a pound of dry cannabis plant material into a big bucket, covered it with solvent and started crushing it down to a pulpy, soupy looking green liquid. After that, he poured it through a coffee filter and put it through various stages of boiling in a rice cooker until nothing remained but approximately two ounces of thick, greenish black oil.

Talking while working, the man in the video claimed that his oil would cure most forms of cancer within ninety days. At that moment, Tessa and Andrew looked at each other and, without saying anything, knew they would try this for her father.

"A pound of weed, though, Andrew, to make that little amount of oil. I don't know what a pound of weed goes for, but it can't be cheap," Tessa said.

"No worries about that, Tessa. Leave that up to me," Andrew said. "Take these books home. I've only skimmed them so far, but there's stuff in here that will make more and more sense once we read it all closely. It adds up. More importantly, it's worth a shot."

When Tessa got to her father's house that Friday evening, Mémère was in the kitchen and Dad was in his bedroom. She stuck her head around his partially open door and saw that he was asleep. Over the past three days, Tessa had read both books, all the articles, and watched numerous testimonials online and was eager to share what she and Andrew were learning. *This will be easier for Mémère,* Tessa thought. *There's no drastic dietary changes to adhere to. And there's more scientific research behind this than anything I've tried to get him to do so far.*

But Mémère wouldn't hear it. "It's complete quackery, Tessa. Have you lost your mind?"

"No, Mem. There's science behind this. I've done my research. It seems all I do these days is research ways to help him. I know what I'm talking about. What harm can anything natural do at this point? It could be our last chance to save him, or at least help him feel better while he's still with us...for however long he's got left. Don't you want that?"

Mémère put both her hands down on the table, flat

palmed and serious. "Cancer is the devil, Tessa. The good man in this world cannot always win a fight with the devil. We need to let him go with his dignity and morality intact. God will provide eternal life in Heaven. He's been a good man all these years. After your mother left, he worked hard for you and he never divorced her even after how she treated him, leaving him with a young girl to raise and a business to run and nobody to help him but me. Everything he did was out of love for you."

"I understand that, Mem. And that's why I want to help him now. He needs *me* now."

"He's told me and he's told you he's all done with doctors. You think I haven't tried to talk him into trying again. One more round. One more attempt. Keep your appointments, I always said to him. Let the doctors do their work. He sometimes listened, sometimes not. He'd rather be in that restaurant than in the hospital, Tessa. What can I do?"

"This, Mem. You can listen to me now. The chemo. The radiation. It did more harm than good. That's most likely what's killing him now. I have pages and pages of research on this. Legitimate research, not quackery, Mem." Tessa pulled the packet out of her bag and laid it on the table before her grandmother. "He's still young. His body could respond very well to this. Just imagine his immune system getting back its function."

She spread the articles out on the table in front of Mémère and wondered which one her grandmother would pick up first.

Mémère did nothing more than give them a cursory glance from her side of the table. "So you printed some stories, Tessa. You have to be careful about what you find on the internet. Everybody knows that. It's always on the news. Every Tom, Dick and Harry can write something and put it on the internet."

"Of course I know that, Mem. But this is..."

"It's nonsense, Tessa. It's some crazy idea that these drug pushers are trying to brainwash you into believing."

"A lot of this is laboratory and university research. I'll read it aloud to you, okay? It's been on the news a lot lately. You must've seen it on the news or *60 Minutes* by now."

"Yes, of course I've seen it on the news. It seems to be all the rage nowadays. They show all these idiots out in Colorado, the girls sitting on the men's shoulders and getting high out in the middle of the day at a park. And there are people pushing for looser laws here too. Good Lord, Tessa. I've been around long enough to know what this stuff is and what it isn't. I saw all those crazy hippies in the sixties. People getting high and stupid. That stuff made people psychotic. Believe *me*, Tessa. You don't know what these nuts, these druggies, put in that stuff. Whatever it is you're reading about...it's not true," she said, ruffling the articles on the table for emphasis.

Tessa picked them back up and stacked them neatly again before slipping them back into her tote bag.

"Now I'm going to tell you a story. Sit down," Mem ordered.

Even though Tessa's body didn't want to sit down, she did. She wanted to remain upright and strong, shoulders back and head high, but she pulled out a kitchen chair and plopped into it.

"You never knew your grandfather, my husband, your father's father. Your father hardly knew him either, not since he was a very little boy. My husband was a very sociable man, always inviting his buddies over, always off playing pool and going out for rides with these guys. We were young, so I just tolerated it. I had a young child to take care of. He was working and providing for us, but he liked to indulge on the weekends." She paused and told Tessa to put the kettle on, get the cream from the fridge and the cookies from the cupboard. "One night, I'll never forget this as long as I live, Fourth of July, 1968, I had put your father to bed just before the knock on the door came. I thought it was him, you know, my husband, forgot his keys or was tanked from being out with his buddies. So I opened the door, ready to throw something at him, but it wasn't my husband standing there in the doorway. It was a policeman, very somber and serious. 'Ma'am,' he said, 'Ma'am, I have some bad news for you.' And then he told me about the accident. Car full of guys, all friends, full of beer and *marijuana* and who knows what else. All dead. As soon as your father was old enough to understand, I told him how his father died." She paused. "And he promised me he'd never touch that stuff. It's evil, that *marijuana*. And cancer is evil, but you can't fix evil with more evil."

The kettle whistled loudly.

Tessa stood and switched it off. The click of the knob was so loud, louder than her grandmother's elevated breathing and louder than the crunch of gravel in the driveway and the slam of Frankie's truck door closing.

Tessa poured the hot water into two cups. Mémère liked to dip the tea bag in slowly and deliberately, as she watched the clear, steamy water turn orange-red with bergamot, then set it on her saucer once the perfect strength and color was achieved. Tessa didn't care. Tea was tea. She typically didn't even remove her tea bag, just let it steep continuously as she drank. Mémère just shook her head at it, as if she must teach the girl everything.

"Now you listen to me. I will not tolerate this, Tessa. Do you understand me? You will not, *will not* bring that stuff into this house," Mémère stated. "Don't be a stupid girl. For God's sake, you could get yourself arrested. Then what good are you to your father?"

Before Tessa could even sit again, Frankie was at the back door. He never bothered knocking.

"How are my ladies today?" He burst in and set a warm loaf of sweet bread from the Portuguese bakery on the table.

Tessa grabbed her full tote bag and slung it over her shoulder.

"Mrs. T, you look upset. What's going on?" He turned to Tessa. "Things okay, Tessie?"

"No, Frankie, nothing is okay," Tessa snapped. "And damn it, Frankie, *it's Tessa!*"

"Never mind, Frankie. Just one of Tessa's crazy ideas," Mémère hastily said. "Are you hungry?"

"Always," Frankie said, unwrapping the sweet bread.

When Tessa got to her father's door, she peeked in. He was tossing around in his bed sheets again. This was how he woke up—cold sweats and disorientation. She went in, sat beside him. It took several minutes for him to acknowledge her. They held hands the way they did when she was young and scared. That is, his own strong masculine hand atop her small quivering one. It was opposite now. She had trouble looking at how bony his hands had become. Every brittle internal element had come to the surface—purple and gray knuckles and veins. The soft pads of fingertips were gone.

"Daddy?" She hadn't called him Daddy in years, but it came out easily, as if it had only been a day since she'd used that name for him.

He looked up at her. "Tessa, baby. What day is it?"

"Friday, Dad. Friday night. I'm here for the weekend. I'm here for you...to stay with you."

"Help me up, baby. I need the bathroom."

The remainder of the weekend went much the same. He mainly stayed in his bed and she checked on him. By Saturday afternoon, she was able to get a twenty-ounce green drink into him and a scoopful of fruit salad. On Sunday, he told her to go down to Tremblay's Place and air it out a little. He declined going with her, preferring instead to slump on the couch. Tessa put another green drink on the end table before heading down the street to check on her father's restaurant.

I will help you, Dad. Always. She thought as she backed out of the driveway.

NINETEEN

It had become Tessa's routine to leave work an hour or so early on Friday afternoons so she could pick up groceries and get an early start on her drive. At 4:00 PM, she took a walk to the library's third floor reference department, hoping to see Andrew before the weekend took over her time and energy. *Maybe he's back from Vermont by now and got busy with work. I'll surprise him before I head out.*

He'd left for Vermont more than a week ago and Tessa hadn't heard whether or not the house sale had been successful. She remembered him initially telling her two or three days should do it. *Two or three days and nights in his house with Heather.* Tessa had tried not to obsess over that, while also trying to wrap her head around the fact that all the while she'd been trying to save for her own place, Andrew had an extra one that he was trying to sell. As she pulled open the library's heavy glass door, she realized it had been ten days with no word from Andrew about the house sale or when he was coming back to work—or to her. She didn't want to admit how much she missed him. It was a strange feeling not to see Andrew during the day, either at lunch or in the evening. Their routine had become consistent and safe until now. Then she caught herself with this thought. *Safe! What a concept.* What a crazy way of seeing her time with him, as safe. She reached the third floor landing and turned toward the hall where Andrew's office was located. Upon finding it closed and locked, she slipped her hand off the door knob and turned to go. *No Andrew today either,* she thought sadly. *Maybe I conjured him up. Maybe he's my imaginary lover.*

"May I help you?" one of the librarians, a tall brunette woman who was dressed in a long, straight navy skirt and matching blazer, asked.

"I'm all set. Thank you," Tessa managed, then hesitated for a moment. "I was just wondering if Andrew might be in." *If Andrew is just a fantasy, a figment of my imagination, this woman will surely tell me.*

"No, he's not in. He's on vacation. Is there something I can help you with? A project you're working on?"

"No. I'm not a student. He's a friend. I was just passing through and thought I'd say hi," Tessa said, falsely cheerful. "Okay, thanks. No big deal. I'll stop in next week and catch up with him then. I actually wanted to thank him for his help with something, but it can wait until Monday."

"Oh, he won't be back on Monday. Family trip or something, he said when he left," the librarian said. "Do you want to write him a message or something? I could leave it in his mailbox...if you want."

"No, that's okay. Like I said, it's no big deal," Tessa lied and turned to go.

"Have a good evening," the woman said.

"Yes, you, too," Tessa reciprocated blandly without looking back.

A family trip or something? Goddamn it. He isn't my figment. A family trip!

As she approached her car, Tessa checked the time on her phone. 4:17 PM, still early, but she was in no mood for grocery shopping. She wanted only to shut off her phone, get in her car and drive—and drive. *Loud music would be good, too.* She flipped through her CD stash and pulled out an old favorite, a Pat Benatar greatest hits disc that she hadn't listened to in months—years, maybe. *No sappy, sentimental tunes today.* Pat Benatar was her heart-thumping, sweating, running music. And Tessa was running today, running from her artificial life on this campus so far from home that it felt like another world entirely. She remembered reading an interview once in which Pat Benatar mentioned her need to be tough and strong because she was only five feet tall. If she was wimpy, she came across as a child. If she was emotionally strong, it elevated her. *Good stuff.* Tessa could aspire to this attitude. *Definitely.* But first, one more peek at the phone before shutting it off and tossing it into her tote. *No new voicemail or texts,* despite the several she'd left for Andrew. Hers had been simple, cheery ones like: *See you soon. Good luck with the house. xo, Tessa.* This one was days old already. And, *Not trying to pester you, just thinking about you. It's Wednesday and you know what we like to do on Wednesday nights.* That was two days ago. Light and fun and likely to get a light and fun response, but no. There had been no response. Then yesterday, *Hi, just catch up with me when you can. Miss your sweet hugs and all other methods of non-verbal communication. Words are good too, Andrew. Hope you are okay. Tessa.* No response. After that one, she stopped. Three messages was enough, too much perhaps. Any more and she might look like a ridiculous lovesick girl, which she was not. She was absolutely not.

It was Friday, 4:21 PM. Tessa sent one more message before shutting off her phone and burying it deep inside her big bag. *Feels like a roller coaster to me.* She tapped the send button and instantly hated the cheesy cliché. Then, she looked into the rearview mirror, winced at the vividness of her facial scar, and backed out of her parking space. The music was cranked up loud as she drove to the highway ramp.

She would not allow herself to miss him. Her mother's words pounded in her ears. This was no subtle whispering. *Just turn your feelings off. Your heart, Tessa. You have to manage it, turn it on and off as necessary. Otherwise, it's time to go.* The trouble was, every time she tried to turn it off, she felt dead. *Whatever. Maybe numbness is a good thing after all. No feelings. No pain.* She merged into the high speed lane and turned up the music even louder.

Tessa drove until 6:00 PM and stopped at Market Basket for the groceries she hadn't felt like getting earlier. The store was mobbed, as usual, and was testing what remained of her patience.

Spinach. Kale. Pineapple. Red raspberries. Carrots. Pears. Everything organic. It all had to be organic to even do any good. This was according to all the research she had done so far. Pomegranate juice. *He actually likes this.* She did, too. Fresh ginger to steep in boiling water for an infusion. *He doesn't like this,* she remembered, and put the ginger back. Japanese green tea. Nothing with refined sugar. That was critical. Refined sugar, according to every holistic guru, was toxic. Her father's body was toxic enough already. She needed to purge the toxicity out with her recipes and had to make enough to last him the week while she was at work. Kate—God bless Kate—was helping her.

At the check-out counter, Tessa impulsively grabbed two overflowing handfuls of candy from the display. All her old standbys, Snickers, Milky Way, York Peppermint Patties, Starburst and peanut M&Ms, of course, and a twenty-ounce bottle of lemonade to wash it all down. She didn't make eye contact with the cashier, as she carefully unloaded her basketful of organic produce onto the conveyer belt, then quickly dumped the toxic handful of sugar and fat and chemicals on as well. This was her old strategy of dealing when she didn't want to deal. It had been her way of getting through her teens and even her earlier years with Frankie. Nowadays, she was more of a runner than a binge eater, which had the added benefit of keeping her slim. But running, physically running with her feet in sneakers on the road, was the furthest thing from her mind. The only running she was doing was the kind where she got in her car, turned off her phone and shoveled cheap, overly sweet chocolate into her mouth. She was bolting.

By the time Tessa pulled into her father's driveway on Friday evening, there was a light mist hovering in the air. She popped her trunk open and grabbed the three Market Basket bags and headed in by the back door. The candy stash had kept her company on the passenger seat and was now sitting very uncomfortably in her stomach. *All of it. Damn it.* She felt gross. The sweets binge had left her with a tightness in her waistband and a heaviness inside her that made her feel as if she'd eaten a brick instead of digestible food.

Blackness of the soul. Blackness of the heart.

Mémère was in the kitchen washing the dishes when Tessa walked in.

"Good that you got home before the storm," she said, without turning her head away from the sink.

Tessa laid her grocery bags down on the table.

"How's my dad? Is he sleeping already?"

"He's on the couch in the living room. I think he's got the *Wheel of Fortune* on," she said. "Go in, Tessa. He's been asking about you all day today."

She could smell that Mémère had cooked pork chops and home fries for dinner and verified this when she lifted the lid of the big cast iron pan that was atop the stove's front burner.

"That's for you. You should eat something," Mémère said, as she dried her hands on a dish towel and turned to face Tessa. "You just missed Frankie. He ate supper with us, but then he got a call and had to go change a flat tire or something. I told him to stop by again later when he's done working and said that you should be home soon."

"Mem, I really don't want to see Frankie tonight. I'm tired and not in the mood."

"He doesn't want to take you out dancing, Tessa. He just wants to see you," she said. "Might be nice to have someone...a man...who can soothe you."

"Frankie doesn't soothe me," she snapped. "He adds to my stress."

"You should be nice to him, Tessa. He's very good to us. Just this week, he went to the pharmacy for my blood pressure medicine. And he fixed the toilet."

"What was wrong with the toilet?"

"It wouldn't flush. We had water all over the floor. It was awful."

"So he came and plunged it?" Tessa asked.

"It was more than just plunging. It needed a new part. He went out and bought the part and came back and installed it. You should thank him for all he does when you're not here."

"Mmm, I'll be sure to," she replied. The smell of the fried pork was doing her in. The junk food she'd inhaled on the highway was a hard clump in her stomach, where it undoubtedly would remain until morning. "Mem, we talked about this, remember? Dad can't eat meat and fried things now."

"Nonsense, Tessa. He needs protein. He needs nutrients."

"That's what Kate and I are trying to do with the recipes I've been making him and the green drinks."

"Yes, herbs and spices and all those greens. I'm afraid

it'll give him the runs. He's already so weak."

"There's research behind it. I've talked to experts and listened to their advice. His body will respond. It takes time..."

"He doesn't have time," Mem cut her off.

"What do we have to lose by trying? Can't we get on the same page, Mem. It's so frustrating."

"Tessa, I'm doing the best I can," her grandmother huffed, turning back to the sink to finish washing the dishes.

"So am I," Tessa said, mostly under her breath, and stepped over to the living room, where the TV hummed in the background.

It was not quite 7:00 PM yet and the face and voice she heard was not that of Pat Sajak, but Brian Williams signing off with his signature line. "And that's our broadcast for this Friday evening. I'm Brian Williams. We hope to see you right back here tomorrow evening. Thank you for joining us and have a good night."

Oh Christ. Brian Williams. As if I need any reminders. It consoled her slightly that Mr. Williams was wearing one of his purple striped neckties, something Andrew wouldn't touch, as his preferences ran more to abstract patterns or multi-colored creations that looked like stained glass windows. *Brilliant.* A man in a necktie on TV could throw Andrew back into her consciousness when she'd done so well blocking him out for the whole drive. That there were no similarities in their appearances—aside from a well-cut suit and good posture—made it all the more frustrating. But once she'd made the connection and she and Andrew had talked and teased each other so much about the journalist, the association was set and she couldn't get rid of it. And in another thirty minutes, *Jeopardy,* and its accompanying theme song, would start. Andrew was already enmeshed in the day-to-day details of her life.

"Hey Dad," she said, sitting on the floor by the couch

and leaning her head against the same pillow her father was resting on.

"Tessie, baby," he said in his weak voice, "what's going on?"

Even sick, he was perceptive to her moods, but she didn't want to go there. There would be no open floodgates tonight.

"Did you eat pork chops and home fries for dinner, Dad?"

"What little I could eat of it. Not much of an appetite anymore."

Tessa could see that her father had no appetite anymore. His skin was stretched tightly over the protruding bones of his face and shoulder blades.

"How about the drinks I make you and put in the freezer every Sunday night? You like those. They're full of all the best stuff, Dad, all the organic produce that I bring here for you. That's what's going to help you now, not fried pork." She was annoyed with Mémère and her father for not taking her suggestions seriously. And yet she was so damn full of sugar at the moment that she could've laughed if she'd been in any mood for laughing. "Is Kate giving you the herbal infusions in the morning?"

"Tessa, I eat what I can."

"I've talked to naturopathic doctors about this, Dad. You have to give it a chance. I want to see you with a little more energy. I want to take a walk with you outside. Remember how well you did last time?" She prompted. "What do you say? It's still light. Just around the block, even a couple houses and back." It was as much for his health as her own that she asked. She felt stifled in the house and wanted to be outside moving around. Anything was better than sitting in this small room with Brian Williams on the TV invoking unwelcome thoughts of Andrew. Her head needed clearing.

"Not right now, Tessa. I don't have it in me. Let's shoot for the morning, baby. Maybe I can even make it around the big block, if you stay right near me and hold me up a bit."

"Of course, Dad. Right near you."

She curled into one end of the couch and watched a trio of strangers spin a giant wheel around and around, while her father dozed on and off at the other end. If she closed her eyes, she might be able to have just enough magical thoughts to get her to the next morning.

TWENTY

"Let's camp, Tessie baby. What do you say?" Tessa's father was full of enthusiasm on Saturday morning, as they walked around the block. It was quite the turnaround from the previous evening when she'd found him slumping on the couch watching the news. It gave her hope.

"Camp? Dad, how and where are we going to camp?"

"Not camp, camp. Like sleeping outside all night. I mean, like we used to do, me and you, kid. Marshmallows, hot dogs, campfire in the backyard. A case of beer. I don't think I've ever had a beer with my daughter. What do you think, love? We could bake a special pie just for the occasion."

Like we used to do? There had been maybe one time each year when Tessa had been in elementary school when they camped together. As she got older, the frequency had tapered off. Once her mother left, the campfires had all but stopped, even though her mother had never participated in them.

"What is the occasion, Dad?" Tessa was cranky. She

didn't want to be cranky, especially when her father was so unusually chipper, so eager for some fun. It had been a rough night with thoughts of Andrew in and out of her head and a series of crazy, disjointed dreams. She'd woken up still tired and fitful.

"I'm dying, Tessa, and I want to spend some time with you. Good time. I don't want you to remember doing my laundry and cleaning up after me and all the errands and shit you do every weekend, baby. I want to put fun memories in you before I go," he said. "Hot dogs, beer, whatever kind you like. No more red wine, baby. It's too goddamn strong for me now with the meds I'm on. One glass and I'll be sleeping in my chair. Not much company, a snoring old skin and bones man who might not even wake up tomorrow."

"Please, Dad. Stop it. You're going to wake up tomorrow," Tessa said. "You have to. I insist."

"I'm doing my best to wake up every morning, baby. But it's getting harder. Sometimes my breathing is...funny."

"Funny?" Tessa repeated her father's word. "You need to use the oxygen tank every night, like Kate said."

"Not funny funny, Tessa. I mean weird. It stops...then starts again. One day, it might just stop," he said. "So go to the store. Get some hot dogs and the good buns, not those whole wheat things."

Her mother's voice played in Tessa's head, as she remembered one of her Mum's more intense quirks. *"Goddamn hot dog buns and white bread. Are you serious, Ben? How can you do this to me? How can you bring this stuff in the house? You know that stuff makes me loony."* Her mother hated when leftovers got brought home from the restaurant, especially certain things that she tried hard to avoid. For her sanity. *"Why can't you just appreciate it? It's less you have to buy at the grocery store. Chop it up and throw it in with the scrambled eggs."* He'd say. *"You have no idea. How many times have I told you I cannot tolerate white bread in my house, Ben?*

It. Makes. Me. Loony." "Just ignore it, then. Tessa and I will eat it. You don't have to touch it." "I'm not supposed to have triggers. No triggers. This," she'd say, holding up the white bread and shaking it at him, *"is a fucking trigger. I might as well just shoot myself now."* And she'd go into her bedroom and lock the door. Of all the memories to come crashing down on Tessa at that moment—*why this one?* Her father might've had the same memory at the mention of white bread hot dog buns, but he was giving nothing away and kept talking, kept adding to his list of items for her to pick up. "Get some marshmallows and chocolate and graham crackers and some figs if you want them. I've grown kind of fond of them, myself."

"I don't think it's peak season for figs anymore." Her Google search had taught her that figs had two seasons— one short, early summer crop and one longer, late summer harvest. "Might not be able to find them today," she said, knowing she would absolutely not buy them even if there was a mountain of them on display at the supermarket.

"Beer, then. Get a whole case of beer. Get a few in me and I'll even sing you some campfire songs."

By 10:00 on Saturday night, Tessa and her father had eaten two hot dogs each, in the big fluffy white bread buns, bunches of massively sticky s'mores and she had lost count of the number of beers she'd popped open for him—but only one for herself, and not Sam Adams. She'd bought an obscure foreign brand that she had never heard of, but was recommended by the guy working the counter at the package store. The night was clear and lucid and so was she. She might be numbing out to any thoughts of Andrew with her belly full of camping food, but she was totally present for her dad—100%.

Her father was dozing in his deck chair, perking up

every now and then to tell her a snippet from her baby days. He was keeping it positive. No sad mama stories. No cancer talk. He had accepted his fate, she could tell, and was working his magic to get her to the same place. "You won't be an orphan, baby girl. I'll always be with you. You know that," he said when he roused from his most recent doze under the stars. She wouldn't be an orphan in the true sense anyway. As far as she knew, her mother was still alive. *Somewhere.*

"Without you, I don't know what I'm going to do. You're the only person I know how to love," she said. She couldn't let him leave this world without hearing her say it.

"Oh come on, Tessa. That's not true."

"Yeah, it is."

"What about Andrew?"

She wanted to forget about Andrew, not talk about him. But she said, "No, not Andrew. I used to think maybe. Maybe if I knew what I was doing. I used to...but..."

"Used to?"

Tessa took another sip of her foreign beer. "I haven't heard from him. I don't know where he is," she admitted. "We used to see each other or talk every day. Like best friends more than anything else." She paused and looked away. "Anyway, it's probably for the best. I'd only end up scaring him off...or I guess I've done that already, right? Better now than years from now when I'd get in my car and drive all the way to who knows where, some little nothing town in the middle of nowhere or to the west coast. Far away, anyway. I've heard the coast of Oregon is nice."

"And what would you do there?" he asked.

"I'll find a place with a really cool downtown with galleries and little one-of-a-kind shops. A place with a cliff by the ocean and I'll think it's where I'm meant to be. Just me. Alone. I'll stay there and I won't have to worry about loving a person because I will just love the place and I will become it." She wiped a bit of smoke out of her eyes. "All I've ever wanted really is a place to call my own." *A place to call home.*

"Sounds awfully lonely to me."

"But seems like something I'd do, doesn't it?" she asked. "Haven't you ever fantasized about finding a place where you could be...be someone new?"

Her father paused, took a breath, before answering her. "No, can't say I have, Tessa."

She listened carefully to his breathing, making sure each breath was not his last.

"You're not her, Tessa. You are *not* her."

"But I am."

"No."

"Dad. I feel it. I feel her in me, all the time lately for the past couple weeks. My urge to run away is so strong. It's only you that's prevented it so far. You've been the magnet that's kept pulling me back...here."

"Home, Tessa. You can use the word *home.*"

"When I was a kid and Mum was...Mum was Mum, so shut off and distant and all the rest, I stopped thinking of this house as home. It was just a place to eat, sleep and shower."

"And now?"

"I don't have warm and fuzzy feelings about it. It's four walls and a roof."

"The restaurant, Tessa. Have you thought about it?

She noticed the way he now referred to it as 'the restaurant,' not *his* restaurant or even Tremblay's Place. "A little," she said.

"Give it a shot, Tessie. Maybe it's just the thing for you. Maybe it's what you need."

"Maybe," *Not likely.* The fear was huge.

"It would be too weird without you. Too weird to even be here, never mind in the restaurant. How could I ever fill the shoes you left, Dad? Everybody loved that place." She realized afterwards that she was speaking in the past tense.

"It was a hell of a little place back in the day, Tessie." He said this with cracks in his already shaky voice. It had been his life. "I made a lot out of it." *And so can you,* was left unsaid. "When I bought it, it was a crummy little hole-in-the-wall diner, but I knew it had potential."

Back in the day? It had only been a couple months since he'd closed its doors.

"But you were the glue that held it together, held me together, Dad."

"Maybe you don't need glue anymore. Maybe you're already strong and solid and...dry." He laughed a little at this. "What do you think of that?"

Tessa's mother had been the broken one who needed someone to piece her together. Her father had failed at this. It was Tessa who got the best of Benjamin Tremblay. She felt a crushing sense of loss for her mother at that moment. She didn't like to think of her mother as someone who needed gluing back together time and again and didn't get it, as a girl/woman who hadn't known how to get from one day to the next without collapsing inward on herself. Had he really not seen it? Had her father been unable or unwilling to find her the tools to heal, to help herself—to stay? Unable or unwilling? It suddenly mattered.

"It's poetic, Dad," she said. *Getting glued back together was poetic. Remaining unglued was poetic.* All at once, Tessa felt the broken pieces of her mother crumbling inside her. There wasn't enough glue for all the sharp chips and shards.

"You want poetic? I've got notebooks full of stuff I wrote, scribbled down, over the years. I had to release it all somehow. That one you found in my bed is just the tip of the iceberg, baby. I'll leave it all for you to read when I'm gone."

"How about before?"

"Before?"

"Before you're gone, Dad?"

"We'll see, baby. We'll see."

"Come on, Dad. I'll get you in the house now. You're getting sensitive to the smoke. I can tell. You're coughing more and breathing hard." She stood from her spot on the deck steps and reached for his hands to pull him up. He walked with more difficulty than he had in the morning when he was newly awake and eager for the day ahead with Tessa. She had to slip both of her arms under his armpits and guide him step-by-step into the house.

Just as she was getting him settled in his bed, she heard the familiar sound of tires crunching over the gravel driveway, then stop. A few seconds later, the headlights went off and she heard the closing of a door. She took her time tucking her father in, stalling her need to go outside and clean up the deck and extinguish the campfire. She avoided the windows and didn't turn lights on.

She didn't want the burden of Frankie tonight. She knew she was vulnerable and raw. Even though she'd spent a wonderful evening with her dad, it was all bittersweet in the end. *The end,* she knew, *isn't far off. Who am I kidding with all the patched together holistic stuff anyway?* One sideways glance from Frankie's coffee brown eyes, one bottle of Sam Adams slipped coolly into her hand or one *'Hey, Tessie baby,'* and she might just give in. She had no defenses left. Then again, maybe Frankie would be just the thing to make her go completely numb. Maybe a quick fuck with Frankie in the back seat of his truck or on his lumpy old sofa bed would help her forget everything that had happened or not happened over the past few months, make her remember who she was. She was not Andrew's lover anymore and he was not hers, had never really been hers. She was not an independent woman with her own life to live or place in the world. She was the girl with the scar on her face. The girl who couldn't think for herself. She was the girl who should be grateful for Frankie. He was a constant at least. He wasn't taking off without communication, dropping her like she meant nothing after months of making her feel exquisite. She knew Frankie would never make her feel exquisite. With Frankie, there was no cliff with red flowers. There were no quivering, powder blue feather fingers on her skin. No dark red voice.

After a minute's thought, though, she knew she'd only feel a greater sense of emptiness afterwards. It was always the same with Frankie, even in the beginning. *Better to be alone than be with Frankie*, she decided.

I need to get away from this place, this house, if only for a little while, she decided, as she made her way to the backdoor. She'd go outside and clean the deck, put out the fire pit and go for a drive to the beach. A long stay wasn't necessary, just a few laps of the tide washing in and out under the moonlight, then she'd come back, peek into her father's room and go to bed.

Frankie probably had his feet up on the concrete blocks of the fire pit, a beer in his hand already, maybe even a second one by this point. She'd ignore him. He would make fun of her foreign beer, snort at it and call her a snob. *What do I care? No more Frankie.*

She stepped outside and said, "Just go. I'm not in the mood tonight. I'm exhausted and I'm...drained. Completely drained."

But it wasn't Frankie waiting for her on the back steps when she emerged from the house.

"I can't believe you showed up here."

"I needed to see you."

"Not so much all last week, though, and half of the week before," she said. "Your co-worker told me you're off on a family vacation. You could've told me that, Andrew."

"I was in Vermont dealing with the house. I told you

that. I didn't feel like telling people at work my personal business, so I said I was visiting family."

"I thought you would be gone for two days, not almost two weeks," Tessa said. "It's uncharacteristic of you not to reply to my messages. I was worried." *I thought you had vanished,* she thought.

"It was an intense few days. I'm sorry."

"Did you sell your house?"

"Yes, it's a big relief to finally not have to think about that house anymore...or try not to anyway."

"What do you mean *try not to?* It's over now, right?"

He leaned against the side of the house and looked down at his shoes. "Heather and I spent a bit of time together, Tessa. We have some...*had* some, I guess, personal business too...a connection still, I guess you could say," Andrew said, stepping closer to Tessa. "I need to talk to you and I need you to be calm. Please, Tessa."

"Do I want to hear this?"

"I don't know. Maybe you don't, especially given your father's health, but I want to finally tell you. I probably owe it to you at this point."

"You probably owe it to me at this point?" *Breathe. Breathe. Breathe.*

"Tessa, you and I have been...sleeping together for a while now, a couple months. We've been enjoying each other's company immensely, I think it's fair to say, not just sleeping together. That was just..."

"Just the first thing to come to your mind," she finished his sentence. It was what they did together more than anything else.

"I suppose, yes, and it's been very nice. Our time together..."

"Very nice?"

"It's been brilliant, actually," he said.

"Brilliant?" *That word!*

"Let me finish, Tessa. Please," he said, putting both his hands firmly on each of her shoulders to keep her still.

"Not sure I want to let you finish this. I'm thinking maybe I should take the initiative and save you the trouble, Andrew. I'll finish it, if that's what you came here to do," Tessa said, as she slipped away from him and began gathering the odds and ends from her campfire picnic with her father. "Over and done, if that's what you want. No need to drag it out. I'm a big girl. I can handle it." She put her hands up to stop him from talking before she was finished. "Let me just say one more thing, Andrew. One more thing," she continued. "You...you made me feel...you made me feel exquisite. I'd never felt exquisite before I met you. Really, I've never felt much of anything. Certainly not exquisite." Both of her hands were now on her face, covering it almost completely. The jaggedness of her scar pressed hotly into her palms. She was determined not to cry.

"No, Tessa. That's not what I drove all the way from northern Vermont to tell you. Is that what you thought?"

"I've tried not to have too many thoughts about you since I got here yesterday. I just put my father to bed. He's declining, deteriorating. He's not interested in my help anymore, if he ever was. The whole holistic approach. It's all bullshit. It's too late, he says, and I have to face it. He wanted to have a campfire tonight and eat hot dogs and marshmallows. Drink beer with me. So we did. I sat with him out here like we used to do when I was a little girl. Just the two of us. We told stories and ate crappy junk food and didn't care that we'd have belly aches in the morning, just like we used to. What difference does tomorrow make when there aren't that many left?" she said. "You kind of interrupted that...showing up here now. You could've called first." Her movement around the deck as she spoke prevented the tears from starting. If she just stayed dynamic, the tears could be kept away. *Perhaps.*

"I'm sorry, I really am. I'm sorry I didn't call you. I had a lot to deal with this week, too. Yes, with Heather. I want to tell you. I came here to tell you what I've been wanting to tell you but haven't been able to find the words. It's difficult. Have patience, please." His voice cracked a little, just a little. "Could we sit down?"

Tessa didn't want to sit down. Her body fought the suggestion by tightening up in the shoulders and neck, while her hands kept picking things up only to put them back down in a different spot. Andrew took a step closer to her.

"Okay," she said, and let her body slide down the deck rail until she was sitting. "Talk to me. Seems as though this thing between us is not about simplicity anymore."

"It never was for me," he said. "Would it be all right if I...if I touched you while we talk? I know it's a lot to ask and I know you're mad at me right now, but I could use the comfort of it and I think you probably could, too."

"Where?" she asked. "Where do you want to touch me?"

"You decide."

"Not my knee. Not my shoulders. Not my neck." She was far too raw for any of that.

He slid behind her and hesitantly put his arms lightly around her waist. "Is this okay?"

She nodded her consent. *Damn.* If she felt his fingertips on her skin, she had no idea how she would react. *Neutral. Just remain neutral,* she told herself, *and breathe.* It was the body that remembered. The mind was logic. The heart was a mechanical thing, a pump. *That's all.* It was the rest of the body that was sensation, bunches of nerves that sent and received feeling. *Oh Lord, what a system.*

"I married Heather when I was about your age. A little older than you, actually, I was twenty-nine. We both were. After about a year, she got pregnant, but a couple months in, she lost it. Miscarried. The doctors said it was just one of those things. Happens all the time. No specific reason. It just wasn't viable." He paused, breathed. "Anyway, she wanted to try again. So we did. It took a little longer and I have to admit I wasn't 100% on board for it. I kind of took the more casual 'if it happens, it happens' approach, as guys usually do, I suppose. Well, it happened and it was viable. Then our daughter Annabelle was born on July 24, 2010. That's the other reason I went to Vermont. It was her birthday."

It had never occurred to Tessa that Andrew was a father. Although she knew he was older and had been married for several years.

He paused, breathed. Then he moved his right hand a little, searching for skin to touch. Tessa found it floundering between the night air and the hem of her t-shirt. She took hold of it and steadied it.

"When Annabelle was three months old, Heather was invited to a party for a friend of hers who was getting married. It was at a resort in upstate New York. A bachelorette thing. I told her to go. It would be good for her to have fun. A night away. I could handle the baby on my own for a night. I remember that night. It was the first weekend of November and already quite chilly. I played with her well into the evening. We were both tired by the time she took her bottle, but she drank all of it. I remember. Then I cleaned her up. I kissed her and put her in the crib with her favorite pink blanket that Heather's mother had made. She was already asleep, her breathing sweet and steady. Then I went back to the living room and collapsed on the couch. I had the TV on some dumb-ass comedy movie and I just zoned out and fell asleep. I was exhausted. By the time I woke up, it was eight o'clock in the morning and I was disconcerted. I'd forgotten that Heather wasn't there, then remembered, and I jumped up. Annabelle hadn't cried yet, but it was late so I got a bottle ready and brought it with me." He paused, took a deep breath in and held it for several heartbeats. He continued, "When I got to her room...she was...she was still and, oh God, I'll never forget this...she was...gray. She was gray. I picked her up, but it was too late. My sweet little baby was gone. She was lifeless." His whole body was shaking and his dark red voice cracked and faded to watery orange.

Tessa grabbed hold of both his hands and squeezed them into hers, then into her chest in an attempt to hold his grief. She knew she had to say something, but didn't know what. "Oh God, Andrew. I'm so sorry. I don't know what else to say. I can't imagine how awful..." *How awful. How unexpected.* "I don't understand, though. I mean, what happened? Had she been sick? I don't know much about babies."

"Apparently, I didn't either. It was my fault. I put her down the wrong way. She smothered. She couldn't roll over yet. I was her father. I was supposed to check on her. Flip her onto her back...or put her that way in the first place. Not use the blanket in the crib. Heather usually...Heather always put her down. Heather was the one who checked on her. I was that arrogant, stupid father who just assumed it was easy and intuitive. She seemed comfortable on her stomach. I mean, she slept on my chest like that sometimes. And I didn't want her to be cold. It seemed okay."

"What did you do? After you found her, what did you do?"

"I called 911. It was too late, of course, but I still called. It was all I could think to do." His hands were trembling within hers, but she locked them into her chest. "Then I called Heather. She was three hours away at her friend's party. Then I sat in the rocking chair with my baby girl in my arms and looked at the bottle that I'd put down on her dresser when I walked into the room. And I cried and cried."

Tessa had no words. Her mind went places, but her

mouth remained still. She thought of the beach her mother ran away to when Tessa herself was the age of Andrew's daughter. She thought of the home pregnancy test she took nearly eight months ago. Her father's poetry journal then came into her mind. The words, rhyming and non-rhyming, scribbled out in bursts and crossed out in big scratches across the page. The finished poem she'd read appeared in the back of her eye. *Bodies remember even when our minds fail us...the skin feels whispers smooth as pale sunbeams through stained glass windows. When bodies fail and minds must complete us, memory and love become hurried and chaotic. Quick, quick love before it's too late.*

She recited it ghost quiet into the night air, as Andrew held her on the back deck of her father's house. A very mild heat emanated from the fire pit's soft gray and bright orange embers and she knew the flames could easily be extinguished or reignited.

"Say that again, Tessa. What you just said. Say it again, please."

She repeated the poem, a little louder this time, and gave credit to its author. They were not her words, but they were soothing Andrew. She told him about the notebook she'd found in her father's pillow case.

"She blamed me, of course. Heather, I mean. How could I have been so careless? So stupid? Hadn't I seen her put Annabelle down on her back a hundred times? Why didn't I know this? I don't know. I just didn't. And then the autopsy. The God awful autopsy they made us have done to prove I hadn't dropped her or drugged her or worse. You don't know shame until you've got a team of people looking at you like you may have just killed your own child. Guilty until proven innocent."

"That must have been horrendous," Tessa's first thought came out her mouth.

"In a word, yes. Horrendous. In the end, they called it

Sudden Infant Death Syndrome. I was exonerated...in their eyes anyway. But I could feel Heather's blame and agony that she hadn't been there, had trusted me. And look what had happened."

He went on to tell her that after some time Heather had started going to a bereaved parents support group.

"I couldn't bring myself to go. Hell, there wasn't a support group for neglectful fathers and insensitive husbands. I didn't feel I deserved to be in a bereaved parents group, sitting there with her when she still couldn't get past it being my fault. And I couldn't either. All I could do was work—day in, day out. Even little tasks to occupy my mind. I became hyper aware of every little thing in my environment. Every small thing became enormous to me," Andrew said, relaxing his grip around Tessa's waist. "She asked me to go with her once, just once, and it was on a night I worked. She did it on purpose to see which I would choose, knowing, I think, that I'd choose work. It was my escape, my place to get out of my head and get absorbed by the problems of others, even if their biggest problem was not knowing how to operate the self-service copier or the microfilm reader. Such simple problems and I could be useful to someone. Then I started noticing how important the small stuff was and feeling like I needed to know how to save someone's life if I had to. That's when I became more...more..."

Tessa could feel him struggling. "Detail oriented," she finished for him.

"Yes, more detail oriented." His tears dripped onto her hands.

"It's not for everyone, I guess. Support groups. Spilling your guts out to random people and hoping it helps," Tessa said.

"It seemed to help her. She grieved in a way that I couldn't understand. It seemed so linear, so neat, her process, I mean, which I'm sure it wasn't but it seemed that way to me. She's stronger than me. As for myself, I've been in a state of...I don't know...limbo. My grieving has been haphazard. It goes on and off. I've never felt a decent sense of closure over her death. I still blame myself."

He went on to tell Tessa that Heather had met another guy, a guy from her therapy group of all things, and got together with him. Within a year of her splitting up with Andrew, she was pregnant and, as soon as their divorce was final, re-married.

"She couldn't wait. She was getting into her late thirties and didn't want to face other issues." He shook his head. "I'm telling you all this, Tessa, because I want you to know about me. Sorry it took this long."

"It hasn't taken that long," she said. "It's a lot to think about, a lot to say. I'm kind of at a loss for a response."

"I needed you to know what you're getting with...well...with me. You, you're young still and you may want...oh, never mind. I'm getting ahead of myself. It's just the way I feel about you, Tessa, is...intense, to put it mildly. These weekends when I can't see you because you're here...these weekends break my heart, especially knowing what you're dealing with here with your father. I didn't want to wait until Monday. Didn't want to think of you being upset with me or hurt by me. The last time we saw each other, you were so glad to see me."

"I'm always glad to see you. You know that."

"Yeah, I do. But that Tuesday before I went to Vermont you were cheerful, optimistic even. You were happy that your dad seemed more energetic and was showing signs of...hope, is how you said it."

"And now he's crashing again. Don't know if he'll have another wave like that one." Today had been an anomaly and Tessa knew it. It was astounding that her father went for a walk with her and had it in him to re-play one of their traditional campfires. She knew he was mustering all of it just for her sake, good memories and all that.

"You're right. Who knows with these situations? And the last time we saw each other, I wanted, really wanted to talk to you then, but the night got away from us, as it has a way of doing when we're together and I guess I didn't want to go to that place in my head...or take you there. My God, Tessa. The way you feel in my hands, your skin under my fingertips, you make my sadness go away, my grief...it's fading. When I'm with you, it's nearly nonexistent." He paused. "And to be honest, I didn't want to tell you then because I...well, because..." He stopped talking.

"Because why, Andrew?" Her tears were starting, stinging her just behind her eyelids. It was only slight at first, but picking up the momentum of all that he'd just told her.

"Because in my mind I didn't want to be that guy to you," he spoke quickly. "That middle-aged guy with an ex-wife and a...dead baby. I wanted to be younger and...starting fresh." He then added just as quickly, "I didn't want to be the irresponsible guy, the arrogant guy, the guy with a dead baby, the guy whose fault it was...I didn't...I don't want you to see me in that way."

Andrew tightened his arms around Tessa's waist. She leaned her head back on him and let the night air—with its frog and cricket sounds and dying campfire smell—penetrate her senses. He was quiet after his revelation about his daughter and kept mostly still. Tessa reached around, rested her own hands atop his and lightly rubbed them with her fingertips from his wrists, across his knuckles and to the ends of his fingers. Then she turned his hands around, lifted them one at a time to her face and pressed his palms to her mouth. The taste of his skin on her tongue was strange and familiar at the same time, but mostly familiar.

"My God, Tessa. For a long time, I never expected to tell that story to anyone. I wanted to start over. Forget, I suppose. That's why I came here. Not here specifically tonight. I mean, it's why I left Vermont and moved to Massachusetts. I grew up, went to school, settled down, for a little while anyway, all within a rather small radius. People knew me. I knew people. I couldn't take the constant reminders every time I bumped into some acquaintance in the bank or the grocery store. So I ran away, but it was the best thing for me to do at the time. I needed it."

"So, you left then?" she asked.

"It took a while for it to come to that."

"But you said she left you."

"Yes, she did. She left the marriage. I left...geographically."

"Oh," Tessa said and was quiet for a long moment. "What was her other news, besides the house?" She'd suddenly remembered the motel room phone call from Heather.

"She's leaving the country for a couple years. Her new husband got a contract over in London and they're moving there for his job. She's very excited about it. Also..." he paused, "also...they're expecting their second child together. She's in her fourth month. Her doctor says everything looks great."

"Are you all right?"

"I'm all right," he replied, letting his fingers dance over her face. "I'm more than all right. She wanted to tell me because she won't be around for Annabelle's birthday memorial next year and so forth. That's really the reason we've stayed in contact the past few years. That, and trying to sell the house."

Tessa let a few minutes pass before she spoke. They sat quietly, absorbing their surroundings. The night air held them in its blanket of humidity and the frog sounds lulled them with a peaceful repetition. Their words were sinking into their collective beings like rain into the earth.

"I could go with you next year. You could introduce me to Annabelle," Tessa said tentatively, trying to keep her voice steady and hoping she wasn't out of line.

"I've already introduced you to Annabelle. Where she's buried is just where she's buried. She lives here," he said, bringing Tessa's hand to his heart.

She turned to face him, opened the top three buttons of his shirt and pressed her mouth onto his chest. Her lips caressed his heart gently and lovingly, as though it was a sweet and perfect newborn.

He held her head in place and exhaled the breath he had been holding. "Thank you, Tessa, for...for everything. For understanding me. Yes, you can come with me next year. I'd like that very much. I'll always keep her in my memory, my angel baby. That's what she'll always be," he said. "And you...well...I'm so in love with you, Tessa. That must be obvious to you by now. Tell me the rest of this...about how this happened to you. The accident. Can you let out the details and free yourself of what happened? I think we have enough trust between us now." He said this all in one breath. Annabelle was his angel baby. He was in love with Tessa. And he wanted her scar story. One breath.

"Tomorrow," she said, attempting to collect herself, "I'll tell you tomorrow. Will you stay here with me tonight?"

"In your dad's house? Before I've properly met him?"

"It's okay," she answered, standing up from the deck, "he's been wanting to meet you."

"Perhaps on the couch."

"No, Andrew, not on the couch. My grandmother gets up early, especially on Sundays. You won't be able to relax knowing she may see you before the sun rises. Besides, I need to be near you."

She led Andrew upstairs to her childhood bedroom, conscious of the white painted bureau which still had sparkly stickers on its drawers and the pastel ruffled curtains on her window, but he didn't seem to take notice. If he did, she hoped it was in an endearing way, as though he'd always thought of her as a girl who decorated her bedroom with sparkles and ruffles.

"I'll try my best to behave myself in here tonight," he said, as Tessa closed the door.

"Sorry I don't have a proper grown-up bed," she said.

"Looks proper enough to me," he said. "We'll be very cozy."

"And I've only got the one pillow."

"Quite all right, love. It's good to share with you, Tessa. Very good."

She let Andrew have the pillow and rested her head on his chest. She heard swishing and pumping and kindness. She even heard love. Then her thoughts turned to her own heart, the heart that had for so long been absent of color and light.

She pressed her head against his heartbeat. She liked the steady thump-thumping sound it made in her ear. She whispered *thank you* into the little envelope of air that enclosed them in her single bed of her childhood room. He didn't respond either verbally or non-verbally and she assumed he was already in deep sleep, exhausted from the burden he'd just released.

With her head on top of him on this little bed, she not only heard his heartbeat in her ear, but felt it as though it was her own. His lungs rose and fell with each breath and slow exhale. She was becoming molten on the inside. Could he sense it? Or feel how liquid she was when he touched her? Since her mother left, Tessa had always feared turning liquid on the inside—for surely the liquid would then become vapor and disperse too quickly to be caught and contained. If her mother's departure had taught her anything, it was that remaining a solid was the safest way to live. *But solid is stagnant. Safe is changing, moving. Safe is this. This.*

TWENTY-ONE

Tessa woke before 6:00 AM when she heard Mémère puttering around downstairs, doing her Sunday morning prayers. She poked her head into her father's room and found that he was still sleeping. With a bit of time left before she had to be up and active, she went back to her own bedroom and curled up with Andrew, who wrapped her into him and kissed her on the temple. He was partially awake and talkative again. "You know how it is, Tessa, with some people, you just love them instantly. Seems like that anyway," Andrew said. "The first time I saw you, that winter day when you came into the greenhouse and you had on a red wool coat with that huge hood...I don't think you saw me because of that hood. But then you took it off and you noticed me sitting there. You apologized for interrupting my privacy and turned to go, but I didn't mind. Didn't mind at all. I hoped you wouldn't go right away. And then you asked me if I knew the name of the plant to my left. I didn't, of course."

"I thought you might be a horticulturist," she said.

210

He snorted an *as if* kind of snort.

"Really, I was just looking for something to say."

"Then you asked my name and I told you and you said you'd call the plant an Andrew plant."

"Wow, you remember all that?" she asked, kissing him softly and lightly on his earlobe.

He smiled. "Yeah, I do. I'm Mister Detail, remember?" he said, bringing a hand to her face for one of his feather light touches.

"I held her in my arms, this little baby, and she looked at me. She even wrapped her little hand around my thumb. Sometimes, she just stared at me. After she was fed, I'd take her and hold her and we looked at each other. And you know how when you look into someone's eyes and they look into yours and you can see your face in their eyes..."

"Yeah, I know," Tessa said, closing her own eyes for a moment.

"Well, I saw myself there...in Annabelle's eyes, and it was really something."

"You bonded."

"Yes, we bonded," Andrew said. "I know this is going to sound terrible, but after she died, a while after, I used to wonder if it would've been easier on me if we hadn't bonded."

"It's not terrible. Anyone would probably wonder that."

"I suppose."

"That you bonded with her shows the kind of person you are. It shows that you had...have...a soul connection with her, that she has a place within you," Tessa said, as his fingers danced lightly over her face and neck. "It's a good thing. Not all parents and kids have it. Plenty don't."

Andrew paused for a moment. "I've told you how I feel about you, Tessa. You can tell me anything."

"It's good to be loved, Andrew. So good. Really. I have such a hard time with it, though...with accepting that I'm..."

She turned the other way in her little girl bed, away from Andrew.

"That you're what, Tessa? That you're lovable?"

"That I'm worthy of it, yes. I don't have much experience with it. I've never known anyone like you."

"Hey, turn around, baby. You are so worthy of it. So very worthy. I can make you a list of reasons why, if you'd like."

"I don't feel that way about myself and I didn't want you to know that," she said, pressing her fingers above her lips and feeling the jagged bumpiness there. "That's why I'm silly around you and I try to be funny...to make up for my...I don't know how to put it...to make up for the sense that I don't deserve it. Don't deserve...you."

He tightened his arms around her. She kept her own fingers on her face to prevent his from meandering there.

"It's just us in here, Tessa. Just you. Just me. I won't let go of you. It's okay," he said gently.

"Your hands, Andrew. Your touch. I get lost in it and I feel so good, *so good.* I forget everything else. It transcends anything I ever thought I'd feel...or have." She paused before adding, "I feel happy and at peace...almost like I'm somebody else." She closed her eyes.

"I better keep touching you then. Happy and at peace are good places to be," Andrew said. His hands felt warm on her belly. "But don't turn into someone else. Just stay Tessa. *My* Tessa."

"Your Tessa? Yeah, I'll be *your* Tessa."

"You've been my Tessa for a while now, my sweet Tessa," he said. "Notice how I'm saying your name over and over again. Tessa. Tessa. Tessa. I love to say it. I love to hear it. I love to think it. I'm like a love struck teenage boy around you, Tessa, not a forty-year-old man."

"Not yet, right?" she asked. "Forty, I mean. Did your birthday come and go without you telling me?"

"No. Technically I'm still thirty-nine—until November."

"November what? I need to know so I can surpass the amazing fig picnic."

"Don't know if there's any surpassing the amazing fig picnic, Tessa," he teased.

"Oh, yes there is, Andrew, my Andrew. That was a very cool birthday. Best yet, but it can be topped. I have ideas already. So tell me, November what?"

"You're changing the subject here, Tessa."

"November what?" she persisted.

"November seventeenth."

"Nice time of year. Lots of choices. I'll keep you in suspense until then."

"No clues?"

"Not sure what it'll be yet. But no...no clues. It'll be awesome, though. I can promise you that."

"I have no doubt it will be, Tessa."

"You only get one fortieth birthday, after all."

"Thankfully, 'cuz I'm feeling a bit old despite the teenage emotional and hormonal surge you inspire in me," he said, glancing around the room at all the remnants of Tessa's childhood.

"Must be my silly, girly bedroom. Must be the sparkles and the ruffles. I haven't updated it since I was ten."

"You have sparkles and ruffles in here? I hardly noticed."

"What happened to Mister Detail?" she teased.

"Mister Detail just slept very peacefully in this little bed with you and woke up...woke up happy to be here." He smiled. "And as far as birthdays go, just remember whatever you do for mine, I get lots more advance planning time to outdo it for yours."

She turned around, kissed him and rubbed both her hands on his unshaven Sunday morning face. She'd never seen him on a Sunday morning until now. *Better than love. Better than love.*

With no warning, his fingers slid down from her belly and into her.

"Oh God, Andrew. Oh God. Not now," she said, though she didn't take his hand away. "Not here. You know how loud I can get."

"Bite the pillow," he said and slipped it out from under his head. "Bite the pillow, baby. This is just for you right now. You say you love my hands. Let my hands love you, please."

"We'll talk more later, I promise," she said before biting into the corner of the pillow to silence herself under Andrew's hot blue touch.

When Tessa and Andrew got downstairs, Mémère was in her recliner watching the 7:00 AM live broadcast Catholic Mass. Tessa didn't dare interrupt and went straight to the kitchen to brew coffee for herself and Andrew, and tea for her dad and Mémère. She pulled fruits and vegetables from the fridge, cracked eggs into a bowl to scramble and sliced her dad's favorite cinnamon raisin English muffins to grill on the stove top. She even went onto the back deck to pluck a few basil leaves from the one successful herb plant she'd been able to keep thriving over the summer. Then she set Andrew up with the chopping board and the tomatoes and peppers, asking him to dice them for the omelet.

By the time Mémère's Mass was half over, the table was set, the skillet was sizzling and Tessa could hear her father shuffling into the bathroom down the hall. There was no Kate on early Sunday mornings. An aide came by, but not until mid-morning. "I can manage," her dad had told her. He did just fine with his routine. No need to worry. But she couldn't help it. He'd lost his balance and fallen in the bathroom in the past and she knew it could easily happen again. So she asked Andrew to keep watch over the omelet and popped into the hallway to listen for his footsteps. He was using his cane today. She could hear the distinct thumping it made. It was one of those three-pronged things—"like an extra foot," he'd said. Tessa pictured him trying to maneuver himself around the small bathroom with the three-pronged cane. If he gripped it too tightly, the skin on his hand would open up and bleed. Not only that, but he'd get wrist pain from the stress of trying to hold onto it. She knew by now that he was blood and bone weary. His declines came in cycles, she'd noticed, each one getting closer and closer to the previous one. It was like watching a spiral that got narrower and slipperier with each rotation.

The toilet flushed. The faucet started, then stopped. There was a clattering of some sort and fumbling. She knocked lightly on the door, which he'd left slightly ajar.

"Dad, are you all right? Need help?"

No response.

"Can I open the door, Dad?"

"I'm okay, Tessie. I knocked the soap over with this damn cane. It fell in the toilet. I can't get it."

He was wearing his pajama bottoms and a flannel shirt, unbuttoned. His clothes hung loosely on his withered frame. He needed a shower and a shave, but that would wait for the aide.

"I got it," she said, reaching into the toilet and grabbing the bottle of Softsoap. She gave it a rinse under the hot tap and wiped it off before setting it back onto the countertop. She washed her hands and touched his face. "How did you sleep last night? I didn't hear you after I brought you in."

"Not too bad. Tossed and turned a bit, but nothing out of the ordinary."

"How's your pain this morning? Did you take your first dose already?" He'd acquiesced and started taking vitamin and herbal supplements that she'd researched in addition to the pain medication that he took as needed. The need was becoming greater and more frequent and there had been some talk from Kate about a morphine drip which would require constant care and monitoring. Still a few weeks off, Kate seemed to think, but one never knew. Sometimes, the need to manage his pain snuck up with little warning. He already wasn't the same man he was yesterday morning, as she laced up his sneakers and took him around the big block.

"Is Kate here yet? I usually hear her by now," he asked.

"No, Dad. It's Sunday. Kate doesn't come on Sundays, remember? One of the aides will be here later though, around ten."

"Oh, okay baby. Help me back into the bed, will you? My legs are no good today."

He had overdone it yesterday. She felt a pang of guilt for going along with the walk around the block, then the campfire. And all that beer. Maybe it interfered with his medication and made his pain worse. *Shit. I should've known that. I shouldn't have let him drink it. Or at least not so many.*

"I'm making breakfast. Why don't we go to the kitchen. I'll get you to the table, Dad. Come on," she said. "I found the most beautiful sweet red peppers at the farmers' market yesterday, just like the ones you always used at the restaurant. And our basil plant has been good to us this summer so far."

But it wasn't peppers and basil that her father wanted. He just wanted his bed. "No, Tessa, not just yet. I want to be in my room for a little while. Just let me be," he said. As they crossed the hallway to his bedroom, his whole body was drooping.

She settled him back into his bed and sat beside him for a minute. "I'm making all your favorite things. I'll keep them warm for you for later," she said and her eyes stung for a moment.

"Thank you, baby. That's my girl."

"Dad?"

"Yes, baby."

"Andrew's here. He's in the kitchen."

"Andrew? Here? Did you know he was coming?"

"No, he surprised me."

"Things okay then? Hearts and all that?" He still had it in him to tease her.

"Yeah, Dad. Hearts and all that." She smiled.

"Is he staying all day? I'll meet him later, okay? After the aide comes and goes. Don't let him leave before I meet him, okay, baby?"

She left his door ajar and headed back to the kitchen. By the time she got there, Andrew was introducing himself to Mémère.

"Kind of early for a social call. I would've gotten dressed if I'd known we were having a visitor," Mémère said. She was still in her housecoat and slippers, her hair unbrushed. She peered over at Tessa, clearly pissed.

"Sorry ma'am. I didn't mean to surprise you. Tessa let me in last night."

"Last night? Did you sleep in Tessa's bedroom with her last night? A man like you?" she scoffed, looking him up and down, no doubt noticing his crumpled shirt, gray sprinkled stubble and bare feet.

A man like you. A man like you.

She then uttered something about Tessa being a good girl, a good Catholic girl.

"Mémère," Tessa interjected, "it's fine. Everything's fine here. You've met Andrew, I see. My boyfriend. He helped make breakfast. Come sit down. It's ready."

"Your boyfriend?"

"Mmm hmm." Boyfriend was the best word to use in this context, though she definitely felt weird saying it out loud, especially with Andrew right there in the room.

"This is not your boyfriend, Tessa," she said a bit softer, but surely loud enough for Andrew to hear.

"Yes. I assure you, he is," Tessa said, looking at Andrew for some help.

He stepped closer to her and wrapped an arm around her waist, then kissed her on the cheek.

"Let me pour the coffee, ladies. Sit, please," he said, pulling out two chairs.

"I don't drink coffee. I drink tea," Mémère said, then turned to speak directly to her granddaughter. "Tessa, I'm too old and set in my ways to deal with unfamiliar men coming out of your bedroom on a Sunday morning."

"I'll be going then. I don't want to cause any strife here," Andrew said. "I'll call your cell phone, Tessa. Keep it on."

"No, Andrew, please stay," Tessa implored. "My dad wants to meet you, remember?"

"Tessa, my presence is upsetting your grandmother."

"You'll upset *me* if you leave right now," she said and instantly regretted it. *Damn. What a way to put him on the spot.*

"I'll be out in the yard. I won't leave," Andrew said. He grabbed his shoes and walked out the back door, bowing his head slightly at the two women in the kitchen. "I'm sorry if I've upset you, Mrs. Tremblay. Terribly sorry," he added and Tessa knew he meant it sincerely.

"That was rude, Mémère. That was very rude of you."

"Rude of me? Rude of me, Tessa? I know this is the twenty-first century, but where's the respect for your father and his house? For me? And isn't he a bit old for you?"

"He's the real deal, Mem. We've known each other for a while now. He loves me," she added for good measure and because it felt kind of good to say it out loud. "I'm sure of it."

"And...you love him, too? You gonna break Frankie's heart again for a man who sneaks into your sick father's house to sleep with you?"

Tessa took a deep breath. "I'm a grown-up, Mem. A grown-up. I am twenty-five years old. I could be married with babies by now."

"You could be, yes, but you're not," Mémère said, as she made her way to the stove top to pour boiling water over her tea bag.

"...and he didn't sneak in here to sleep with me. He drove here last night, a long way to see me, to talk to me about some personal stuff that he's been wanting to tell me." She tried to keep her voice even. "It was very late when we were done talking and he was exhausted, too exhausted to drive back again."

"You make Frankie sleep in his truck in the driveway, but this strange man gets to sleep in your bed with you? And what personal stuff, Tessa? Is he running away from a wife? Looking for a young girl to play with? He will get tired of you, believe me. The ones who leave one woman for another always do. That's how they operate. They don't know what they want." She put her tea down on the table and maneuvered herself into her chair. "But he'll wait 'til you're thirty something or even forty with kids and a house payment and gray hairs."

"Stop it, Mem. You don't know what you're talking about," Tessa said, peeking out the window at Andrew. She would join him in a minute.

"I know very well what I'm talking about. People leave each other all the time." Tessa's mother's name was unspoken, but vividly in the air. "I didn't get to seventy-five years old without learning a few things about people."

"Maybe so, but you're not talking about Andrew. He's not leaving anyone for me. He's single...and he's outside right now probably feeling awkward and uncomfortable...and hungry," she said, reaching for the screen door handle.

"He's a bachelor, then?" Mem asked.

"He's divorced," Tessa said, instantly regretting it. She should've lied and said he was a bachelor.

"Oh, Tessa. You're not thinking. Divorced men are trouble."

"No, Mem."

"You shouldn't have let him in here last night. We don't know this man."

"I know him. I've known him since last winter. It's not as if I just met him yesterday."

"Since last winter. Last winter," she dismissed it, as if those months meant nothing. "Frankie comes here a couple times a week when you're working at that job that's so far away. He brings me stuff from the store if I need anything and we talk about a lot of things. He's been in your life for years. *Years.* He's the real deal, Tessa. Frankie is the real deal and I can't understand why you treat him the way you do. He's stable and smart. He runs a successful business and has ideas on how to help you with your father's restaurant. Above all, we know him. Your father and I know him and his family. He'll never leave you and he knows this house inside and out with all he's done for us over the past year or so." She dipped a piece of toast into her tea and ate it. "You'll need someone to help you with the house once your father is gone. You and I can't do it ourselves. With Frankie, you wouldn't have to worry."

Tessa took a deep breath before opening the back door. She could see Andrew wandering around in the yard. "Eat breakfast, Mem, before it gets cold. Let me know how delicious the omelet is and I'll thank Andrew for you. He made it himself with his own very capable hands."

"Are you running out now, then? Aren't you going to help your father?"

"He's tired. I'll be back soon."

TWENTY-TWO

"Let's go, Andrew. I need to cool off after that. Get in my car with me."

"Through all that, how is your dad? I mean, when you checked on him, how did he seem?"

"Awful. He was drooping," she said. "But he wants to meet you. He made me promise that you wouldn't leave until he met you."

"I hope he's not expecting Brian Williams," he teased.

"Nope, he's expecting Andrew Hartigan," Tessa replied. She didn't have it in her to joke.

They drove down to the end of the block and turned toward the beach. Once there, they could get out and walk.

"Anyway, I have some of that oil we talked about—the cannabis oil—two different strains. One for daytime. One for nighttime. I'll give it to you. That's the other reason I came down here last night. I didn't want him to have to wait any longer."

"Where did you get it?" she asked.

"I found someone in Vermont while I was up there, an

alternative medicine provider who grows good quality strains in his basement and makes the oil himself. I bought a two month supply and know how to find him when we need more. He told me exactly how to dose it, plus with everything I've read, I feel very comfortable with it."

"I don't know if he'll do it, Andrew." She told him an abbreviated version of the story her grandmother had told her when she tried to inform her about medical cannabis.

"Leave it to me. I'll explain it. You know me, Tessa. Mister detail. I will tell him everything I've learned about it. You and I have read the reports. There is now solid, fact-based evidence that it can and does kill cancer cells. I'll show him testimonials. I'll break it down for him."

Mister detail. Yes. She knew Andrew was capable of learning all the ways of saving someone's life or even just the one way that would work. "I hope he listens," she said.

"Me, too."

When they got to the beach, Tessa parked and jumped out of the car. She needed to move quickly while she told the story of her long ago accident. Andrew followed her.

"We went away on a girl's weekend, my mum and I. It was the week after I turned fourteen and I was finishing up eighth grade. She'd been around, been back for a few months—since Christmas—she'd been home with us and it seemed like she might be better. And it was good...good to have her around. No guessing where she might be or when she might return and I so craved that stability." She could feel herself starting to shake a little. "When she was gone, the void just sucked. I was sick of it. And when she was well, or seemed well, she was wild and fun, cool to hang out with. But then she'd disappear, not right away. First, she'd shut down, withdraw into herself like a hibernating animal. There was no talking to her when she got like that. No nothing with her. It was like she didn't exist and we didn't exist either. But she'd pass it off by saying she was tired, that she

had insomnia at night and had to sleep during the day."
Tessa let herself ramble it out, realizing only after she started
talking that she hadn't given any background information.
She hoped it made sense to Andrew.

He reached for her hand as they made their way to the
shoreline. "Where was she back from?" he asked.

"She used to run away a lot. She called them
treatments. I just called it running away."

The beach was cool and breezy, blue-gray.

"Treatments for?"

"It was always so vague to me. To this day, I don't
know. All kinds of stuff. Depression. Anxiety. What I
overheard her call 'deep black moods' when she didn't know
I could hear her talking to my father." Tessa slipped her
hand out of his. "Mental illness. I don't know." She could
feel herself tensing up and starting to filter her words, which
she didn't want to do—not anymore. She would tell Andrew
this story. *I have to tell him this story.*

"Do you want to stop and sit down somewhere?" he
asked.

"No, just hold my hand," she said, reaching for his
again. "Let's keep walking. I need to keep moving."

"Okay," he said, taking hold of her hand and weaving
his fingers around hers.

"So anyway, when I turned fourteen, she said she
wanted to take me with her on an adventure, just the two of
us. Of course I wanted to go. All my life, I'd been trying to
get her to do stuff with me and here she was volunteering. I
envisioned all kinds of cool stuff," Tessa began. "We left on
a Friday morning and drove into Boston to see a show and
stayed at the Four Seasons. Absolute luxury like nothing I'd
ever seen. I still don't know how she afforded it. Just a
splurge, maybe. In the morning, we ate a big breakfast. Well,
I ate. My mother doesn't eat much. Didn't. Doesn't. I don't
know at this point. Food made her too nervous, she used to

say. Gave her tantrums...God-awful tantrums. She had tea and a fruit cup or some ridiculous thing. We checked out and drove some more, through New Hampshire and the White Mountains, into the northern part of Vermont, all the way to the Canadian border. It was fun just driving and talking, telling stories. All the way up, she was surprisingly calm and I started fantasizing that maybe she could just be a normal mother after all. She told me she wanted to take me to Montreal to show me around. She said she'd been when she was my age and loved it. There was a pastry shop that she loved. Pastry. Can you imagine? My mother who hardly ate—ever—who was so obsessed with...not eating, drove to Canada to take me to a pastry shop. It was completely ridiculous and exciting and wild. Oh God, Andrew. Do you want the long story or the shortened version?" Tessa asked.

"Whichever one you want to tell, love."

"Okay, I think I need to be brief now. We got to the border and they wouldn't let us cross. I didn't have any identification on me. No birth certificate. No driver's license. I didn't have it yet. No passport. I'd never had any need for one. She blamed me, of course. How could I have left the house with no I.D? What kind of person left the house with no I.D? A kid, I said, a kid who didn't have an I.D. and didn't know I was being taken on a road trip where we might cross an international border. This was not like anything we'd ever done before and she was my mother. She was supposed to teach me these things. We argued and fought right there at the border until they made us turn around. She could've seen to it that I'd packed what I'd need to cross the border, slipped a copy of my birth certificate into her bag or whatever. But she was spontaneous or...more likely...out of her senses, and just assumed," Tessa continued. "On the way back, she didn't even talk to me, just blasted the radio. I thought she'd calm down after a while, but she just got more and more erratic, like a switch was flipped and it went from a fun adventure to a nightmare. I told her it was okay. We didn't need to go to Montreal. We didn't need to. If I shut the radio off, she turned it back on even louder. She wouldn't even stop to let me go to the bathroom...said if I didn't eat and drink so much, I wouldn't need to go to the bathroom so often. That's when I shut down inside and I felt like everything I said or did didn't matter to her." Tessa and Andrew walked along the big, gray-white boulders that jutted out from the sand at the ocean's edge. She told herself that she was being brave and took another deep breath before continuing. "The accident happened right after sunset. We'd just crossed back into Massachusetts from New Hampshire. It was just us, I mean, no other cars involved. She went around that big loop when we got onto 495 in Methuen...crazy fast. Didn't slow down at all. On purpose. When the car flipped onto the passenger side where I was sitting, I heard my mother scream, *I killed my girl. I killed my girl.* The ambulance came, of course. I'd smashed my head pretty badly, had a concussion and some pretty major bruising along my ribs and right hip—and a broken arm. Eight weeks in a cast. The whole goddamn summer. And my face...I didn't even feel my face. It was as if it had stayed there while the rest of me got into the ambulance. Didn't feel the blood dripping down. Not at first. I didn't know until they held a towel over my face to stop the bleeding. But I was in one piece, essentially. My head was still attached to my spine. I must not have moved or made any noises because again I heard her say, *I killed my girl.*"

Andrew wrapped his right arm around Tessa's shoulder and ran his hand up and down her arm. He didn't speak. They continued to walk. She didn't cry—just walked and talked. Always moving. Always. There had to be motion. Her mind went back and forth between the night of the accident and the big triangle she traveled every week. She knew in her bones that they were connected. The difference was that Tessa drove in straight lines and angles, carefully placed angles, not loops. Never crazy fast loops.

"I don't have any scars on my arm. They were able to set it and I didn't need surgery, just a cast and it healed. This," she said, touching the jagged, bumpy line on her face as they walked along, "this is the only scar I got. When the car flipped over, the broken glass flew at me. I was lucky, the doctor told me, lucky that I didn't swallow any or get it in my eyes. A shard stuck there and I swear there's a little sliver in me that they couldn't get out. I've felt it there for years."

She paused on the rock and looked out at the water. Andrew started to say something, but she stopped him.

"I had a big gaping gash right in the middle of my face. I was swallowing my own blood. It took nineteen stitches to close it up. I looked like the Bride of Frankenstein's monster...for a while, but my mum never saw that. She left the hospital before I was released. My dad took her home when she got discharged. A day later, he came back to get me and left her home. She was exhausted, he'd said, still on pain meds and wanted to sleep. When we got back home, she was gone. I've always assumed that someone must've picked her up or she got on a bus. The car had been totaled in the accident. The day she left the hospital was the last time I saw her. She stood in the hallway outside my room, while my father came in to tell me he'd be back for me. Of course, I didn't know it would be the last time I'd see her. That was eleven years ago." Tessa looked straight at the ocean, not at Andrew's face. "She thought she'd killed me and never came to see me once they told her I'd survived."

"Oh sweet, beautiful Tessa. My Tessa," Andrew said, wrapping her up in him. "You've had no contact with her all these years?" he asked after several minutes.

"No actual contact. I do have her words, though. Her words live in me. They live in me and I can't get them out." She didn't want to cry, but started to anyway.

226

They stopped walking, first Andrew, then Tessa, and stood on the rocks.

"She liked the beach, too. This beach, in fact. The first time she ran away, she came here." Tessa relayed the story her father had told her a few weeks ago. "I've tried to make sense of her leaving. Tried all these years. Tried to figure her out. Tried to analyze the hell out of it, actually. All the things that pop into my head at any given time, stuff she used to tell me," Tessa said. "Especially recently."

"Because of your dad being sick?"

"Yes and no. There's that, of course. But mainly...mainly I'm trying to figure out if I'm like her. You know, similar in my," she took a deep breath before continuing. "In my...personal characteristics."

"Do you think you are?"

"Yes, I think I am. In some ways," Tessa said, wiping her eyes with her shirt. She looked down at their dirty feet. *In a lot of ways.*

"Such as?" he asked.

She didn't want to answer him, was too afraid of what would come out of her mouth.

"Such as?" he asked again. "How do you feel you're like her?"

Oh God. Why is he pestering me now? Can't he see how upset I am? When did he turn into a therapist anyway? She wanted to retract the whole story, lighten it up. But what would come of lightening it up? That's what she'd done for eleven years in her own head and in her relationship with her father. She'd glossed it over, made it less important than it was. And to what effect?

"Just everything, okay. I'm like her because she's my mother and I came from her. Then she left me hanging. And I've been just hanging and hanging for eleven years, unable to make a fucking decision on anything." And now she was losing her father, the glue that held her together when the pieces of herself popped out of place, as they invariably did.

That's when she shut down, turned off her voice and walked away from him. The beach was still largely deserted and she wondered if her father was still in his bedroom or if the health aide had turned up yet. She was sorry she'd said as much as she had. *Oh hell. His story is so much more heartbreaking than mine and yet he told me.*

She carried her sandals, one in each hand, as she climbed down from the rock, then made her way down the beach. She thought about climbing up the lifeguard station like she used to do when she was a teenager seeking perspective, but changed her mind and kept walking. When she got to the jetty, she stopped to scoop up some stones at the shoreline and throw them one by one at it. As they clanged and smashed, Tessa could feel her anger increase. She didn't know how much time had passed when she turned around and found Andrew sitting on the sand a little distance off. Her stride was quick and purposeful as she approached him.

"Why did you have to come here? Why, Andrew? It's just fucking everything all up. I wanted to keep things simple with you and me. Simple. I didn't want you to see all this shit. All my stupid shit that lives in me." *He isn't supposed to be here. It's throwing the delicate balance way off.* All the shifting corners of her life, her world, had lost their distance from each other and merged into one big mess.

He didn't say anything, just sat on the sand and looked out at the ocean.

"Can you hear me? Can you hear me, Andrew?" Her voice got louder.

"I can hear you," he replied, without turning his head. "Things can't stay simple. They evolve. Grow. If they're good, they do. After a while, simple becomes another word for superficial. Is that what you want?"

"What if I said I hated you for interrupting my weekend

with him? That I wished you hadn't come last night? Would you just leave and let me have some time with him, whatever time I have left?" she shouted. "I'm asking you, Andrew, asking you to leave now. Go!"

"I won't go. Not like this, Tessa." He was calm and not looking at her, but at the water. There were a few early morning fishing boats out.

"Why? I'm asking you to go. To leave me...alone. Just leave me, Andrew. Can't you just let me deal with all my bullshit without burdening you? It's too much. This..." she said, and gestured wildly with her arms. "This is too much for me."

"That's just it. You're asking me. Everything you're saying is a question. You're asking me, not telling me. And I'm answering you," he said. "You don't hate me, Tessa. It hurts me that you said that, but I know it's not true. Think about who it is you're taking me to be. Who do you hate? It's not me, Tessa. It sure as hell isn't me," Andrew said, finally breaking his gaze at the water and turning to look at her.

"You expect too much from me. You know that. Too damn much, Andrew." She'd run out of stones to throw at the jetty and let her arms hang limply by her sides, useless.

She could see him breathing, his chest rising high three times, yet visibly quivering, before he exhaled and stood. He was fragile, too, she knew. He took the few steps necessary to reach her, dropped his shoes with a thump into the sand and reached his hands out to her.

"Do you remember that night in the motel a few weeks ago? And then another time in my office when you asked me if you were real? If *this* was real?"

She nodded.

"Do you feel this sand under our feet? Do you feel the breeze coming off the ocean? Do you see me here in front of you on the beach where you grew up? Feel my hands on your skin?"

She looked up from the ground and saw his perfect face covered in sea salt mist, saw his dark hair being whipped wildly by the breeze.

"I know you need time with him while you're here. I know that, Tessa. I know it's a lot for you that I'm here now, but I'm not here to be a burden or to intrude. I'm here because I need you. I needed to release my story to you, finally. And I'm here to help you...and your father. We'll go back whenever you're ready and I'll explain this cannabis oil to him. I'll use every detail I know about this stuff to convince him to at least try it. It's worth a shot, right? Nothing to lose at this point. It might not cure him, let's not assume it will, but let's be hopeful that it will help him in some way. Get him out of the house more. Give him less pain and a better quality of life while he's still with us." He said all this with both his hands on the sides of her face, forcing her to keep her gaze tilted up at him.

A small flock of seagulls circled and squawked over their heads. The tide was coming in and lapping at their bare feet along the shoreline. Several more fishing boats were in the water now. An old couple who appeared to be in their eighties approached slowly with a pair of dogs on leashes. Tessa heard the couple say something about how nice it was to see young people up with the sun on a summer's day. She just stood in place amidst the chaos of the awakening day and let herself feel Andrew's hands on her face. She'd heard everything he said.

"I love your hands, Andrew. I love them." This was all she could say, all that would come out of her.

"That's what got the story out of me last night. These hands...you holding them," he started before pausing and stuttering a little. "These hands that you love so much, these hands that touch you and love you...these were neglectful hands, cold, non-protective hands. Hands that have held a dead child, a child who died because of my lack of attention, my lack of nearness, of attention to detail, my stupidity, my arrogance, my assumptions, my fatigue, my desire to be alone, to zone out and forget I had responsibilities. These are my hands, Tessa," he said, looking away from her.

"They aren't those hands, Andrew. They are things of beauty. Of tenderness. Of gentleness...to me. Can you see that?"

"I'm trying."

"What do you want to feel?" she asked, but didn't await the answer. "That's not who you are, Andrew. You're none of those things to me. You're sweet and beautiful and dignified. You make me feel important. You make me feel special and at peace and...real. It's your hands that do that. Mostly. Your hands that day with the wine and the towel. Your hands. Your touch. You." There was so much more, but it was still trapped inside her without adequate words.

"You need me," he said it in a soft, almost whisper, but she heard him. "And I need you."

They sat down on the first big rock of the jetty. Tessa curled into Andrew's lap. He wrapped himself around her against the spray of water and she felt safe, almost embryonic. The incoming tide splashed onto the jetty, creating little deaths and rebirths every four seconds.

"You're very important to me. More important than anyone's ever been," she said into his shoulder, as she leaned on him. "It scares me, okay. It scares me to death, Andrew."

"I'm in love with you, Tessa."

"That's what scares me. That's how I'm like my mother," she said, unfolding herself from him to hug her own knees and rock back and forth.

"I don't understand," Andrew said.

"She didn't know how to stick around with those who loved her. She ran away. She was...is...I don't know anymore...flighty. Unpredictable. Volatile. Selfish, like me. And there's so much about her I don't understand. Things that would be impossible for me to explain to you...or anyone."

"Selfish? You? You're the least selfish person I know. Look at what you do."

"Yes. What do I do every Friday afternoon and every Monday morning?" she asked.

"Well, you're usually driving at those times, right?"

"Right, driving back and forth from one life to another. Always driving, just like she does...or did. It's been a while, so I don't know if it's still one of her escape mechanisms." Tessa knew she would always love to drive despite her history with cars and the accident and her erratic mother. Driving calmed her. She could never explain it. It just did.

"Tessa, it's not an escape mechanism for you. It's a necessity."

"Really? Is it a necessity that I have a job that's so far from my dying father? A necessity that I do what I do? I could stay here with him full time. He doesn't have much longer. It would be a small sacrifice to give up my job and do something else afterwards. Or take a leave of absence. But, no. I'm selfish. I like having my independence. I like having my own income, however small, it's enough for me—or it almost is. I'm scared of giving that up and then being stuck—stuck with nothing. I've been trying to save for a while and one of these days I'll be able to afford a place of my own—an apartment or something where I'd only have myself to worry about. And this...this is really selfish of me. I could go shopping and buy stuff to decorate my place. I could spend hours looking for vases or cheap little sculptures at antique shops or painting my walls turquoise, if I want to. Whatever. I could just be in my own place in this world— just be myself, if I can ever figure out who that is." She paused and looked out at the waves. "And then...then I could cook something or order something, or not, depending on how I feel and invite my incredibly awesome lover to come over and spend the night in my bed with me, making me feel alive and amazing and free. And we would talk and think about living, not about anyone dying." She said this last part quietly, almost to herself.

He reached out to touch her hand. She took hold of his and held it tightly.

"Tessa, that doesn't make you selfish. It makes you human. And if I'm the incredibly awesome lover..." He laughed a little and put his mouth on her neck for a moment. "Then it sounds pretty good to me. Not selfish. Just a human need for one's own space in the world. But maybe it's still forthcoming for you. It might not be time for that yet."

"I'm really ready to be unstuck, Andrew. This limbo place sucks."

"I know, believe me. I know about limbo places."

"I hate the anticipation of it. I know he's dying, but I'm not ready for it."

"Nobody's ever ready, love," Andrew said. "Time is precious and little, Tessa. Precious and little."

She leaned into him and let herself melt a bit. *Precious and little, indeed.* She thought then about when she first met Andrew. It had been less than six months since that day in the greenhouse. She silently thanked God for the presence of this human being on her path that day and for how he continued to stay on her path up until this day—this summer day on a rock at her childhood beach amid the spray of salt water and scurrying sand crabs and hovering seabirds.

"Where is this oil...this cannabis oil you have for him?" Tessa asked after several minutes.

"In my pocket."

"Show me."

Andrew reached into his pocket and pulled out a small plastic bag containing two syringe droppers full of a greenish black substance.

"That's what it looks like?" she asked.

"Yeah, that's what it looks like."

"I somehow expected a bottle or...I don't know...a jar maybe."

"It's very concentrated. It only takes a tiny amount to have benefits," he explained.

"Right. But why the syringe? He's not injecting it, right?"

Andrew opened the cap of one of the syringes and showed Tessa the tip of the syringe. It had a small opening to expel the oil. No needle.

"He will put it on his finger, like this," Andrew said, pushing a rice grain-sized amount of the thick black substance onto his finger. "Stick it in his mouth, under his tongue. That's it. We'll see how he responds and then up the dosage, especially at night."

Tessa picked up his hand and tentatively licked the bit of oil with just the tip of her tongue. It tasted like a pine tree.

⚘

It was mid-morning by the time Tessa and Andrew made their way back to the car. Her father would most likely be up with the aide by now. The sun was heating up the beach and families had started to arrive with beach blankets and coolers and armloads of plastic shovels and pails for making sandcastles. They watched a couple with two young kids clatter by with all their essentials for a day at the beach. The father carried the umbrella and two sand chairs. The mother had a kid's hand in each of hers, a floral printed sarong around her waist, and a gigantic canvas tote bag slung crosswise over her body. The kids screeched when they saw the tide come in, broke free and ran for the wave.

It was time for Tessa and Andrew to go, time for her to introduce Andrew to her father.

"I want to stop somewhere first and show you

234

something," she said, as they backed out of their parking spot. "A place."

"Sure. Your grandmother's probably not too keen to see me again anyway. A detour sounds good," he said, touching her right shoulder with his fingertips.

"Don't let her bother you. She can be difficult. I know. But I don't play by her rules. She doesn't like it, but she'll deal. Eventually." Tessa was making this up as she spoke, hoping it was true.

They drove out of the beach parking lot and down the road that ran parallel to the shoreline.

"This is a nice area, where you grew up," Andrew said.

"Yup, I grew up here and lived here all my life until last year, but I actually prefer where you live."

"A fourth floor apartment in a brick building on the edge of a college town?"

"Yeah. Sounds good to me." She hoped she didn't sound like she was looking to live with him. She wasn't.

"I only live there because it's close to work," he said.

When they got to their destination a minute later, she parked behind the building, off the street. The dumpster was overflowing. Her father must have canceled the service, but it appeared that some of the neighbors were still using it to toss their trash. After making a mental note to call the company and request a pick up, she got out of the car and nodded her head at Andrew to follow her.

"If I had the key on me, I'd let you in. Show you around." Tessa put her hands above her eyes, visor style, to narrow her view into the window. Andrew joined her and wrapped his arm around her shoulder.

"This is...was...Tremblay's Place, my father's restaurant. It was a hell of a little place back in its day," she said, quoting her father and his love of his place. "I grew up *here* more than anywhere else." She nodded. "It meant so much to him, more than anything else in the world. I know it broke his heart to close this door, put this sign up." The sign on the door told customers that Tremblay's Place was temporarily closed. "This is how he related to the world around him. This place. This was his world. His family was this place. I was here. A lot. My mother wasn't. She couldn't fit into his world. Didn't want to. It didn't suit her...and he didn't know how to deal with her. She was so volatile. So unpredictable. Nothing he said was right. Nothing she did made sense to him. I never realized it, but they were as incompatible as two people could be. Both stubborn. Neither willing to listen to the other for very long. And now...now he sits in the house all day, dying and thinking about the past. Trying to figure out where he went wrong. How to make peace with it. With her." She turned to look at the water, walked out toward the boardwalk and left Andrew standing at the window.

"Thank you for sharing that with me, Tessa, you know, before I meet him. Gives me a bit of a picture of him," Andrew said when he'd caught up with her.

"He's giving it to me," she said to the ocean. "This place. His restaurant. He wants me to take it over. To run it."

"What do *you* want?" Andrew asked.

"I want him to get well enough to go back to it," she said. "Even if it's just part-time. Even if he has to take a business partner."

"What about you as his business partner?"

"Geez, you sound like him now and you haven't even met yet," Tessa said.

"Looks like it was a cozy, everybody-knows-your-name sort of place," Andrew said, turning his gaze back toward Tremblay's Place.

"Yeah, that's just the sort of place it was," she confirmed. "Sometimes, it was a little too much, a lot too much...for a kid. I could never just be anonymous. I was

Benjamin's daughter. All the regulars knew all my business, pretty much all the time. It wasn't that *he* talked about me, it was just small town gossip. People talked and they were paying customers and mostly his friends so he just let it go. Carried on. When my mother left for the last time, that was the worst. I didn't want all the attention. The pity. The advice from some of the mother hens."

"How'd you handle it?"

"I learned to ignore them for the most part, if I was feeling rude. If I wanted to look gracious, I'd smile, tell them school was going well and thank them for asking. There were a couple of them who were troubled, actually troubled they said, by this," she said, touching the scar on her face. *You could be so pretty, Tessa. You should take care of that before it becomes permanent.'* And they'd give me phone numbers of dermatologists and plastic surgeons. I never went to see them—obviously. One time, I overheard them talking about me, saying how they just didn't understand why I didn't take them seriously. They even criticized my father for not insisting I take their advice. *'She'll regret it, if she leaves it untreated for too long.'* I used to have a boyfriend who did the same thing, but then denied saying it, as if I'd just imagined it." She added the final sentence quietly.

"Oh good Lord, Tessa. What gives people the right to..."

"...to insult. I know. To hurt?" she finished for him. "I just always had hope that there would come a day when I wouldn't care about it anymore. That I would accept it as part of who I am."

He put his fingers on it—lightly, as always. "I'm glad you didn't have plastic surgery."

She closed her eyes.

"And I'm glad you didn't know me when I was...when I was...well...before," he said.

She knew he couldn't finish his sentence. He couldn't

say, *'before I lost my child. Before my wife left me.'* But she knew what he meant and what this meant to her. She wouldn't have wanted to meet him before he was the man she met in the campus greenhouse that cold February day.

"This place is my past. It's not my future," she said. "Are you ready to go?"

"If you are," he said, reaching out for her hand to hold.

"I do love these hands of yours and what they do," she said, as she took hold of his hand and they walked back to the car. Perhaps they could simply have a moment of tactile simplicity after all they'd just said to each other.

"What else do you love, Tessa? I want to know more."

"Your mouth. Your weight on top of me," she answered. "That you drove all the way here to see me and to help my father," she added quietly. *The gift of your heartbeat in my ear when you're sleeping and I'm resting my head on your chest,* she thought. *Yeah, that.*

"You know, in all the time we've known each other, we haven't been out on an actual, proper date," Andrew said. "What do you say? Would you like to?"

"Well, it's kind of a time issue. I'm here every weekend."

"Yes, but there's Monday, Tuesday, Wednesday and Thursday," he replied

"Thursday's out. You work 'til eleven," she said.

"Monday, Tuesday or Wednesday then. Pick a day."

"I like our Mondays and Wednesdays as they are, Andrew. I think you know that."

"Mmm, yes. That leaves Tuesday. We'll go out on a real date like a lady and a gentleman. You'll wear a very long skirt so I won't be too distracted. We'll eat. We'll laugh. We'll tell each other stories. Maybe I'll even hold your hand," he chirped, smiling broadly at her. "Then I'll take you home."

"Sounds good, but which home will you take me to?"

"Back to your cousin's."

"It's thirty-seven miles from campus. How will I get myself to work on Wednesday?"

"Thirty-seven miles is nothing, Tessa. I'll come back and pick you up in the morning. We'll go to breakfast before work. What do you think?"

"I like driving. It helps me process things," she protested.

"Tessa, I want to drop you off and pick you up—just this once. Your car will be fine at work. You could park it in the overnight lot."

"You know Charlotte's house is not really home to me. I just crash there, for now."

"I know. Maybe you can introduce me to her. You have told her about me, right? She must wonder where you stay on Mondays and Wednesdays."

"I've told her about you. She's kind of absorbed in her own world most of the time. I don't know if she really notices my absence too much when I'm not there."

"Still, you could introduce me, right?"

"Okay, Tuesday we'll go on a proper date." She'd straighten up the cottage when she got back tonight. She'd tell Charlotte more about Andrew. All she'd said so far was that he was her lover, and this had been primarily to keep Charlotte from hooking her up with anyone. She'd tell her cousin that Andrew was dignified and a bit older. She wouldn't tell her about his baby, wouldn't tell her about his sadness. She wanted to hold that close for him.

Tessa was a little giddy at the thought of Tuesday. She felt hot inside, like boiling liquid that was evaporating into steam. She much preferred being a solid state of matter. It was easier to get around as a solid. Gases were too unpredictable with their molecules bouncing randomly about, and escaping.

She squeezed her own shoulders to feel for muscle and bone, to ground herself, and said, "Tuesday. Okay. Where will you take me on our date?"

"Somewhere elegant," he answered. "So dress accordingly. No rickety bridges and bare feet."

"Oh bummer, I like rickety bridges and bare feet."

"Well, maybe I'll work that in then," he winked at her and squeezed her close to him, as they approached Tessa's car behind her father's restaurant.

It was good to have that lightness back in their conversations, but Tessa knew something had shifted with Andrew—something major. She would have to be more open to him, more willing to allow herself to feel whatever was emerging within her.

TWENTY-THREE

Mémère was in her bedroom when Tessa and Andrew arrived back at the house. It was close to noon and they were both starving and warm. The day had turned out to be a hot one. Momentarily she thought of the families at the beach, but then turned her attention back to her growling stomach. She pulled Andrew straight into the kitchen to whip up a quick tuna salad for sandwiches. While he was doing that, Tessa grabbed the fresh spinach and cucumbers from the fridge. She sliced a lemon for tanginess, which her dad liked, and chopped an apple to give the green drink a little more substance and pulp. Then she tossed it all into the blender with a cup and a half of mineral water.

"Dad," she called into his always ajar bedroom door a few minutes later. "Dad, how are you feeling now?"

She found him knee deep in his closet, his flannel shirt unbuttoned and his sleeves rolled up past the elbows. The sound of her entering the room must have startled him because he twitched a little and said, "Tess, Tessie, Tessa. Tess, Tessie, Tessa."

"What's going on? Did the health aide come?" She could never remember the names of the rotating Sunday aides, just knew that it was never Kate on Sundays.

"Yeah, yeah, she came. She left," he replied from inside his closet.

"Why are you on the floor? Did you fall?" Tessa asked, stepping in closer and noticing that he couldn't have fallen because he was sitting on a pillow. "Why didn't she shave you?"

"I'm letting it grow. Not much there anyway," he replied without looking up.

It was true. The chemo had left him scrawny and bald. He didn't have hair on his chest or forearms anymore. The little that had grown back had trickled in slowly and sparingly, just a bit of soft fuzz on his chin and cheeks. He didn't even have eyebrows anymore. When he was younger and healthy, his beard had been a rich, deep copper color and his face had been full and soft. Now his face was sunken and sallow, his beard a yellow-white tinge.

"What did she do? Did you eat at all?"

"I ate a little. It was a good omelet that you made," he said. "She took some boxes down for me. That's what I'm doing now. I'm looking through boxes."

He was indeed surrounded by boxes of various sorts: Old shoe boxes. Plastic totes. A metal safe that she'd never seen before.

"I could've taken those down for you, Dad. Do you want to sit in your chair? I could put the boxes on your footstool or something. Make it easier on you. Or the kitchen table, so you don't have to be crouched down on the floor."

He didn't answer.

"Dad?"

"It's all right, Tessa," he nearly shouted, "I'm doing okay. Just looking for some old pictures...and stuff."

She let it pass for a moment. Andrew was in the kitchen and she didn't want him to have to face her grandmother alone again.

"Anyway Dad, Andrew's still here. Do you want to come out and meet him before he drives back? We're having tuna sandwiches, if you want one. And I made you a green drink."

"Yeah, Andrew. Of course I want to meet him. Help me up, baby," he said, extending both his hands to her. "Is he doing anything to your heart yet?"

"Yeah, a bit," she said, pulling him from the floor to a shaky standing position. She grabbed the three-pronged cane and set it in front of him.

"A bit's good, baby. Let's go. I'm dying to meet him."

"Can you not use that expression, Dad? Please."

He straightened himself against the cane and started for the bedroom door.

"I could help you with whatever you're doing with these boxes," she suggested.

"No, no, no, baby. It's mostly boring old paperwork I'm trying to sort out before...before my time's up."

Tessa tapped on Mémère's bedroom door before walking her father to the kitchen.

"Come in," her grandmother's voice answered.

Tessa stepped into the room and found Mémère's rocking chair facing the single window that looked out onto the front yard. She had a romance novel in her lap and her Bible on the nightstand.

"I talked to Frankie on the phone while you were out," she said to the window. "Is that man still here...or did he go home yet?"

"Andrew, Mem. Not *that man,* and he's in the kitchen if you want to apologize to him...or get to know him."

"Well, I told Frankie to stop by when he can. Are you making lunch for your father or should I?"

"I'm making lunch. That's what I came to tell you...to ask you if you want a tuna sandwich."

"I'm not hungry just now. I'll stay in my room," she said. "Close the door all the way, Tessa. I feel like I need to rest my eyes."

⁂

Andrew didn't bother shaking Benjamin's hand, but went straight for a hug.

"Andrew, my man. Good to meet you finally."

"And you as well, sir," Andrew replied.

"None of this sir business. I'm Ben. That's it. Just Ben. Got it?"

"Got it."

"Dad, let's go sit down on the deck," Tessa suggested. She wanted to get him outside where they could talk free of worry that Mémère would overhear anything. "It's nice out. I'll bring lunch outside."

When she got outside with the sandwiches and salad and green drinks for everyone, Tessa found her father and Andrew in deck chairs, talking. They both looked happy to see her approach with food.

"I'm getting to know your friend here, Tessa. Very bright, open-minded person. Like you, baby girl. I can see why you like him so much," he said, winking at her. "Tells me he wants to save my life. Asks me how I want to feel and if I want to choose getting well."

Tessa looked at Andrew, then at her dad. Of course this is what they had talked about, while she spent ten minutes in the kitchen. *Of course. No time wasted.*

After they'd eaten, her father started telling stories. *Maybe he's missed male companionship since he closed Tremblay's Place.* She breathed in, sat back in her chair and listened to him talk about everything from his *little diner* to Tessa's first attempt to ride a bike. He talked about the beach. He talked about his life and how he wanted to settle things up, make everything right. At that, Andrew shook his head and told him there was still time. *There was still time.* Ben reached out and put a hand atop Andrew's, tapping it several times. Tessa wasn't sure if it was in agreement or contradiction. Either way, he seemed at peace. Either way, there was something new at work. Her father took a deep breath, so did Tessa and Andrew.

Between the three of them, there was a palpable vibe, an optimistic vibe that flowed through the late July air. It was not something any of them could've had individually, but collectively they each brought something. She remembered back to the first bunch of articles and holistic resources Andrew had found for her. *Successful eradication of disease or even a period of remission is dependent on the total mental, physical and spiritual belief in a cure.* She pictured a triangle, her driving triangle, and thought of the three points. Point A was her father's house. Point B was Charlotte's cottage. Point C was the campus where she worked. The miles between all her transitory places merged on the back deck that day. *Mental. Physical. Spiritual. Andrew. Ben. Tessa.*

"Tessa," her father said suddenly. "Leave him with me will you, baby. Just for a little while. I won't torture him, I promise."

Tessa got up, clearing their plates and cups from the deck.

"Do you think you could go to the market now? See if you can get some figs while you're there, baby. I'm in the mood for them for later."

She kissed her dad's cheek first, then Andrew's, before grabbing her keys and tote bag and heading off to look for more figs. She had a feeling she may even find them in the first store she tried, even though that had not been her experience in looking for them so far. It was often hit or miss with the little darlings.

When she came up the back steps with grocery bags in each hand an hour and a half later, Tessa found Andrew puttering around the fire pit, collecting wood and stray beer cans she hadn't seen the night before. She briefly wondered if Frankie had shown up while she was out, but didn't let the thought linger. There was no need to worry about how Andrew would handle Frankie.

"Hi, what's going on? Is he in the house now?" she asked.

"Mmm hmm. He said he wanted to do another campout tonight...with us. With you and me. I know it's hours away from getting dark, but I'm trying to make myself useful while he sleeps."

"Did you wear him out with all the conversation?"

"Perhaps. More likely it was the dose of cannabis oil and the bit of indica brownie I gave him."

"He actually took the oil?"

"He did. Yeah. And the brownie for his pain. He'll take a long nap and be up in a few hours," Andrew said, making his way up to the back door to open it for Tessa. "What's left in the car, love?"

"Nothing. This is all of it."

"He's not done with life yet, Tessa."

"He told you that?"

"He didn't need to tell me," Andrew said. "When I took him to his room, he gave me a notebook full of his poems and told me to read them with you."

"Shall we?" Tessa asked, as she deposited the bags on the counter.

"Let's stick around, though. I want to be here when he wakes up. I want to know how he feels. He fell asleep very peacefully."

"That's a relief. Usually, he...he tosses around, sweats and grimaces in pain and tells us to let him be," Tessa said. "Where's the poetry notebook?"

She was a little shocked that he had given it to Andrew instead of directly to her.

"On the couch. I haven't opened it yet."

She padded down the hall to her father's bedroom, peeked in and saw him quiet and still under the fresh sheet she'd put on his bed before their campout the previous night. The door to his bedroom perfectly ajar, Tessa walked back to the living room to join Andrew and her father's poetry on the couch.

She picked up the black composition notebook, the same one she'd found in his pillow case a few weeks back. There were a few pages dog-eared, making it easy to find the poems that her dad had marked. Nothing was dated.

Sometimes she dreams
Dreams with the August moon
Closes her eyes
She'll be sleeping soon
Escaping on her nightly trips
A shimmering moonbeam her ship

But stay here tonight
Remain
Take me to the warmth of your light
To that softly shadowed place in your breath
Where we can exhale
And most of all, stay
Most of all
Stay
Barefooted child
Sweetly dancing girl
Alone beneath the stars

The moonbeams gripping her baby toes
And pulling, pulling her to shore

This one was close to the beginning of the journal. She flipped to the next folded page and read her father's next poem.

I awake in night
Realize I sleep alone
Starlight is my foe
Sleep, come back again

She then flipped to the center of the notebook where another dog-eared page revealed this bittersweet one.

One by one 'til none remember
Except the moon and the sun
Death's voracious hands take us one by one
One by one we all succumb
So celebrate this good hour
This hour of memories
Until it's time to rest with angels

She quickly flipped to the next poem, which was accompanied by a pencil sketch of a tree.

In the soft soil around the tree by the bay
Acorns fall, take root and sprout
The grand daddy tree shelters them
Embraces in thick arms, then shows them the sun
The boy and the girl pluck new leaves to hold
As they lean their backs on the roots
And rest their bare feet in the cool of the bay

Though there were plenty more, after four poems she

needed to put the notebook down. Her father's poetry was of loneliness and wistful longing. Despair and hope. Life and death. And love. Tessa closed the notebook and leaned her head onto Andrew's shoulder as they waited for her dad to wake up and spend the remainder of the weekend with them.

TWENTY-FOUR

By the time Andrew and Tessa finally had their long anticipated Tuesday night date, it was mid-August. Ever since Andrew's surprise visit to her dad's house several weeks prior, Tessa had been checking in at home more and more, often getting there early on Friday morning and staying until late on Monday evening. It was a partial leave of absence, a trial that she was able to manage. She finally let herself feel the necessity of her real work—helping her father feel the best he possibly could—and he wasn't pushing her out the door and back to her far away job nearly as vigorously. She read and reread all the articles and books Andrew had given her on medicinal cannabis, especially the one by Rick Simpson, the man who had made a name for himself with the oil, and the one about the endocannabinoid system. It all made an amazing amount of sense.

Tessa's father had been using the oil and the infused edibles that Andrew had brought for just over three weeks. He was sleeping at night and, he told Tessa, having great, vivid dreams—dreams that made him feel serene and enthusiastic at the same time. He reported less pain and Kate had cut down on his opiate pain medications and stopped talking about a morphine drip. The swelling in his feet had improved and he was spending fewer daytime hours in his bedroom. He had even gone to Tremblay's Place with Tessa over the weekend to help her air it out.

On the Tuesday of their date, Tessa called home at 5:00 PM to check in. Mémère answered and told her that her father was in the kitchen, playing with new recipe ideas.

"God works in mysterious ways, Tessa. He got up early today with more energy than he's had in a long time and made some kind of zucchini bread with cinnamon in it. Three loaves. Best I've ever tasted."

"Mmm. Put a piece in the freezer for me for this weekend," Tessa said. "Let me talk to him, Mem."

"He's up to his elbows in flour at the moment."

"Please. Tell him to wipe his hands off. I just need to talk to him quickly."

She waited for her father to come to the phone.

"Tessie baby, I'm cooking up a surprise for you and Andrew."

"Yes, Mem told me you made a nice zucchini cinnamon bread. Save me some, okay."

"No, no. I'll make another one by this weekend and then some. Bring Andrew home with you, baby girl. I'm planning something big for Saturday night."

"Something big?"

"Can't say anymore. It's a surprise."

"Okay, Dad. Take it easy on yourself. Don't overdo it. I'll call you again tomorrow," she said, as she shut down her computer and waved goodbye to Paula in the opposite corner of the office.

Date night. Tessa was half solid, half liquid.

She had worn a shimmering silver skirt that reached her ankles and a pale green v-neck blouse with half-length sleeves. Her hair was down and simple, and her shoes were flat and comfortable just in case excess walking was in store for her.

As promised, Andrew met her at her office door and drove to a Japanese restaurant two towns away where they walked over a foot bridge that crossed a koi pond and took notice of the scattered picnic tables around the grounds.

"That's for after," he said.

"I'm not following you, Mr. Dignified Man. What's for after?"

"Those picnic tables. Well, just one. We'll find the most secluded one so we can, well, you'll see, Tessa..."

"On a picnic table? Really, Andrew? How about your apartment instead?"

"Nope, my apartment's too boring. Too enclosed."

"Mmm, okay. But let's eat first, mister. I'm starving."

"Thank you, Andrew. That was the best date I've ever had," Tessa said when they got to Charlotte's cottage.

Andrew parked on the side of the unpaved road out front and turned to face her.

"I mean it. It really was," she repeated.

"I agree. It was great. I feel like I know you better. You beat the Scrabble master in our very first game." A Scrabble match was the reason he'd found a place with picnic tables on its grounds. "And I got to look at you in that blouse for several hours. Hey, perhaps that's why I lost the game. Too distracted to come up with words." He then flipped her hand over to trace her lifeline with his index finger. "Good night, love. I'll come fetch you again in the morning. I'm thinking early. Six o'clock, if we're going to have breakfast before work."

"I'll probably still be full from that awesome dinner by then."

"Well, maybe just coffee. We'll see."

"Are you coming in? You could meet Charlotte. All the lights are on, I'm sure she's still up."

"It's late, Tessa. I'll meet her in the morning."

"You could still come in, though." Tessa had made her tiny bedroom impeccably neat and didn't want to waste the short time it would stay that way. They could even go straight to her room, avoiding Charlotte's studio, if they went in through the back door.

"It's tempting, Tessa, believe me. But if I come in, we won't sleep. I know we won't and I want you to sleep tonight. You deserve the rest," Andrew said. "Have sweet dreams."

"Oh, by the way, my dad is planning some kind of surprise for us this weekend. Something with zucchini and cinnamon. He was feeling good when I talked to him earlier," she said, leaning over a bit to kiss him before heading into the cottage. "Goodnight, sweet Andrew. You're a beautiful man. Such a beautiful man," she said in the darkness of his car, as she leaned her head onto his shoulder.

He ran his fingertips up and down her arm a few times before insisting that she go in and rest.

Charlotte was packing Rubbermaid totes when Tessa unlocked the door and stepped into the cottage.

"Is he coming in? I have herbal tea on the stove?"

"Herbal tea? Is Marcus here?"

"No. No Marcus tonight. Too much to do," she said, snapping a lid onto a full tote. "So is he coming in? I could use a short break from this."

"He'll be back in the morning. He wanted to let me sleep. What are you doing?"

"Tomorrow's my workshop day. I'm packing my car tonight, so I can just take off in the morning."

Charlotte had started teaching beginner level pottery workshops across the area twice a month. She'd traveled to a

couple summer camps and community centers so far. She
was testing it out over the summer with the hope of creating
a more organized program in the coming year. She'd told
Tessa it was because she needed to get out of the house more
and boost her income a bit. Tessa got the feeling that
Charlotte liked working with people, liked teaching. She
could see Charlotte's enthusiasm for creation when she told
the stories of her various pieces. Her inspiration poured
through her heart via her fingers and produced brilliance.
That was what likely got her out of the house.

"What time are you leaving in the morning?" Tessa
asked.

"Around 7:30, I think. That should be early enough."

"Andrew is picking me up at six to take me to breakfast
before work," Tessa said, feeling silly at the idea of being
picked up and taken to breakfast after just being taken to
dinner.

"Has he forgotten that you know how to drive?"
Charlotte asked.

Tessa laughed. "Maybe. Really, though, I think he's just
trying to be sweet...to be an old fashioned gentleman."

"Well, that's something, I guess. I'll meet him in the
morning then," Charlotte said. "It's good to see you like this,
Tessa."

"Like what?" she said, her face flushing.

"Like you're happy about something."

By the time Tessa got to her bedroom, it was nearly
midnight. She switched the bedside lamp on low. It cast a
dim light on the piece of pottery that she had pulled down
from Charlotte's shelf of early creations. It was heavy and
solid, the perfect paper weight, and she had started stacking
her drawings under it. There was quite an eclectic collection
now. Nothing she would show anyone yet—just whimsical
little pictures, mostly of what the moon looked like when she
was driving from one place to another. Her drawings were

silver and dark blue and hazy orange with drops of burgundy and yellow.

It had been almost an hour since Andrew had dropped her off. She pulled out her phone and typed up a quick text.

Going to sleep now. Thanks again for the beautiful date, beautiful Andrew. See you soon, xo.

As her head sank into her pillow, her phone buzzed a new message. She reached over to grab it from her little table, picked it up and read it.

My pleasure, love. Go to sleep. See you at sunrise, xo.

"You want a Scrabble rematch, don't you?" Tessa said into her phone when it rang and woke her.

"What? Scrabble? No. Tessa?"

"Frankie?"

"Yeah. Who did you think it was?"

"Sorry, Frankie. I was dreaming, I guess. What is it? Is it my dad? What Frankie? Tell me." She felt her panic escalate.

"He collapsed. Your grandmother called me first because..."

"I know why she called you first. Just tell me if he's okay right now. Where is he?"

"The hospital. He was admitted an hour ago," Frankie said. "You should get here as soon as possible."

"He's not on any type of machine, is he?" she asked. She hadn't wanted to ask this, but needed to know what to expect when she got there.

"I don't know. They put him in a room. I'm in the parking lot. Get here, Tessa," he urged. "He was at Tremblay's by himself tonight. Your grandmother got worried when he didn't come home. I got there and he was passed out on the floor. Looked like he was making pies."

Making pies. Crap. Her car was thirty-seven miles away

in the overnight lot of the college and Charlotte's was packed with her workshop supplies, unavailable. She was stranded in this in-between place.

There was no choice but to call Andrew and ask him to come back a couple hours early. "Now, please." It was 3:18 AM. She knew it would be 4:00 AM by the time he got to the cottage and that was if he left immediately.

She hung up and waited.

"I'm sorry. I'm so sorry to ask you to take me there, but I have to go. I have to go, Andrew." She'd already lost nearly an hour between the phone call from Frankie and Andrew's arrival at Charlotte's. And it was another eighty plus miles to the hospital.

He hugged her before opening the car door for her. They let some time pass in silence as Andrew pulled out of the driveway, made his way to the southbound highway ramp and proceeded down the dark stretch of road.

"I'll get your car back to you by the end of the day. I'll do my very best," he said, after they had settled into the trip.

"How, Andrew? How can you possibly get my car to me? You have to work today and I have to be there. I need to be there."

"They can manage without me today. This is more important."

"Then how will you get back? I won't be able to drive you. It's far and I'll be there for who knows how long. A while, maybe." She had to put everything else aside now. Being there for her father was all that mattered.

"Don't worry about me, Tessa. You will have your car. Let me have your key, and I'll see to it," Andrew said. "I'm sorry I created this problem in the first place."

"You only wanted to be sweet...to be a gentleman," she said. "It was nice of you," she added quietly.

"Yeah, but I guess I was a bit selfish. I never considered this possibility, especially with all his recent good days."

Tessa dug through her bag until she felt the familiar jumble of keys and key rings, detached her car key and slipped it to him. She watched as he connected it to his own set of keys.

For the rest of the drive, they talked about practical things. He said he would inform Tessa's supervisor about the situation, freeing her to not worry about making phone calls from the hospital. She babbled on about what her grandmother would need, thought out loud, made a list of trivialities to occupy her mind. Her favorite tea bags. Tea bags. It was not even dawn yet, Tessa was on a nearly deserted highway, and she was having thoughts about her grandmother's tea bags. She hadn't been able to find Mémère's favorite flavor on Sunday when she did her grocery run. *Double Bergamot Earl Grey black tea. So specific. Like a cupful of flowers.* Tessa didn't like it, but bought it every week. She had the box memorized. It was purple and blue with gold letters and little black stars. The store had been out of them on Sunday. That meant that Mémère was going into her third day without it. Her father was in a hospital room, she was sitting with her head in her hands in Andrew's car on the way to him, thinking about Double Bergamot Earl Grey tea bags. *For Mémère.* If she thought about anything else she would break down. *Not yet.*

When they got to the hospital, Tessa told Andrew not to come upstairs with her. "They only let in immediate family at this time of day. They told me that over the phone. The nurse told him I was on my way."

"We could say I'm immediate family."

"No, Andrew. It's better this way," she said without looking at him.

"Do you think your grandmother's here with him?"

"No, she's not."

"I could go get her. Bring her."

"She doesn't want to be here. Doesn't want to see him

257

like this. Thank you for offering, though."

"Tessa, I want to walk you up, even if I don't go into the room. Someone should walk with you, hold your hand along the way from my car to the room."

"The best thing you could do for me now is get my car and bring it back to me."

"I've already promised you that," he said, while opening the driver's side door and getting out. He walked swiftly to her side, but she had clicked the door latch open before he got there to do it for her.

"I will be too distracted, if you go in with me. I need to walk into this building alone, try to be strong and go see my father."

"Okay, just to the door then...of the building. Then I'll go. I'll get your car."

"I appreciate everything you've done for me, Andrew. Really, I do. Everything. Thank you." Her mind was not in a place to say or do anything beyond express gratitude.

Tessa had not been in this hospital since before her father had stopped chemotherapy and radiation months ago. When she got to the nurse's station on the oncology floor, she stopped to give her name and ask for the room number. The floor was eerily quiet; it was not yet dawn. There were no laundry or food service carts lining the halls, just the speckled white and green linoleum stretching from the nurse's station to the single window at the end of the corridor. She avoided peeking into the rooms, glancing only at the numbers beside them, as she looked for her father. It was close to the desk, room 403, third room down on the right. The door was partially open, just as he kept it at home, but this was the staff's doing, not his. She went in slowly and saw him lying flat in the bed with an IV attached to his left hand and oxygen tubes in his nostrils.

"Tessie baby? Come sit with me, Tessa."

She wordlessly obeyed and pulled a yellow plastic chair from the corner of the room up to his bedside. She planned to stay as long as he was here.

"There's a button here somewhere to make this thing go up. Can you find it? I want to sit up a little so I can see you."

She found the button and adjusted the back of the bed until he told her to stop.

"Guess I couldn't stay away from that little diner for very long after all, hmm?" he said.

"Yes, Frankie told me that's where you were. That you were making pies in the middle of the night."

"I was feeling good, you know. Good enough to be back down there a little at a time. Just sorting stuff and breathing the place in. Trying to keep the feel of it in my bones." He started to cry, but quickly wiped his eyes with the edge of the sheet. "Anyway, baby, I was planning a surprise. I wanted to do a special dinner for you and Andrew on Saturday. So, yes, I was making pie crusts. Silly old man, right?"

"No, not silly, Dad." She left it at that. If she said any more, she'd start crying, too.

"Anyway, baby girl, I need to go over some important stuff with you in case I don't make it out of this place this time."

She reached mutely for his hand and held it.

"I have three things I want you to do," he began, then spoke quickly. "First, contact your mother..."

"No, Dad." Tessa protested immediately. She hadn't expected it. They'd lived eleven years without her, with barely a mention of her, except for the few exchanges over the summer. She lived in both their heads and in their ways of perceiving the world, but actual interaction with her had been absent. Tessa was just starting to feel like she wasn't fourteen years old anymore. She was letting go of the influence her mother had on her—or damn well trying to, anyway. She felt it in her feelings for Andrew. She could come around, be at peace with letting go after all this time of being afraid.

"Just listen, baby. I wrote her a letter on Sunday night. It's on my bureau. You'll find her address on an envelope in my top drawer. Please send it when you're ready. You can read it first, if you'd like." He paused briefly, but not long enough for Tessa to say anything. "Second thing. Do something with my restaurant. If you want to sell it, I understand. But do something soon. Don't let it sit vacant too long. I've organized all the paperwork that you'll need. It's in the metal box in my bedroom closet. I even called my lawyer on Monday morning to bring him up to speed."

He closed his eyes and she thought he might have slipped from consciousness. His grip on her hand went slack and his head rolled away from her.

He stayed like that for a while. She patiently waited for the third thing.

"Dad?"

"Baby girl?"

"Yes, Dad. I'm here. I'm here."

"Tessa, baby."

"What's the third thing, Dad? You said you had three things for me to do."

"Keep Andrew. He's a gem, baby. He's done wonders for your heart...and mine. That's all. That's the third thing. Probably the most important. Keep Andrew."

His eyes closed and he drifted off. Tessa remained in the yellow chair, her head resting on the edge of the hospital bed. A nurse came in and checked his vitals, looked at his IV and smiled gently at Tessa.

She heard her father's voice, just as the sun was rising and poking shafts of pink-orange light through the slats of the blinds. She started to sit up to listen, but he told her to stay as she was.

"For a long time, I didn't let much pass through me. I've thought and felt more this past year than I ever have. The thoughts and feelings that I used to block, they all passed through...that I was an inattentive, lousy husband, that I cared more about my work than my family, that I hadn't earned the right to have this cancer leave my body, that I somehow deserved terminal cancer and trying to rid myself of it after the chemo had failed was pointless. I convinced myself that nothing would work. Why bother? You, Tessa, came bounding in all energy and will to help me, but I pushed you out, only half-heartedly, or less, listening to your suggestions. But you kept at it every weekend, all your vacation days spent for me or with me. I let you down over and over again by not trying, not fighting to live.

"I admit it was something about Andrew that made me focus on getting well again...or at least trying to get well. He told me the same story he told you about losing his baby girl and how he grieved and blamed himself for years. I saw myself in him, in his story. I saw that my giving up was about my own grief, my own blame for not helping your mother. And for closing myself off to your help for so long. Real help comes from real love. I had to face that. I saw Andrew as a beautiful, giving soul. As he wept his way through the telling of his daughter's death, I began to see him as an angel who was sent to me. And he came to me *through you.* You found him, loved him and brought him into my remaining life. He's like a thousand stars in your hands, baby—at least a thousand.

"We sat on the deck that day, two guys connected through you, and he looked me straight in the eye and told me how much you wanted to help me get better and how he felt pulled to help me live. I knew he meant live longer and better. When he gave me the two syringes of the oil and explained in great detail what it was and how it could help me, I didn't even hesitate. I just knew, finally, that I would do whatever I could to help myself."

Tessa sat up fully in the yellow chair and looked at her father.

His gaze was tilted toward the window, then back to her face. "And here I am in the hospital. I don't know, Tessa, I just don't. But I do want to try. I *am* trying." Several minutes passed. "I don't know how long they'll keep me here, Tessie, or if I'll even make it out alive."

She climbed onto the bed with him, careful not to disturb any of the tubes and wires that were connecting him to air and nourishment and drugs.

"Oh, I have one more thing for you to do for me, please. Go home tonight and open the windows in my bedroom. Let some fresh air in, and maybe, if there's any left, you could clip some of those red roses in the front yard and put them in a jar on my nightstand."

TWENTY-FIVE

Your car is in Visitor Lot B, row G, space 8. I'm downstairs. See you in a minute or two.

The text came late afternoon. Tessa had been by her father's bedside all day. By the time she looked up from reading it, Andrew was standing in the doorway with Subway sandwiches.

"What are they feeding you in this place, Ben?" he asked after hugging Tessa.

"Liquid through my veins," Tessa's father answered.

"You up for a chicken wrap, my friend? I had them put three kinds of peppers in it. You'll love it. Got one for you, too, Tessa. Extra parmesan and tomatoes on yours," he winked at her and handed it over.

By 8:00 PM, the hospital staff told Tessa and Andrew to go home. "Nothing was imminent," the nurse on duty assured her. She could go home and sleep and come back tomorrow. They promised to call her should he take a turn for the

worse, but doubted he would. He was a fighter again and it showed in his eyes—the sky blue eyes that had regained a certain lucidity that had been lacking for months.

"I'm staying here for now, Andrew," Tessa said. She was pacing in her father's backyard, from the deck to the edge of the woods—back and forth. After sitting in the hospital room all day, she needed to move. Andrew walked beside her, listening when she felt like talking. He occasionally stopped and plucked a weed out of the grass. When he had a handful, he tossed them into the woods.

"I wish you weren't so far away," she said.

"I'm right here."

"I mean when you go and I'm here all the time with him. It's hard to be here. I think that's part of the reason I couldn't stay here full time while he was getting treatment...getting worse. It's too hard to be here, alone."

"Spend as much time with him as you can. Be here. Be fully here," he paused, stepped closer to her. "And we're not so far from each other—really. Just 155 miles, right? And we both know how to drive," he said. "Besides, you're strong and caring and so good for him right now. Plus, you're brilliant. You can handle anything."

That word. "Why do you say I'm brilliant, Andrew? I'm not brilliant. I'm hardly brilliant," she argued.

"You are, Tessa. Look what you've done for me," he started. "A year ago, even less than a year ago, I was chronically depressed. I hardly talked to anyone. Nobody outside of my hometown knew me. I mean, the current me...the year-ago-me. You know what I mean. Then one day, as winter was ending, I saw a brilliant young woman in a red coat walk into the greenhouse where I sat nearly every day on the same bench, eating the same kind of sandwich and you...*you* asked me my name and told me yours. And I told you exactly where I worked and spent the next few weeks hoping to look up from my desk one day and see you standing there. Or in the greenhouse. Or walking on the path that goes through the quad. If you were not brilliant, you would've just walked out without saying anything."

"I almost did." *But I couldn't. Couldn't just walk out. I knew I would be missing something if I did.* "It's funny how you remembered that it's exactly 155 miles."

"Actually it's 155.2. I've driven it a few times now," Andrew said. "But you know what that is between us...those miles?"

"A long stretch of road," Tessa answered.

"Air."

"What?"

"It's air. Put your hands up," he said.

She did as he asked. He held his own hands up at a distance from hers. Then slowly, inch-by-inch, moved them toward hers.

"Air. This right here is air," he said of the narrowing space between their hands. "Breathe it in. Go ahead. Inhale. Exhale. Air. Oxygen, baby. That's what it is."

The world was air according to Andrew. Her world. Air. Indeed, if she thought about it, she could see it this way. The long stretches of road that she drove were all interconnected by the air they all breathed in and exhaled out every day.

She felt her chest fill up and rise with air as Andrew's hands got closer and closer to her own. Then, his hands made contact with hers, not lightly or subtly. It was instant. Just like that. The air between them became merged with their cells. Oxygen and skin, blood and bone—all at once. All at once.

What does he do to your heart? That's mainly what I want to know, she remembered her dad asking.

This. God above and God within. This is what he does. Indeed, in the grand scheme, it was all air. *How silly to think of the miles as an obstacle or even a gap between us.* She felt like she was grounded and flying at the same time. "That's why I love you...because of that," she said.

"That's the first time you've said that to me, Tessa. It feels good," Andrew said, his hands pressed tightly against hers.

"I have trouble with it. You know that. I'm not as detail-oriented as you are."

"That's not a detail, baby. That's the big picture. Say it again, please."

"I feel so...thrilled and terrified by it. Every time I'm near you, I'm thrilled and happy beyond belief. I know it doesn't always look that way or seem that way to you. And I'm terrified of how I'll feel if I'm ever not able to be near you, if I can't feel your hands on me. Your nearness. It just is. It's just there. It feels weird, but good, that I'm saying this actually out loud to you. I've tried telling you in my head as practice and it doesn't come out like this. In my head, it's more fluid, more elegant, not this choppy disaster of words all coming out like a broken-up jigsaw puzzle. I should just stop talking now, but I don't know what else to do if I stop. You know when we first met how I was the talker? Yap, yap, yap about everything but my real, actual feelings, which I tried not to have. All a cover up. A superficial glossing over of trivial stuff. Chit chat just to be near you, to make myself seem like I existed. If I was talking, am talking to you, I must be actually here near you. Alive. Breathing. Feeling like this. So thrilled and terrified, but a little less terrified now. Not quite sure why that is. I think it's your face right now. Your face is so beautiful right now. The way you're looking at me as I babble on. Oh God, I bet *my* face is really red right now. Is it?"

"Yeah," he said, touching her face. His hands felt cool because her face was so warm. "And your heart is beating like crazy. I can actually hear it...and feel it."

"I feel so silly, so utterly silly."

"Why?"

"I should've said all this sooner. Much sooner."

"It's okay. You've said it now."

She snuggled up to him, nuzzled herself into his neck and put his earlobe between her lips. "I love you. I love you. I love you," she repeated in a whisper over and over again until all the air from within her had transformed into those words.

"We found each other at the right time, Tessa," Andrew said. "The two of us found each other at the right time."

They were holding hands, tightly; tight enough to feel bone and muscle and nerves, all the internal workings of the body. Blood racing through veins. The pump of the heart. Andrew wasn't her escape anymore. He wasn't the place she went to be silly and frivolous. Andrew was real. And here. She had once seen him as she'd seen the warm and misty greenhouse, that beautiful, distant, faraway spot on their campus. Her playground. When she pressed rewind in her head, Andrew would always be that. It was his point of origin in her life. The magical place. But now, he was more of a cliff, a big open cliff with a field of scattered red wildflowers and a little house where she could sleep if she got tired, where they could sleep. Andrew was the shaded orange world, the view from the top of the highest rock, the waves below that held all the coins dropped over the edge as wishes. She squeezed his hand a bit tighter, tight enough to feel his pulse.

He reciprocated. "Listen, love," he began, "I called one of my neighbors to come get me and take me back to my apartment. He should be here within an hour. Call me tomorrow with any news about your dad. Oh, and before I come down this weekend, I'm going to try to get back to Vermont to see my new friend. He texted that he's got plants harvested and dried and ready to make more oil this week. If he gets a batch made, I'll go up there and buy it."

"Is it expensive? It must be, Andrew. How much did you pay for the amount you already bought?"

"Never mind," he said. "I just sold my house, remember?"

"Andrew!"

"Tessa, let me do this for him...for you. I want to save his life, or at least make him feel better for as long as possible. I need to," Andrew said. "You heard the nurse tonight. Nothing is imminent and he has that fight back in him. Your dad has the will to live. He does." Andrew paused for a minute and squeezed her hand a little tighter. "And anyway, the price is reasonable. No dispensary. No middle man."

She wished he could stay the night with her, but knew he couldn't take another day off. *I'll see him on the weekend. Maybe Dad will be back home by then,* she thought. She hoped.

Just after 9:00 PM, Andrew's neighbor arrived to bring him back to his apartment. Once they had gone, Tessa went back into the house to look for the letter her father had written to her mother. She found it, written in his favorite blue Paper Mate ink, on three sheets of neatly clipped notebook paper. With a deep breath, she picked it up.

Dear Lila,

As you know, I have never been a man of many words. I lived with my hands in my work and my heart stayed quietly (mostly) out of the way as far as you were concerned. I'm not proud of this, not at all. I wish things could've been different for us, for you and me and Tessa, but I didn't fight hard enough, or maybe I should say I didn't fight gentle enough. Oh hell, fight is probably the wrong word. Anyway, I've tried over the years to set you free from me and set myself free from all the negative stuff that happened with us. We are just people, humans, after all.

So here's what I need to put out there to you now. It's about Tessa. After the accident, when you left us, Tessa was left quite raw and vulnerable and with a scar on her face (and in her heart, I imagine). I decided at some point not to talk to her about her scar, to just be normal with her like it wasn't there, like it didn't matter. I didn't want to make an issue of it, or of your absence. Thought it might help her to not focus too much on what I perceived as the negative. Maybe she thought I didn't care, when really I didn't know what to say. But she was a young girl and I know now that it must have bothered her a lot. She must've thought about it constantly at that age. She had to grow into a woman with a scar on her face. But I tried not to see it and after a little time, I didn't see it. I heard what people said about her. They said it was such a shame on such a beautiful girl, that she was disfigured. It ruined her and so on. People said these things, and more. There was stuff said about you, of course. I filtered it all out. Didn't care and just went about my business. I wanted to try to raise her up, not let anything tear her down, but what did I know of teenage girls? It was a day-to-day effort. I did my best with her, but surely made mistakes along the way—mistakes of omission.

I want you to know that Tessa is not ruined or disfigured and that she is the most beautiful person I know, despite my fumbles and your absence. I'm not blaming you. I know I failed you on the highest level. I didn't show up for your needs. I was selfish and closed off to what you tried to tell me over and over again. You needed help. You were sick and I didn't believe you. And now it is me who is sick. Tessa has been the one to help me. She's put her life on hold, spent her time and resources to help me, but quite possibly it's too late. The doctors say I'm dying, and a lot of the time I feel like they're right.

Please know that I loved you. I did. I know now that I was not enough for you. You needed so much more than what I could offer. I just wanted a normal, simple life with a normal, uncomplicated family. But that's just an illusion. It's only since I've been sick that I've realized that. I went years after you left ignoring what I didn't want to face in myself. Now I have seen what it means to truly need another person, to depend on others for everything. I'm sorry for how long it took me to see this. We cannot go back and do anything differently. It all either happened or it didn't. Tessa has shown me what it all means. She has shown me unconditional love. I've learned a lot in the last year.

I truly hope you've found what you were looking for, what I couldn't give you. I hope you've found peace.

It would be a beautiful and important gesture to reach out to Tessa. Now is as good a time as any. I don't know if she feels the same way, but it's worth a try to find out.

Peace,
Benjamin

With wet eyes, Tessa refolded the letter and found the envelope that her father had mentioned in his top drawer. It was an empty, dark green, card-sized envelope addressed to her father with a California return address in the upper left corner. The postmark was from two years ago—December. *Could Mum have been sending him Christmas cards all along? Or was this a one-time thing? Oh, what does it matter anyway?* She copied out the address on a new envelope. Name. Number. Street. Town. State. Zip code. Then she looked at it. It was completely unfamiliar—almost foreign.

In eleven years, Tessa had never Googled her or plugged her name into whitepages.com or tried any other method of locating her. And here it was, her mother's location in her father's top drawer. She thought about driving straight to the hospital and asking him why he hadn't shared this information with her sooner, but already knew what he'd say. *'You never asked, Tessa.'*

I could get in my car and drive to California. I could just go.

But she could feel herself disappearing at the thought. She felt like vapor, as though every part of her body was dissipating faster than she could put a lid on and contain herself into one solid piece of matter. Mailing the letter, she feared, would feel like too much of a loss—all over again. Another loss. She wanted to hold onto her father's words, not share them with their other intended recipient. *I can't do it. Not yet.* She slipped the letter into the envelope, left it unsealed so she could read it again whenever she needed, and tossed it to the bottom of her tote bag.

TWENTY-SIX

Once Labor Day weekend had passed and the beach was starting to settle into the cooler weather, Tessa decided to spend an entire Saturday inside Tremblay's Place cleaning and sorting and making it ready for the next chapter in its life. Just before dawn, she peeked around her father's door and saw that he was still asleep. She took comfort in the knowledge that Kate would soon arrive and be with him for most of the day. Kate had been unwavering in her support and was, to Tessa's surprise, completely on board with his new lifestyle and medicine choices. When Ben was sent home from the hospital, Andrew had sat down with her and given Kate a thorough description of what Ben was doing. He spent hours explaining cannabis strain information, along with expected and experienced results and side effects, exact dosing and when it was appropriate to increase dosages for maximum benefit. Both Tessa and Andrew, and most importantly, Ben, felt comfortable with Kate in their little circle.

The sunrise was a bold pink along the shore as Tessa

parked outside her father's diner. Ten minutes ago it was dark. She liked the way light had a way of happening all of a sudden. As she worked the key into the door, she remembered how this place had especially thrived during summers. Its appeal had always been its proprietor above all else, and Dad had always maintained reasonable prices and simple home-cooked fare. The beach was a block away. Customers could both smell and see the ocean. Lobster rolls. Ice cream. Cheeseburgers and hot dogs. Clam chowder. Fried clams and scallops in red checkered take-out cartons. Tuna melts. Spicy linguica served in big, fluffy bulkie rolls. Pickles on the side. Onion rings. Watermelon slices as a garnish on every plate when they were in season.

And then there were the pies and cakes. Mémère had started the dessert take-out portion of Tremblay's and it hadn't taken long to build a regular customer base with the word-of-mouth, small town way of advertising. People talked about the beach. They talked about little places to hang out, to stop and eat. And they talked about sweets. Way back when Tessa was very young, her grandmother would go into the restaurant in the morning and bake whatever struck her fancy on a given day.

Apple walnut pie. Cinnamon crusted coffee cake. Raspberry swirl bread. Lemon pastries sprinkled with confectioner's sugar. Strawberry rhubarb pie in early summer. Blueberry and blackberry pies in late summer. Mémère would stay just long enough to bake for the day and when her various pastry items were gone, they were gone. Sometimes, all the desserts were gone by noon. Rarely, there would be one or two left by the time Ben closed up in the evening and he would take them home. After a while, the customers started requesting special occasion treats from Mémère—custom birthday cakes and pies for retirement parties and so forth. She indulged them and grew it into a little side thing, a little something extra that Tremblay's could become known for. It got to a point where Ben had to start baking too. Then Tessa.

For the first time, Tessa wondered what the reaction to Tremblay's being closed over the past summer had meant to the community. *Did they mourn the loss of this little dot on the map, this place that Dad had so lovingly created in this, his, corner of the planet? Did they shake their heads and say things like, 'That poor man. He's been through so much. Such a shame?' Or did they simply move on, see that Tremblay's Place was closed and go to the next little clam shack or lunch spot down the road?*

Once through the door, Tessa didn't sit down, not even to get her bearings. She hardly knew where to begin, so she decided to open the blinds a bit to let the September morning sunshine filter in. She flittered about, opening window blinds all around the restaurant and even kept the front door open to let the air in. If someone popped in, she'd offer them a cup of coffee or tea. It's what her father had always done. Then she surveyed it all. It was not a big place by any standard. There were twelve small tables in the dining area. The ones by the windows had booth benches; the ones in the center had straight-back, wooden chairs. A long counter with stools, for customers who came in alone or just wanted something quick before heading out to the beach, ran the length of one wall. Many of the stools were worn out from everyday use by the weekday regulars who lingered over coffee and pastry and conversation.

The windows needed washing inside and out. Then there were the floors, the kitchen and her father's office in the back. The last time Tessa opened the mop closet had been several months ago when her father had given up his chemo treatments and resigned himself to an early death. The thought of him here in his little corner of the world in a pie crust making frenzy in the middle of the night was never far from Tessa's mind. She visualized him up to his elbows in flour and butter. *Was it really a month ago that he was busy planning the surprise dinner that never happened? A month ago that he drove himself to Tremblay's late at night to have a few precious hours in the place he'd loved for so many years?*

When she got the call from Frankie that night, Tessa couldn't have imagined she would be in this place now, her father out of the hospital and letting himself be helped. She didn't dare say or even think he was improving, as she knew he had refused all lab tests and told the doctors and nurses he didn't want to know the level of anything in his body anymore. He wanted to live out his remaining time on his own terms, knowing there would be good days and bad days and days that fell somewhere in between on the spectrum.

Tessa thought of him now on this crisp September morning and wondered if he had gotten out of bed yet to wait for Kate or to attempt a new recipe if he'd woken up feeling like what he called, *a normal person.* She remembered their conversation of a week ago in which her father told her that he would be Tessa's helper now. Tremblay's was hers and he would teach her whatever he could and be who she needed him to be for her, as she'd done for him since she was fourteen years old.

She propped the closet door open with the mop bucket and gathered what she needed to get started. By the time she'd worked her way through the dining room and gotten to the back corner of the kitchen, Tessa was exhausted and hungry. The battery-operated clock above the counter had long since stopped, but she could tell by the way the sun was shining over and around the windows rather than through them, that it had to be at least 4:00 PM. It was a late afternoon sun.

She opened the door to her father's office and peered in from the threshold. It was probably an eight-by-ten foot room. Nothing much. Unadorned always. It held only his old desk and a pull-out sofa bed that Tessa had occasionally slept on when she was younger. It used to be a treat to sleep in her father's office if he was working later than usual and she didn't want to be home alone. She stretched her arms out and took several deep breaths. The scent of this room was part of her soul.

Looking at it now, she had visions for it. It needed to be completely stripped, cleaned, painted and decorated. Fancy was in the details and she could add those herself. She sat on the pull-out sofa in the corner and made a quick sketch of her ideas. She knew exactly where to go for the cobalt love seat and dark red area rug. The rest of the furniture could easily by gotten at Ikea.

Tessa stepped over to her father's desk and really looked at it for the first time in years. It was an old desk, something he probably bought at a second hand shop or garage sale when he was her age and just starting his business. The top left corner had a chrome desk lamp, a tray for pencils and paper clips and a single, framed four by six inch photograph. In it, she was five years old, wrapped up in a gigantic red Tremblay's Place apron and elbow deep in flour and chopped fruit. Her hair was pulled into a ponytail and her face was smiling and happy, dusted in flour and sugar with bits of fruit pulp on her lips that she had been eating as she filled up the pie crust. She touched every bit of her little girl face in the photograph behind the glass frame, relishing the smoothness of it before carefully wrapping it in a cloth and placing it in her tote.

As her stomach grumbled more and she noticed the daylight slipping away, Tessa decided to have a look in the walk-in freezer for anything to eat—anything at all. A frost bitten loaf of bread would do. She could toast a couple slices and call it dinner. But there was nothing in the freezer— nothing except a plain white bakery box on the middle shelf. She looked inside, eager for it to be something she could defrost and eat immediately. In the box was an envelope with her name on it atop a plate spread with figs that had been cut in half and covered with clear plastic wrap. Beneath the figs was a handmade pie crust with her father's fingertip impressions pressed into the edges. Tessa lifted it out and admired it. Then she opened the envelope and read the letter it contained.

My dear baby girl,

Oh that's such a silly way to start a letter to you. Dear Tessa. There, that's better. Dear Tessa, I am sitting in the corner booth looking out the window. It's a Monday and I've asked Kate to drive me here. You're back at work for the week and won't be back home until Friday. I have a little time here. I know at some point you will be here, probably alone, thinking about stuff. This place. Your plans. Maybe even me, your old man. I love you, baby. Every time I see you, I see the magic in you. I see the little girl who bakes the sweetest, most magical pies and is afraid of nothing. Thank you for everything. I wish I had more time with you, but I'll always be here with you, or wherever you decide to stay.

There's one more thing I want you to do. Kate just took me to the farmers market for these figs. I bought up the rest of the display. I guess fig season is almost over. Before you go, today, right now, make a pie, baby. A fig pie. Sprinkle it with sweetness and think of me while you eat it.

Love, Dad

She wiped her eyes with the backs of her hands and wondered which Monday he could've left the box and letter for her. He might've written it back when it seemed that fig season would end just as quickly as it had started and the perfectly sweet, inverted flowers would no longer be available. *Wait too long to enjoy them and you miss your chance.* No chance of that happening. Her dad had preserved them, kept them available and sweet. Like her father and herself and Andrew, the little darlings weren't so delicate or fragile after all.

Tessa lifted the plate of frozen figs and the pie crust from the freezer shelf and carried them to the long counter where she'd first made a pie in this place—this little place by the sea with her own name above the door. She took her time assembling the figs atop the crust, sprinkled it with sweetness and popped it into the oven. When it was done, she planned on taking it back to her father's house to enjoy there. What a treasure that she found the plate of figs and her father's letter while she could still go home to him and share the sweet creation. *It's not too late.*

While it was baking, she put away all her cleaning supplies, pulled the window blinds back down for the night and got ready to close up. *There's more to do tomorrow...so much more.*

When she got back out to the dining area, Frankie was perched on top of the counter, surveying the place.

"It's a goldmine, Tessa. You do know that, right? We should turn it into a club," he said, as soon as she came through the door that connected the kitchen to the dining area.

"We? What *we*, Frankie?" She practiced her calm breathing—the breathing that became necessary whenever Frankie was around—and walked away from him.

He jumped down from the counter, followed her and kept talking. "It's yours now, right? He gave it to you. Signed it over. I know he did," Frankie said. "So what are your plans for it?"

She didn't respond. Her plans were taking shape in her mind, but there was no need to share any of her ideas with Frankie.

"How about this? I'll buy half, you keep half. We'll get a lawyer. Work that out. Think of it, Tessie baby. We're a block from the ocean. There's parking. There's room to expand. We could build up. We'll turn that old lunch counter into a bar. This old dining room will be the dance floor. We'll build an outdoor stage and patio area." He went on and on. "This is what the people want. I know it."

"People? What people?" Tessa asked.

"Oh, come on. You're not that naive, are you? The public, Tessie," he said. "There's no place like it around here. It's a need in this location. Think about it. Boaters would see the lights from the shoreline. They'd dock and come have a drink. Stay a while. Have a few more."

There were dollar signs peeking through Frankie's eyes, but all she could see was liability. Boaters stopping at her establishment and drinking, people driving, getting into fights. She didn't want all the headaches that went along with serving alcohol. She didn't want any of it. *A club. A bar. No way.* They'd have to stay open half the night. *And then what?* Frankie would expect her to start going home with him again. Those lumpy sofa nights in Frankie's apartment were long since over.

"The parking would overflow to the street. An outdoor stage area would be too noisy, too chaotic." *It was a quiet area with a few businesses, a nice little serene beach at the end of a fingertip of land that curled out into the blue.*

They'd have to build docks. It would disrupt the calm and the view. The neighbors would hate her. She wouldn't be able to live with herself. Most importantly, turning Tremblay's Place into a nightclub—*goldmine or not*—was not something that had ever entered her mind. Not even once.

"No, Frankie. No. I'm not interested," she said firmly, as she pulled the last window blind down. *And I won't be bullied into it!*

"Not interested? Don't be a fool, Tessie. This place has goldmine written all over it. I'm willing to help you. I know how to run a business and you...well, you know how to work in a restaurant. You've worked here enough over the years," he said. "I'm telling you. This is the answer."

"It's not the answer, Frankie," she said calmly, and got a feeling in the pit of her stomach that he'd been hatching this plan for a while. He'd stayed friendly with her dad. He'd gotten her grandmother to believe in him as the rescuer of poor little Tessa, the guy who could fix problems and set her straight. She breathed in, held it and exhaled. Then she faced him. "In case you hadn't noticed, he's still alive, Frankie. My father is alive. Nobody knows for how much longer. Could be a month. Could be a year. Could be longer. We don't know. He's trying to live one day at a time, one precious day at a time." When she got to the door, she held it open. "This is *my* place and my father's place. Notice the name above the door on your way out."

"Are you selling it? I just need to know if you're planning to sell it, Tessie."

"Frankie, I grew up in this place with a father who loves me and the smell of coffee and pastry in my bones. This view. This beach. This worn linoleum floor and this faded green counter. This salt air when I open the windows. Air. Everything here is mine. Everything here is part of me," she said. "No. I'm not selling."

TWENTY-SEVEN

"We could use the whole space," Marcus suggested. "What do you think?"

"No, I'm thinking just this side, the side closest to the beach," Tessa answered.

"It'll be smallish."

"Smallish is okay. I need the rest of the place for tables and chairs and wall space, of course."

With his stage design experience, Marcus was perfect to help Tessa build her idea, her vision for Tremblay's.

"It'll be awesome. Do you mind if I take a few pictures while it's in process to put up on my Facebook page?" Charlotte asked the two of them, as she sat in a corner booth and sketched.

"Go for it. How many followers do you have now?" Tessa replied.

"A bunch." The pottery workshops had really expanded Charlotte's exposure and had even led her to creating an entire program of offerings. Drawing. Painting. Simple sculpture with clay and wire. She traveled two days every week now and kept the other days for her custom work. "Over two thousand, last time I checked."

"Sweet. It's a win-win. You'll get new customers and so will I. When everything's done and ready to go, you'll have to come down and teach some classes," Tessa said.

"Definitely," Charlotte said, looking up from her sketch and replacing the pencil she'd been using in favor of a Grass Green Primsacolor marker.

Marcus was walking back and forth between the big front window and the door that led to the kitchen with a tape measure and a clip board. He stopped every few steps, measured, made notes and moved on, all the while mumbling thoughts that he told Tessa and Charlotte to ignore. "Plywood. Rocks. Artificial turf, no, actual grass, no, too much maintenance. Lighting. Structural support. More rocks. Padding. Velvet. Deep greens and blues. White. Velvet, yes, definitely velvet." His uttering was almost poetic in its practicality.

While Charlotte was making sketches of the details, all of the specifics from inside Tessa's mind were materializing onto a piece of paper, from pencil gray to glorious color. She could hardly wait to show the renderings to her father.

TWENTY-EIGHT

"Happy birthday, Mr. Dignified Man. I know it's not until tomorrow, but I want to start celebrating today...tonight. Are you coming down here after work?" Tessa was almost bursting with her surprise for Andrew's fortieth birthday.

"I'm out of here at five. Heading straight to you. Shall I bring my good shoes and a bottle of merlot so we can revisit our origins?" he asked from 155.2 miles away.

"No need, I have everything," she replied.

"Undoubtedly you do, Tessa." She could hear the grin in his dark red voice.

"I meant corkscrew, glasses, wine...and then some. Just bring yourself."

She met him outside, as soon as she heard his car. It was nearly 8:00 PM and had been dark for hours already.

"So, you'll have to close your eyes," she said, while standing in front of the doorway, blocking his view into Tremblay's.

"I just got here. Can't I look at you for a minute first?"

he asked from under the door light.

"Okay, look," she said, winking her Silly Girl wink and spinning around for his enjoyment. "But I need to get inside soon. I'm freezing in this little skirt. It's not exactly mid-November attire."

"But you wore it just for me. I do appreciate that. Let's go in. I'll warm you up," he said, wrapping both his arms around her. "Did you make me a birthday cake?"

"Better."

She loved how Andrew looked in the doorway of her place, like he belonged there as much as she did. He was wearing one of his black suits and her favorite of all his neckties, the silk one that looked like stained glass dragonflies. It was the one he'd worn when he'd created her birthday picnic on a warm early June day nearly six months ago. She couldn't wait to get her fingers into the knot and loosen it. Removing his neckties had become one of her little pleasures. They were works of art; little works of touchable, wearable, silk art that could be molded to perfection and then brilliantly dismantled with only hands—her hands. The whole process, however simple or lengthy she made it, was a greeting and sensual promise at the same time.

Tessa pressed her hands onto the glass door and led him in while trying to divert his eyes from the main attraction of the room. To save the best for last, she spun Andrew around and began showing him what she'd done with each and every corner of the little restaurant by the sea. The space had been opened up. More wall space. Fewer booths. She had replaced those clunky wall-hugging booths with a few round bistro tables, making the interior of Tremblay's Place look nearly twice as large and much more maneuverable.

After a minute or two of this, she couldn't contain herself any longer and let Andrew see what she'd done to the other side. "So, it's not as high as an actual cliff with rocks and crashing waves, but it's my cliff. Our cliff. The place, the one of many places that I see, that I feel, that I become..."

"I love it," he said. "It's brilliant. Come show me. I want to get a close up look."

"I kind of love it, too," she said. "I mean, I don't kind of love it. I absolutely, really love it. Very much."

"There are actual rocks in here, big rocks," he said, touching them. "Rocks. How did you get them in here?"

"With help. Look at the top. We can actually sleep, or do whatever we want, up there. It's padded. It doesn't look it, but it is."

Marcus and Charlotte had helped her build a stage at one end of the restaurant big enough to turn into Tessa's vision of the misty green and gray cliff of her imagination. There were red flowers, real ones for today, and whimsical painted creations that she and Charlotte had made to replace the fresh ones after Andrew's birthday celebration.

It was a cliff. *A cliff.* Her shaded orange world.

The beach and waves were below them, just out the window and a block away. From the top, though, the water looked immediate. It was just beneath them, lapping at the base of the cliff. They had brought in jagged, salt and seaweed dusted, ocean-worn rocks. The cliff was mostly open space where they could sit and enjoy the view of the ocean through the big front window. Marcus and Charlotte had made the cliff just high enough to climb, with a discreet set of steps off to the side and large enough to stretch out on. There was a cot mattress beneath a green velvet fabric that was arranged to look like hilly terrain. The small house of Tessa's imagination was a pillow decorated like a serene little spot where they could sleep, if they wanted to sleep. They'd hand painted it down to the smallest detail. It had all turned out with more than a touch of whimsy.

"So, this is what you feel," he said, touching her face, "when I touch you? This is the place you feel, Tessa. You created it!"

"You created it, Andrew," she said. "I wanted it to exist, to actually be tangible. Tactile. For both of us. We can come here whenever we want."

"You're amazing," Andrew said and began exploring the cliff.

"I had help...professional help."

Tessa climbed the steps with him, up to the top of the cliff and stretched out. She was too excited to be quiet and relax. She needed to talk, share her ideas.

"So this is what I'm planning," she started. "I'll be here. I'll start a gallery. A studio and gallery...for kids...and beginners...and people who don't know what they want to create until they dive into different things—people like me. I'm still working out the details, of course, but I can absolutely visualize it. Can't you visualize it, love? Charlotte will teach a class or two every week—whatever she wants. All kinds of stuff. It will vary and never be boring or predictable. And I'll bake all sorts of things, of course. Cheese pastries. Fancy fig pies. Chocolate raspberry tarts. Everything."

Tessa's dad promised to be by her side at Tremblay's as much as possible, for as long as possible.

"Oh, and guess what?"

"What, love?" Andrew asked, as he wrapped her into him atop the cliff. "Tell me."

She let herself melt into him first before telling him. "I slept here last night—on this cliff—and it felt so good. So unbelievably whole and perfect. Well, almost." She kissed him. "Almost. Now I want to share it with you. I want you to sleep here with me tonight, to feel this place with me—within me."

"Best birthday ever and it's not even until tomorrow," he said, reciprocating her kiss.

"Yeah. That's the idea."

"You know what I want to do with you, love?" Andrew asked in the morning after they'd woken atop their cliff, tangled around each other.

"Mmm. Again, Andrew? Well, I did promise to surpass my birthday," she teased him. "Out here with all the blinds open or shall we go to the bedroom in the back?"

Tessa had created a bedroom out of her dad's old office. It was just the right size for a proper grown-up bed, a chest of drawers from Ikea, and her antique cobalt blue loveseat. She'd painted the walls her favorite shade of sea wave turquoise and spread a dark red area rug on the floor.

"The bedroom, please. I'm not really a blinds open on Main Street kind of guy...at least not in daylight."

Tessa just laughed.

"But later. Definitely. There's something else I want to do first," Andrew said.

"Okay. It's your day. Whatever you want."

"Let's walk down to the beach and build a sandcastle. It's been too long since I've built a sandcastle...and I've never built one on my birthday."

She didn't say, *It's the third week of November. It might be a bit chilly, or let's stay in my cozy, little art gallery bakery and drink hot cocoa under a blanket on top of our cliff.*

"I'll grab my coat and be right with you," she said instead.

Tessa went back to the bedroom and grabbed her red woolen coat, the only coat she ever wore. Then she slung her tote bag over her shoulder and met Andrew at the glass door of her place by the sea.

"Ready?" he asked.

"What will we use to build our sandcastle?" Tessa wondered aloud. She had no pails or shovels for such a project.

"Our hands, love. Just our hands. Then we'll take a picture of it and you can hang it in your new gallery. It will be the first work of art you display."

"I'll keep it up always. It'll be a permanent feature." She already knew where she'd hang it—on the wall facing the cliff. It would be perfect there.

"A permanent feature. Yeah, that's what I'm thinking, too," Andrew said, taking her hand.

"You go ahead, Andrew. Find the best sandcastle making spot on the beach. I'll meet you there in a minute."

Tessa watched him walk down the sidewalk, his beautiful hands swinging at his sides, ready to go to the beach and build a sandcastle in chilly November. When she turned the corner and approached the mailbox, she reached down to the bottom of her tote bag and pulled out the envelope. With one final glance at the address, she licked it sealed and slipped it through the slot. There was no need to wait for the sound of the little metal flap swinging closed before racing down to the beach to find Andrew.

ABOUT THE AUTHOR

Pamie Roy earned a BA in English from Bridgewater State University. *Fig Season* is her first novel. She lives in Lakeville, Massachusetts with her family.

To contact the author:

Email: figseason17@gmail.com
Facebook: www.facebook.com/pamieroy

Made in the USA
Columbia, SC
27 June 2017